PRAISE FOR *DARK SPACE*

"Segura and Hart combine space opera with espionage to create a world where the US, Russia, and China showdown is at its zenith, and the human race needs its unlikeliest heroes to answer the call. Packed with action and intrigue and so fast-paced, the pages practically turn themselves."

—ALMA KATSU,
author of *Black Vault*

"Segura and Hart interweave their styles seamlessly in this stellar blend of space opera and spy thriller... The universe feels remarkably well-developed and the tension is palpable. James S. A. Corey fans will want to check this out."

—PUBLISHERS WEEKLY

"A thrilling space adventure that mixes real-world politics and space exploration to dramatic effect...This clever science fiction novel is a perfect choice for readers looking for a perilous adventure with a dash of coziness."

—LIBRARY JOURNAL

"This mix of *Star Trek* themes and a story like Robert Ludlum and Andy Weir had a love child is a blast."

—FIRST CLUE REVIEWS

"The stakes steadily escalate, the action-packed plot consistently entertains, and a ping-ponging third-person narrative kindles suspense and keeps the pages turning...Gritty, bombastic space pulp served with a side of Roddenberry-esque optimism."

—KIRKUS REVIEWS

"This future-espionage tale is a rollicking space adventure full of action, politics, and intergalactic diplomacy on board and back at the station, and will be fun for fans of SF and thrillers."

—BOOKLIST

"This is an intense thriller, with two great authors teaming up, you wouldn't expect anything less. Fans of space adventures will love this one."

—RED CARPET CRASH

"A thrilling spy romp in space...Each chapter propels you forward at warp speed while simultaneously inviting reflection on what it means to be human when confronted with the unknown... A novel well worth your time."

—CAPES & TIGHTS

"A fun space opera."

—TRANSFER ORBIT

"*Dark Space* is the perfect book for fans of John le Carré, a slow-burn yet quick-moving thriller that had me blazing through page after page to find out what the heck is going on."

—FANFIADDICT

"Rob Hart and Alex Segura's sci-fi collaboration *Dark Space* opens with a bang and does not let up... Fun, engaging, and, much like *Star Trek* itself, optimistic to its core."

—PILE BY THE BED

"*Dark Space* is a superior blend of suspense, mystery, and light sci-fi...Authors Rob Hart and Alex Segura combine their prolific talents to produce a book that keeps you up all night and the next day."

—GREAT MYSTERIES & THRILLERS

DARK SPACE

BOOKS BY ROB HART

STANDALONE NOVELS

Dark Space (with Alex Segura)

Assassins Anonymous

The Paradox Hotel

The Warehouse

THE ASH MCKENNA SERIES

New Yorked

City of Rose

South Village

The Woman from Prague

Potter's Field

NOVELLAS

Scott Free (with James Patterson)

Bad Beat (with Alex Segura)

SHORT STORY COLLECTIONS

Take-Out: And Other Tales of Culinary Crime

BOOKS BY ALEX SEGURA

STANDALONE NOVELS

Dark Space (with Rob Hart)

Alter Ego

Encanto: Nightmares and Sueños

Araña and Spider-Man 2099: Dark Tomorrow

Secret Identity

Poe Dameron: Free Fall

THE PETE FERNANDEZ SERIES

Silent City

Down the Darkest Street

Dangerous Ends

Blackout

Miami Midnight

NOVELLAS

Shallow Grave (with Dave White)

Bad Beat (with Rob Hart)

DARK SPACE

ROB HART AND ALEX SEGURA

BLACK STONE
PUBLISHING

Published in 2025 by Blackstone Publishing
Cover and book design by Candice Edwards

Printed in the United States of America
Originally published in hardcover by Blackstone Publishing in 2024

First paperback edition: 2025
ISBN 979-8-228-39626-5
Fiction / Science Fiction / General

Version 1

Blackstone Publishing
31 Mistletoe Rd.
Ashland, OR 97520

www.BlackstonePublishing.com

To Ray Bradbury,
who ignited my love for science fiction.
—Rob

To Gene Roddenberry, D. C. Fontana, and Gene L. Coon—
for introducing me to strange new worlds.
—Alex

“The Earth is a very small stage in a vast cosmic arena . . . our posturings, our imagined self-importance, the delusion that we have some privileged position in the universe, are challenged by this point of pale light.”

—Carl Sagan

“To light a candle is to cast a shadow.”

—Ursula K. Le Guin

FOLD 321-B,
4.1 LIGHT-YEARS FROM EARTH

MOSAIC FLIGHT DECK

Lieutenant Commander Jose Carriles watched as his coffee mug spun at eye level, tendrils of the black liquid spiraling off the white ceramic and shimmering in the flight-deck lights. He figured they had about twenty minutes until every single person on the *Mosaic* was dead.

Carriles felt himself float off his seat. Not good. He nudged himself back and tapped the small button on his wristband that activated the magnets in his boots, clamping him to the iron plates in the floor.

One problem solved.

But his stomach still felt like he'd just gone over the dip on a roller coaster, proof the engines were powering down.

And without those, three things were about to go wrong.

The ship was blasting through a gravity manifold at close to light speed, like a race car barreling down an empty highway. First, with the engines gone, they risked careening off the safety of the track—leaving them stranded in the area between lanes referred to as "dark space." A gray zone too far from rescue, resources, or hope.

Not that it would matter for long. Second, the engines also powered the entire ship—from the artificial gravity that had kept him firmly planted in the chair where he had been dozing, to more important things, like the life-support systems.

That wasn't the real problem, though.

With the engines went the shields. If those dropped at this speed, even a miniscule piece of space debris would cut clean through the ship like a superheated razor.

The console gave a little *ping* every time the shield deflected something of notable size—like a giant asteroid chunk or space trash. The rhythmic tone of it, every few minutes, was actually what had put Carriles to sleep.

Now every *ping* made his shoulders bunch up. Each one could be the last thing he'd ever hear.

That led to the third problem: the alarms weren't going off.

The Klaxons should be blaring, threatening to burst his eardrums—and everyone else's on the damn ship. But the deck was dim and silent. Not that the rest of the crew couldn't tell something was wrong—this early in the morning, a lot of them would probably find out as they floated to the tops of their bunks. But it would be helpful if they knew *how* wrong it was.

He yanked his foot off the floor and threw it forward. It came down in front of him with a hard *clank*, which made him wobble and nearly fall. After he regained his balance, he worked on freeing the other foot.

It was a laborious task—he'd only ever used the magnet boots at the academy, and even then, just for a few minutes, so he didn't really have a feel for them. He tugged and lumbered his way to the next console over, where he could throw himself forward just enough to hit the round maroon button he had hoped he would never have to hit.

BREEEEEEEEEEEEEEEEEEEEEEEEEEEEEEEEEEEEEEE.
BREEEEEEEEEEEEEEEEEEEEEEEEEEEEEEEEEEEEEEE.
BREEEEEEEEEEEEEEEEEEEEEEEEEEEEEEEEEEEEEEE.
BREEEEEEEEEEEEEEEEEEEEEEEEEEEEEEEEEEEEEEE.

A few moments later, the double metal doors whooshed open and Captain Wythe Delmar strode in, buttoning his navy-blue service jacket. If Delmar was feeling the same deep well of terror that was chewing at Carriles's gut, there was no way to tell.

Carriles couldn't tell if the man was already awake, or just efficient. He looked fresh-eyed, his sculpted blonde hair perfectly in place. The man's chest was out and his square chin was high, and he looked like he was surveying a leaky faucet.

Delmar was also having a much easier time with the magnetized boots, and barely slowed down as he weaved around the various chairs and consoles in the cramped space.

"Turn that damn thing off, Carriles," Delmar said, without making eye contact, and Carriles dutifully canceled the alarm. "Anyone who was sleeping certainly isn't sleeping anymore. Gimme a sit-rep, will you?"

"Engines are going fast," Carriles said. "Alarm didn't go off, either. I had to hit it manually."

Delmar surveyed the flight deck, which at this point was mostly lit in blues, yellows, and greens, from the glittering array of switches and console screens. He raised his chin and said, "Lights," and the overheads brightened, washing the space in harsh amber.

The *Mosaic*'s main flight deck was far from luxurious, but not as cramped as some of the ships Carriles had seen in his career. Each major department—from comms to engineering to ship controls—had a terminal, and there was a central command seat behind the dominant terminal. Close enough to smell your neighbor's cologne, but it only got tight when there were more than half a dozen people taking up space.

That would be pretty soon, Carriles thought.

He remembered, a second too late, that he had been projecting his bootleg copy of *The Orbital Children* anime against the porthole window. The sound was off and the subtitles were on, something to keep him entertained on the graveyard shift, but it was also against protocol. It had been easy to forget about when his coffee mug started doing somersaults.

Delmar zoned in on the screen and arched an eyebrow. Carriles swiped away the projection, leaving just the darkness of space and the faint blue glow of their failing shields.

"Sorry, Captain," Jose said.

Delmar didn't say anything, but he certainly filed it away.

"Anything of note happen beforehand? Warning signs?" he asked.

"Nothing."

Delmar finally made eye contact. "And you were awake."

Not a question, but not really a statement, either. More like an accusation. "Of course," Carriles said, which was a half-truth, but Delmar didn't half-believe it.

Delmar leaned forward and hit the comms button as he swiveled the stalk mic over to his face. "This is Captain Delmar. Engineering, I want a status report on the ship's core and shields. First Officer Wu, report to the flight deck immediately. Doctor Liu, please report to the med hall and make sure we're up to speed. Everyone else, await further instruction, and unless you're standing next to that engine, keep the ship-wide comms clear unless it's an emergency."

He ended the communication and turned to Carriles. "How are the shields?"

Carriles pulled up the holo-screen and swiped panels until he landed on the shield integrity display. A schematic of the entire ship popped up, like an X-ray of the *Mosaic*'s hull, with a long sphere around it. Sections of the sphere were in various colors, delineating shield integrity. Some were blue—many were red, which meant those sections were weakening. Fast. There was a lot of data, but the only thing he concerned himself with was the blinking *82 PERCENT* down in the bottom right-hand corner.

Almost immediately, it clicked down to *79 PERCENT.*

"Can we stop the ship?" Delmar asked. "I'd rather sit and lose a few days on our arrival time while we assess the situation."

"It's not that easy, Captain. We're a few days out from Esparar and just started deceleration. Trying to come to a full stop now is either going to rip us apart or send us spinning off into space. We might go so far we can't get back in."

"Dark space, you mean," Delmar said, shaking his head almost imperceptibly.

"Yessir."

"And the chance of us picking up another manifold?" Delmar asked.

"We don't even have charts for this far out," Carriles said.

Delmar nodded, taking it in. He was lost, but Carriles could tell he didn't want to say it. There was a tension in his brow that made Carriles's heart sink.

Humanity's first mission to a livable planet beyond the solar system, and there was only one person qualified to lead it: Captain Wythe Delmar. The man once held his breath for four and a half minutes when his EVA suit malfunctioned during the rescue of a school trip on the lunar surface. Their module was stranded and hissing oxygen, and anyone else would have turned back to the air lock, but Delmar made the save.

Twenty kids and two teachers, alive, thanks to him.

Delmar, the man who'd led expeditions to every corner of the known solar system. Who'd battled Titanian pirates en route to Pluto to deliver much-needed supplies to a stranded French science ship. Delmar, who would surely snag a seat in the Senate, if not the Interstellar Union itself, when he retired. A man so beloved he needed a security detail to get him through the docking bays on New Destiny. The rare blend of ability and fame. People loved him because he was great at what he did.

There was no runner-up pick for this gig. No one else was suggested. Even China was good with it, and China was rarely good with anything the United States wanted.

If Delmar didn't know what to do next, then the mission would be over before it started.

68 PERCENT.

Delmar hit the comms button again, paging engineering directly.

"Awful quiet down there, folks."

Static, and then a voice. Chief Engineer Tommy Robinson responded: "Still not exactly sure what's going on, Captain. According to my readings, the engine just shut off. No issues detected."

"Well, something is quite wrong, Chief," Delmar said. "I want an update in five minutes, if not sooner."

"Copy that."

55 PERCENT.

Delmar let out a long, controlled sigh.

"So, we can't stop, and pretty soon we won't be able to protect ourselves," Delmar said. "Feels like there should have been some kind of contingency plan for this, but we work with what we've got. Suggestions?" Delmar looked around. "And where the hell is Wu?"

Wu was a heavy sleeper, thanks in large part to mixing booze with sleeping pills. The artificial gravity generated by the engines affected everyone differently, and for some people, the constant hum of it made it hard to sleep, so you had to medicate just to get down for the night.

It'd be nice to have Wu in here brainstorming, but fortunately, this was Carriles's wheelhouse. He wasn't some schlub who lucked into piloting the star of the fleet into unknown space. Jose Carriles may not have anything close to a spotless record, but he had the skills to do the job, and everyone knew it. If Delmar was the star power hitter, Carriles was at least the dependable utility infielder—clever and sharp in a pinch. He racked his brain for some kind of answer.

There wasn't any kind of maneuver they could pull at this speed that would help. Rather, the slightest deviation could create a cascading series of problems. Traveling across space via gravity manifolds was a delicate process—like sprinting across a circus high wire, except millions of miles above the surface. They couldn't risk falling off their lane.

He knew engineering would find the problem, but they had to do so carefully and deliberately, especially while they were moving, or they would risk damaging the engines and hastening their demise. But slow and steady didn't sound great right about now.

What they needed was time.

51 PERCENT.

Time.

Like Delmar with those kids.

"Yeah," Carriles said. "I've got an idea."

"Hit me."

"The engines are failing, but they still have some power. If we drop them completely, we would still continue to move due to inertia. So we could divert most of the ship's remaining power to the shields, just to keep the pathway clear until we get this figured out. That way, it's not a sudden stop, and we do it slowly enough to stay in the lane."

"And what's that gonna cost?"

"Pretty much everything else, including life support," Carriles said. "Shifting power drains in the process, so you have to basically assume you'll lose about a third of whatever you're moving over—like a tax. But we should have enough to keep the shields going and stay on track."

"Do it."

"Should we get in suits first?"

Delmar nodded toward the screen. *40 PERCENT.* "Welcome to the burden of leadership. Can't move around worth a damn in those suits anyway. How long can we hold out?"

Jose tried to figure it out in his head—there were fifty-eight people on board, all of them breathing, probably faster from panic, and they had a robust system of CO_2 scrubbers with redundancies built in, but the math eluded him. It was too much to calculate on the fly. "Life support is going to cut out almost immediately. We'll still have whatever oxygen is circulating in the air already, but once that's gone, it's gone."

"If we get everyone into EVA suits, that'll alleviate some of the burden," Delmar said. "They'll be on a contained system, so instead of the entire crew sucking up air, it'll be us and engineering."

Carriles nodded. "That buys us a little more time, yeah."

36 PERCENT.

Delmar clicked on the ship-wide comms again.

"This is your captain speaking," he said. Carriles felt a wave of admiration hit him as he heard the man talk into the mic, his tone flat but reassuring. "I have some tough news to share. We've encountered an unexpected problem that is draining our shields at a level that will not allow us time to diagnose the problem. As you can imagine, at this speed, our shields are literally keeping us alive. We must maintain them at any cost, which means we're diverting all power to them. Including life support. Please begin suiting up in your EVAs as soon as possible. I understand it'll be tough to work in them. On the bright side, you'll be able to breathe for a little while longer. Again, I suggest you get into a suit now. If you or anyone needs an assist, say the word, and I'll come down there myself to figure this out."

Static.

More static.

Then a chime from engineering. It was Robinson: "We've got the whole team present and working on this, Captain. We'll find the fix. Just keep the ship together, you hear?"

"You're a bunch of goddamn heroes," he said. "Gonna make me look bad. Now get to work."

Delmar clicked off as Carriles pulled up the internal systems that would let him divert the power. He glanced up at the screen: *28 PERCENT.*

Diverting power wasn't a simple procedure, and Carriles typed furiously, trying to distract himself from the knowledge that once the shields were down, he was sitting squarely in the ship's point position, which meant a front-row seat to the first projectile to knife through them.

That's if he even saw it. This fast, a speck of dust could do them in.

"Carriles?" Delmar asked.

Carriles shook his head, trying to focus on the task as the shield integrity clicked down.

21 PERCENT.

17 PERCENT.

5 PERCENT.

Damn it, they must have just hit something big. Bad timing.

Carriles pulled up the final screen and entered the necessary commands to divert power, his fingers flying. He hadn't expected the shields to drop so fast. He did some quick and dirty math. He wasn't sure they'd make it—but it was too late for alternatives.

Carriles didn't want to die out here. He had known there was a chance of that happening, but it had seemed worth the risk, to be one of the first humans to step onto an alien planet. To breathe what was supposed to be breathable air, bask in the light of a different sun. To be a part of history after a life spent dodging it.

To accomplish something great, just by being there. Especially when *just being there* was usually what got him into trouble.

Even dying on the surface of Esparar was preferable to dying in a void.

"Carriles . . ."

The final command prompt shined a bright yellow. Jose pushed it as the integrity panel read: *2 PERCENT.* The button lit up under his fingertip. There was a moment of silence, and he held his breath, waiting to die now or live for another few minutes.

The thought that came to him in that moment was Corin Timony, back on New Destiny. He wished he could have one last drink with her. Hear her laugh.

Tell her he was sorry.

The lights on the flight deck dimmed again, in unison with the integrity panel clicking its way back up, all the way to *100 PERCENT.*

Carriles let the accumulated air out of his lungs, but on his next breath, took a shallow one. There wasn't a whole lot to go around at the moment.

"I'm going to hit the wire and report in to New Destiny, see if I can't raise someone with a brain," Delmar said. "You make sure this ship stays straight. Okay, Carriles?"

Carriles turned to the screen, then flinched when a hand landed on his shoulder. It was Delmar, giving him a reassuring squeeze. "You got this, kid," he said.

"Thanks, Captain," Carriles said, and he actually believed that he did, Delmar's praise giving him a little boost of energy. He gripped the steering gimbal tight.

But as Delmar left the deck, and with a very temporary order restored, Carriles raked the stubble on his face and pushed his hair back onto his head so it would stay out of his eyes. He was free to articulate the thought that'd been nagging at him for the last few minutes.

Why didn't the alarm go off?

Of all the things to fail accidentally, that's a hell of a thing to go, especially in conjunction with the gravity engines, which were an entirely separate system. Jose didn't like the shape of the idea that was forming in his head, so he pushed it aside for the moment as the shield integrity clicked down.

97 PERCENT.

NEW DESTINY

BAZAAR HEADQUARTERS

Corin Timony wasn't sure if she heard the alarm at first, the sharp beeping sound coming from the massive, refrigerator-sized wire terminal inside the Bazaar offices on New Destiny.

She wasn't sure because the pounding inside her skull was much louder, the remnants of a long, solitary drinking session that had, unfortunately, become almost mundane.

But still hurt like hell, she thought.

The haze cleared briefly and her senses focused. There was that damn sound. She felt her hands spasm, as if unsure what to do, as if the movement was new to them. And it was, Timony thought. She'd been relegated to this desk-jockey job months ago, and every day still felt like the first day.

The Bazaar offices were on the second floor of a nondescript building on the border between Texas 2 and New Chinatown. The kind of thing most commuters wouldn't even glance at, which is how the leadership liked it.

After all, the Bazaar thrived on secrecy in a time when there were few secrets left.

Timony tapped a few keys on the terminal, logging the alarm and alerting those above her that she was on it. Then she drilled down.

This wasn't the usual yellow flag, she realized. It was coming from the *Mosaic*, and it was on the wire, the only way a ship that far gone in space could communicate with home in anything resembling real time.

At this kind of distance, normal communications could take months to relay—hence the wire, a new piece of bleeding-edge tech that made her brain go sideways whenever she thought about it. It was a quantum entanglement device—the next stage in quantum computing. Take a particle, cut it in half, and whatever happens to one half will be immediately reflected in the other, instantaneously, even if there are entire star systems in between. It was such a wacky idea that even Einstein thought the theory was bullshit.

Turns out, he got that one wrong.

The problem with the system was that all they could do was make a light particle wobble, which created controlled flashes of light, which, at this juncture, limited them to Morse code.

--. .-. .- ...- .. - -.-- / . -. --. .. -. . ... / ..-. .- .. .-.. .. -. --. .-.-.- / -.-. .- ..- ... . / ..- -. -.- -. --- .-- -. .-.-.- / .--. --- .-- . .-. / -.. .. ...- . .-. - . -.. / - --- / ... .-.. -.. ... .-.-.- / ... .. - ..- .- - .. --- -. / -.-. ..- .-. .-. . -. - .-.. -.--/ ... - .- -... .-.. . .-.-.- / .-- .. .-.. .-.. / ..- .--. -.. .- - . / ... . --- .-. - .-.. -.-- .-.-.-

Given her job, Timony had learned to translate on the fly, without waiting for the computer to spit out a translation a few seconds later.

This time, she waited for the confirmation, because what she was reading terrified her.

GRAVITY ENGINES FAILING. CAUSE UNKNOWN. POWER DIVERTED TO SHIELDS. SITUATION CURRENTLY STABLE. WILL UPDATE SHORTLY.

Timony rubbed her eyes to clear away the cobwebs. She read the message again.

Then a moment later.

-.. .. ... .-. . --. .- .-. -.. / .--. .-. . ...- .. --- ..- ... / -- . ...- --. .

DISREGARD PREVIOUS MESSAGE.

". . . the fuck?" she muttered.

She sat back in her chair.

Corin Timony had been an agent with the Bazaar—the international espionage conglomerate that purported to serve the entire solar system and Earth, but in fact was just a confederacy of agents from the US, China, Russia, and whoever else wanted to play—for over a decade.

She couldn't say "an agent in good standing" or "a decorated agent" because that'd be a lie. At least now. If she'd considered it a year ago, she might have been able to milk the statement a bit. "Agent in good standing with a slight drinking problem," or "somewhat decorated agent who hasn't fully lived up to her potential and might be an addict."

She'd still be dancing between the raindrops. *If not for Carriles.*

Timony pushed the thought out of her mind. She didn't have time to dwell on spoiled, entitled assholes like Carriles.

She tapped another series of keys, following the same protocol as before—alerting her bosses and their bosses about the aborted distress signal. This was her job now, on the front line of messages and incoming communiqués—a glorified secretary with little to no input on the information she ferried up the ladder. It was the price she had paid, and Timony was aware it could've been much, much worse.

At least for people like her, who didn't have a powerful parent or a recognizable last name.

She pushed a strand of dirty-blonde hair from her face and felt her eyes widening intentionally, as if trying to will herself to wake the fuck up and pay attention. Deep inside the crevices of her mind, past the fuzz and smoke that amounted to her daily hangover, an internal alarm was going off. An instinct that she'd buried over the last year, dulled through drink and ignorance, was struggling to get to the surface. Something was wrong, it screamed. This was weird.

Fuck, she thought. *Why now?*

There was a time, before Timony had to take breaks from her desk job just to get the blood in her legs pumping again, when she was out there. In the field. An actual agent of the Bazaar. And, hell, she was a pretty damn good one, too. The kind of agent who had sources in every corner of New Destiny.

New Destiny, humanity's shrine to world peace and space exploration. Even if, in the past decade since it'd been built, the cracks were beginning to show. Now it was a dented, rusted trophy. Buildings falling apart, roads cracking—and geopolitical tempers rising between the settlement's conglomerate nations that talked about peace in public and vied for control in private.

Which made her job more necessary than ever.

She sometimes wondered why the seventeen inches of S-glass offering protection from the hostility of the moon's surface wasn't enough to keep everyone cooperating. The precarious environment gave new meaning to the phrase "mutually assured destruction."

But it also meant she got to keep doing her job. Being

a spy was all Timony had ever wanted, and she'd relished it. Thrived on the subterfuge, strategy, and the power of a good double cross.

She'd helped take down the cell trying to assassinate President Warren five years earlier. She'd gone undercover to root out a cabal of vicious cyberhackers running a vile child-trafficking ring just two years back. She'd been part of a task force that eliminated a white supremacist militia group covertly building their own private space station on the other side of Venus.

Which was a long-winded way of saying that sitting in front of a comms terminal in the middle of the night was beyond beneath her—it was offensive, and her bosses knew it.

Hell, they probably liked it.

Worse, she felt useless. Her skill set did not include "troubleshooting gravity engines over the distance of several light-years using only dots and dashes." What if there was still something wrong? She was totally out of her range of experience. And if there was something wrong, why had the *Mosaic* immediately asked her to disregard its message?

The door behind her creaked open. She wheeled her chair around and found Sam Osman's massive frame filling the doorway. He had the same look of slight confusion that he always did, but at least this time it felt warranted.

"Little late for you, isn't it?" Timony asked.

He shrugged. "Forgot the book I was reading. Heard the alarm."

"Didn't take you for a bibliophile," Timony said, immediately regretting it.

Sam was sweet—a giant pile of muscle who would pull on a push door until someone explained the difference. He was a low-level grunt, better with protection details than paperwork. She'd found herself drunkenly making out with him a few times after work events, but it'd never graduated beyond that—and Timony was grateful for it. Osman was nice enough, Timony thought—and attractive. But there was something missing, and Timony was grateful for the iota of restraint that had prevented her from making something awkward into something painfully awkward.

He gave a little shrug and held up a tattered pulp novel. The book featured a typical femme fatale on the painted cover. "Eh, I like them. Keep me entertained."

"Sorry, that was rude of me," Timony said. "And I think everything's okay, but . . ."

Before she could finish, she heard another voice from the hallway.

"What are you doing here?"

Osman turned and his face dropped. "Oh, hey—sorry, boss. I meant to reach out . . ."

Boss? Here we go.

Timony pushed back from the desk and stepped into the hallway, where Derek Sandwyn was leaning against the wall, hands in his pockets, like he was waiting for a bus.

The Bazaar was, on paper, a utopian organization meant to pool intelligence from Earth's remaining superpowers. It was a way for Earth and New Destiny to combine efforts and help each other. The Bazaar was answerable to the Interstellar Union, the governing body housed a few blocks away, and responsible for overseeing all human settlements and colonies outside Earth.

But espionage and intelligence weren't meant to be friendly.

Of course, the whole thing was a charade. All that distrust

the human race was supposed to leave behind on Earth was tucked nicely behind a veneer of friendship and cooperation. Countries still spied on each other. Backroom deals still happened. Sometimes murders were still sanctioned. It reminded Timony of a picture she saw as a kid in school. Back when glaciers existed, how a little bit of ice above the waterline camouflaged a massive collection of it in the depths.

The Iceberg Effect.

The Bazaar was the iceberg.

The reality went so much deeper, and was more jagged.

But in the course of keeping up appearances, each country had a point person. And the office space was meant to promote a collaborative atmosphere. Most countries kept at least a desk here.

Sandwyn was the man in charge of the entire US operation. Anything that touched US interests ran through Sandwyn—which made him a very, very powerful person.

He was also responsible for Timony being demoted a year back. He'd couched it as a mercy to her when it happened. But it felt like anything but kind today.

Timony and Osman stood there, unsure what to say. Sandwyn offered nothing but a humorless smile as he turned his dark gaze toward them. Sandwyn was tall and lithe, pushing sixty, but he still looked like he could throw a punch. His dark, slicked-back hair seemed almost painted on. Everything about Sandwyn screamed "well-crafted." He was a product of his environment, and built to survive the pressures of not only New Destiny but of the Bazaar, too.

After a few awkward seconds of silence, Sandwyn took a small notepad from his pocket and scribbled something on it. Then he ripped off the page and handed it to Osman. "Need you to get something for me. Now."

Osman shuffled in his sneakers. "I'm technically off the clock, just came by to—"

"I wouldn't ask if it wasn't important. Put in for the overtime if it makes you feel better."

Osman gingerly took the paper. "Sounds good." He cast a brief, helpless look at Timony before disappearing down the hallway.

Once he was out of earshot, Sandwyn turned to Timony. "Follow me, Corin."

Sandwyn turned without waiting, power walking down the small aisle that circumvented the cubicle farm. Timony had to hustle to keep up, until he stopped in front of the elevator bank. They rode up the few floors in silence. But Timony knew where they were heading the moment Sandwyn tapped their destination.

The interrogation rooms.

As they entered one of the open rooms, Sandwyn clicked on the lights—the bright, neon kind Timony was used to. The room was barely big enough for the table and two chairs it held.

"Sit," he said with a half-hearted motion.

Timony did, her body running on autopilot. Sandwyn pulled out the chair across from her. He didn't take out his notepad. This was odd. Timony knew Sandwyn was a notes guy. Loved to document everything and then circulate the information to the key stakeholders. The fact that he didn't want to write anything down was an interesting and troubling detail.

"Corin. Good to see you," he said. "Been a while."

Timony bit her tongue. It was inside-voice time. Be friendly until it was time to not be friendly.

"Yes," she said. "It has."

Sandwyn leaned forward, elbows resting on the table.

A sign of intimacy and closeness Timony could've done without. But that was his intent. Make her uncomfortable. She'd played this game before with people much more talented than Sandwyn. She pulled back, feeling the chair's rigid frame pressing into her.

"Talk me through what happened," Sandwyn said.

"What happened?"

"With the alert," he said.

"A distress signal came in and then got canceled. That's all I got."

Sandwyn frowned and drew out his words. "Tell me what happened, Corin."

Timony's mouth opened, but no sound came out. Her mind fluttered back to a year before. In a room like this, Sandwyn looming over her. His words still haunted her dreams and most of her waking hours.

"You think the Bazaar is going to just turn a blind eye to one of our agents running drugs? To being a junkie? Have you completely lost it?"

"Corin?"

Sandwyn's question pulled her back to the present. She shook her head slightly.

"Sorry, sorry, I just needed a minute," she said, looking at the table, figuring at this moment it was best to play ball. "We got a distress call from the *Mosaic*. It came over the wire, so it was terse. Engines were down, power diverted to shields. Then I got a disregard. I followed protocol and reported it. Next thing I know, Osman's in the room."

"Why was Osman there?"

"He forgot his book."

Sandwyn gave a little laugh. "Didn't take Osman for a reader."

"Guy loves pulp novels, apparently."

"Walk me through everything again in detail, okay?"

So she did, even though there wasn't much more to tell.

After the third time explaining it, when it became clear that she had nothing else to offer, Sandwyn simply nodded and stood. "Follow me," he said.

Timony was so tired she didn't even bother hiding the exasperated sigh she let out. She followed Sandwyn back to the elevator bank, where he hit the button.

"I want you to listen to me very, very clearly, Timony, okay? I'm saying this because I know 'listening' is a problem for you."

Timony scowled. "You're a charmer, Sandwyn."

"Again—are you listening?"

"Yes," Timony said through gritted teeth. "I am."

Sandwyn leaned into her.

"Tonight? Everything? Didn't happen," he said. "Forget it."

"Well, that's a hell of a perspective to take when we get a distress signal. Can you at least tell me if the ship is safe?"

"Again, this didn't happen. All you need to know is that it's being handled."

"That's it? Biggest moment for humanity since the moon landing—hell, since we discovered fire—and that's all you can tell me? That it's 'being handled'?"

Sandwyn sighed himself, and seemed to soften for a minute. There was something big going on, big enough to weigh down his shoulders. He was following orders, and Timony knew the feeling—or had, once.

"This is complicated, and I get that it's complicated for you, but the best thing you can do . . ."

The elevator doors chimed open. Sandwyn stuck his hand out to hold the door open.

". . . is to just go home, get some sleep, put this all out of your head. I'm trying to help you here."

"Well, you've always had my back," Timony said, sharpening the words to a fine point.

Not that Sandwyn cared.

"Listen, Corin, I know you've done a lot of good for the Bazaar," he said as he stepped into the elevator. "It's why I let you stay. But you've run out of goodwill. There will be no third chance. So do yourself a favor and take the week off. Clear your head. Forget this happened, or you will be retired, in every sense of the word."

"I hear there are some nice cities on Mars."

Sandwyn's face turned to a flat line.

"Not that kind of retirement," he said.

She didn't need him to explain it; it was pretty clear to Timony what he meant.

Timony followed him onto the elevator, feeling like she was floating, unable to tether herself to the ground.

MOSAIC

FLIGHT DECK

59 PERCENT.

Carriles didn't want to be here, just staring at the numbers. But with power diverted to life support and the lights on the flight deck dimmed, the status screen was the best source of illumination available.

The shields were dropping more slowly than they were before, but whatever relief that offered was erased by the thought of the increasing levels of carbon dioxide in the air around him. That, and the odd sensation of his body trying to float out of its chair, kept in place only by the straps over his shoulders. He considered going for an EVA suit, but he knew that wouldn't fly—he could still make voice commands, but couldn't manage some of the finer buttons in the bulky suit. Plus, it would be a violation of Delmar's order.

Which, when it came down to it, a court-martial or dishonorable discharge was better than dying.

But they'd die faster if he compromised his abilities.

Not that there was anything to do but wait.

And wait.

And wait.

57 PERCENT.

Carriles tried to take fewer, shorter breaths.

He kept the shield status in the lower corner of the screen and switched over to the wire logs. Surely Delmar had reported this on his way down to engineering, and maybe the brainiacs on New Destiny had cooked up some kind of solution. Or at the very least, an acknowledgment.

Except, when Carriles brought up the log, he found a blank screen.

Delmar was the only one who had clearance to use the wire, but any senior staff member could read it. Usually, it was just a series of daily status updates, letting the folks back home know that the mission was proceeding as intended. White noise. Carriles figured the blank screen must be a glitch, but after some basic searches, he discovered the entire day's log had been trashed. That was strange. White noise or not, the wire logs also served as an archive of a ship's behavior and communications. It was important to preserve. Or so Carriles thought.

He pinged Delmar on the comms. "Captain? Did you report back to New Destiny?"

After a few seconds of static, Delmar responded: "Did you hear back? What did they say?"

"Nothing," Carriles said. "There's nothing in the logs. They've been erased."

"God damn it, this ship is failing . . ."

The call cut off. Carriles knew better than to try and raise Delmar again. He was probably in the middle of troubleshooting the issue. Still, that's three system failures. Systems that weren't directly related. One is an anomaly, two could be a coincidence.

Three is a pattern.

His train of thought was halted as the doors behind him hissed open. He turned back, expecting to see First Officer Wu, but instead found Lieutenant Aaron Stegman clomping toward him in his magnetic boots, rubbing the sleep from his eyes.

And not wearing his EVA suit.

"Captain ordered us . . ." Carriles started.

Stegman waved him off as he plopped down on the open seat next to Jose. "I know what the captain said, dude. If we're gonna die, I'm not gonna die in one of those suits."

"Right, but we're supposed to be conserving oxygen . . ."

Stegman shrugged. "Relax, man," he said. "Look, it's simple calculus. We're gonna live through this and it won't matter, or we're gonna die before the air runs out. Here." He handed a metal carafe to Carriles. "Coffee with a touch of the good stuff. Gonna be a short night or a very long day, so may as well be ready."

Carriles took the carafe and sipped. Burnt synthetic beans with a dash of battery acid. A little more booze than he would have liked—he needed to keep his head clear—but it'd take the edge off, and that much was a mercy.

He smiled as he handed the container back. Aaron took it, hoisted it in a "cheers" gesture, and took a deep swig.

If he was going to die, there were worse ways to go. Stegman was his only real friend on the ship, the two of them going back nearly as long as him and Timony back on New Destiny. The difference was that Stegman still spoke to him. Might even like him.

Not that he could blame Timony for shutting him out.

It sucks when the difference between a promotion and a demotion is your last name.

"So how long do you think we got?" Stegman asked.

Carriles tapped the screen. *52 PERCENT.*

"At this rate, I don't know, half hour?" Carriles said. "Unless we hit something big. I gotta say, man, you seem pretty relaxed about all this. I know you're good under pressure, but it's a real struggle to not literally shit myself."

Stegman laughed and handed the carafe back to Carriles. "Have some more coffee, it'll help."

As Carriles took another swig, Stegman sighed. "You know as well as I do, Jose—this mission came with a lot of dangers, a lot of variables. I made my peace with it before we left port. I figured, hell, even if I die, at least I died doing something great. And whatever mistakes we make here, hopefully the next mission will learn from them."

Sure, Carriles thought. If New Destiny even knows something is wrong. If the wire was down, if they couldn't communicate, then this would all be for nothing. The next mission would be starting from the same blank slate they did. There was no scenario where a salvage mission could come out and even examine the wreckage. The ship would either be blasted to pieces or float off into the recesses of dark space, leaving no trail.

The comms lit up. Delmar's voice crackled through the speaker.

"Okay, I think we found the issue. Problem is, we don't know how to fix it."

"What've you got?" Carriles asked.

"The gravity generator stopped spinning. We could restart it manually, but it would take too long to get up to speed. So, me and the boys in engineering are trying to come up with some sort of solution. How are we doing on shields?"

"Forty-eight percent."

Delmar sighed. "Okay. Back with more soon."

Carriles clicked off, ending the call.

"Well, that ain't great," Stegman said.

"No," Carriles replied. "It is not."

Carriles knew the gravity drives pretty well. He was a pilot first, but Carriles prided himself on being versatile—solid on all fronts. Or at least that had been his goal, back when he considered things like a "career" or "dreams."

The drives served a couple of purposes: generating the artificial gravity on the ship, but also allowing them to bend both space and time around their route so they could travel at speeds that combated the effect of time dilation. It meant that by the time they arrived, nearly the same amount of time would have passed on New Destiny. Which gave them the added bonus of reporting back to their friends and family, rather than their ancestors.

Or would it be preceptors?

Whatever. Not important.

Carriles also knew the internal mechanism of the engine was a spinning drive—a mini collider that simultaneously generated and exploded gravitational particles in order to release their energy. But it wasn't something you could just rev up by hand. It moved at impossible speeds, so if the thing was sitting at a dead halt, it'd be at least an hour, maybe two, before it got back up to where it needed to be.

Unless . . .

"You know how bullets work?" Carriles asked. "Like, old bullets, before plasma blasters."

Stegman shrugged. "Sort of. But enlighten me."

"The barrels of old-school guns were rifled. There was a corkscrew spin on the inside. It meant when the bullet left the barrel, it was spinning at a high rate of speed. That makes it more accurate. Keeps it centered on its trajectory."

"I do not like where this is going," Stegman said with a dry laugh.

"You shouldn't, because it's going to suck," Carriles said.

He paged Delmar. "I have an idea."

"Talk to me."

"Keep the drive in an unlocked state. We spin the ship. Get everything on board moving up to speed. But then we stop it, hard and fast. And hopefully, if we're all still alive, the drive will keep spinning."

There was a long pause on the other side.

Finally, Delmar said, "Sounds too risky."

Carriles explained the bullet theory, which would—hopefully—keep them inside the manifold. Delmar was quiet for a beat, then said, "That's a hell of a maneuver. Think you can pull it off?"

Nope, Carriles thought, but then said, "It's the best idea we got."

"Pocket it for now. That's going to be our last resort. We think we have something . . ."

He was interrupted by a crash and a shudder that, if he wasn't strapped down, would have knocked him out of his seat. Carriles looked at the shield status.

22 PERCENT.

"The hell was that?" Delmar asked.

"We just hit something big," Carriles said, his heart slamming in his chest. "Shield integrity just got cut in half."

"Damn it . . ." Delmar said. "Okay, it's Hail Mary time. What do we need to do for this spin maneuver?"

"Everyone needs to brace, right now," Carriles said,

prepping the controls to take over manual steering of the ship. "And we just have to hope I don't pass out before I can stop the spin. Then we all probably pass out or vomit. Maybe both."

"On my signal." Delmar's voice then switched over to the main comms.

"Everyone, this is the captain speaking. Assume brace positions immediately. We're going to attempt a risky maneuver to get the drives back up. I can't say it's going to work, but this is our best option. If it doesn't, well, you were a hell of a crew and I'll see you on the other side. Delmar out."

"I hate you," Stegman muttered. "Can't even get on a carousel with my niece without puking."

17 PERCENT.

"Say you hate me again in ten minutes," Carriles said. "If we're still alive."

Delmar patched into Carriles directly. "Okay. Do it."

Carriles held his breath, gripped the steering gimbal, and turned hard.

There was no easing into it. You went all in or you didn't go in at all.

At the speed the ship was moving, it started to spin fast. So fast that Carriles's vision went blurry almost immediately. And the spin kept picking up speed, until Carriles could barely see in front of him. But he'd already snaked his finger over to the button that would reorient the ship and halt the spin.

At this speed, he wasn't even sure it would work. They might be moving too fast for the mechanism to kick in. It could break. It could rip them to shreds. It could do nothing. And then they'd just die spiraling, nauseous, and upside down.

Stegman was screaming something, but Carriles couldn't hear it. He counted to ten in his head, until darkness began to creep around the edges of his vision.

This was it. He'd be a hero, or he'd be dead.

There were worse things.

He pressed the button.

His head jerked back, his stomach lurched, and there was a massive grinding sound.

Then he passed out.

NEW DESTINY

TEXAS 2

"Want another?"

Timony nodded to the bartender, a short and scruffy Pakistani man she'd seen behind the bar before—Tadeen was his name, maybe?—and he was a decent enough option to take home if no one else in the bar panned out. The idea of that—a distraction—felt so good in her head right about now. Like a vacation from the world. It was a familiar, sad feeling, Timony noted. She let the fantasy play in her mind for a few more seconds.

The truth was, she felt shaken by what had happened with Sandwyn, and she didn't want to be alone.

She gave another sweep around the half-empty dive. Alamo looked bad in the light and somehow worse in the dark, like the shadows were sucking you right into the corners of the tight space. Even worse? In those occasional pools of jaundiced light, she couldn't make out anyone less than thirty years her senior.

Tadeen placed another glass of vodka in front of her, and Timony smiled a knowing smile and mouthed, "Thanks."

Tadeen raised an eyebrow but offered no response beyond that, instead moving toward the opening door, preparing to dole out another drink.

Fine. Timony pulled out her phone and texted Osman: *Done with your errand?*

If she tried really hard, she could convince herself she was reaching out because she needed someone to compare notes with. He'd heard the signal, too.

The truth was, she didn't want to go home by herself. The idea of her empty apartment put her teeth on edge. She didn't have to sleep with him, but Timony knew sitting in the dark alone was less than ideal.

She waited for some kind of response. She spun her mental contact list, thinking of potential colleagues she could talk to. Most of them weren't on speaking terms with her. She considered Slade for a second, her former protégé. Slade was the US's top field agent now.

Slade would definitely know what was going on.

But Timony wasn't willing to sink that low. Not yet. She slapped down her phone.

What the hell was going on at the Bazaar?

She picked up her phone again. If anyone knew, it would be Miranda Slade. Her former protégé, now one of the company's top agents. And there might still be enough goodwill lingering there that Slade would be willing to offer some intel.

Maybe.

But the unbearable pain of going hat in hand to the woman she trained to basically take over her dream job was not something she was ready to consider. No. Not three drinks in.

Four would be better. Probably five.

"How do you drink that stuff?" came a voice from behind her.

"Like this," Timony said, throwing the glass back. It tasted like vinegar mixed with something dead, but it did the job.

She turned to the voice and found Senator Antwan Tobin, his rumpled suit covering his large frame.

Tobin was in his midfifties, and had occupied a seat in the Interstellar Union Senate for close to two decades. His face looked worn and tired, but his eyes were sharp. If Timony was a spy, which she still felt like she was, Tobin was her congressional equivalent—a man who knew the inner workings of government so well he could bend the Interstellar Union to his will with a phone call. No one got elected without Tobin's blessing, and few presidents survived a term without his support. He was the connective tissue that kept New Destiny alive. He also seemed to have a soft spot for her.

Timony didn't recall when they'd become friends. She guessed it was around the time of the failed assassination. Tobin had been part of President Warren's entourage that day, and the bomb that was supposed to take out the leader of the free world would've certainly shredded Tobin in the process. Maybe Tobin felt like he owed Timony something. Maybe Timony had the one thing that seemed to get Tobin's antennae up: intel. For someone in his position, it didn't hurt to have a source in the Bazaar, desk jockey or not.

Still, him being here was a little like seeing a priest in a whorehouse.

"What brings you all the way out here? Just felt like slumming it?" Timony asked. "I imagine you'd prefer a place with a working bathroom."

Tobin smiled.

"A drink is a drink, no matter where you get it." He waved over Tadeen. "Whiskey, neat. Whatever you have from Earth." He nodded toward Timony. "Make it two."

Tadeen whistled, not recognizing Tobin. Timony smiled. It was hard to get good whiskey on New Destiny. Whiskey needed to be aged in barrels, which needed wood, which was almost impossible to find on New Destiny and in dwindling supply on Earth.

Tadeen managed to scare up a dusty bottle from the back end of the top shelf and poured two anemic glasses, sliding them over gently. Tobin threw his back and proffered his glass for another, while Timony savored the woody sting, the notes of citrus and vanilla.

"Hell of a night, huh?" Tobin said. "I'm hearing a lot of things. But first off, how are you holding up? Seems like they kept you for a while."

"I'm fine," Timony said with a shrug before polishing off the rest of the drink. She turned to face Tobin, sizing him up. "Not sure what you're asking me about."

Tobin scoffed.

"Come on, Corin, I'm not some newborn babe. I hear things. I have sources. I know you got cornered at work today," Tobin said, his voice lowering as he leaned in slightly. She could smell the fresh whiskey on his breath. "I don't need you to tell me anything. I need you to confirm it. If you can't, I can find someone who will."

Timony shrugged. She didn't have the energy or desire to spar with Tobin. And fuck Sandwyn.

"It's big, that's all I know," she said.

"A message," Tobin said. "From the *Mosaic*."

"Yup. We got a distress signal, but it got pulled back,

almost immediately. Why the hell would you send out a distress signal and then backtrack with zero explanation?"

Tobin contemplated his drink. He really didn't know what was going on. This was news to him. "Well, the wire is quite rudimentary—"

"It's not smoke signals, Senator," Timony said, her voice slurring slightly on the last word. "They went dead quiet after those two messages, and it left me looking like I didn't know what the fuck I was doing. If I never see Sandwyn again, it'd be too—"

"Sandwyn was there? He questioned you?"

"Yes," Timony said, brow furrowing.

"That's unexpected," Tobin said, smirking to himself. He held his glass in one hand, swirling the last sip. "What did the messages say? What was it about? The black site?"

There'd been rumors swirling around intelligence circles about a secret weapons cache tucked away past Pluto, but Timony had chalked it up to creative gossip. Hearing Tobin mention it so glibly gave her pause. But that was a future Timony problem. She was worried about something else.

Timony recounted as best she could—the messages, but also the interrogation. Probably more than she should offer in one sitting, but she was angry and drunk. And Tobin was trustworthy: besides the friendly-grandpa vibe, he was a man who understood the importance of secrets.

"That's a lot to process," Tobin said. "And I'm always around for a bit of gossip, but I came here for a reason. I need to talk to you."

Timony steeled herself. She felt off-balance. Not just from the drink but from the meeting. Tobin wasn't one to socialize. They weren't friends—their relationship was symbiotic. They each got something from the other. That's as far as it went. If it inched further in either direction, they'd be in trouble. He was here to find her, and that couldn't be good. This was starting to feel a touch more familiar than she was used to.

"What is it?" she asked.

"Adan," Tobin said, his voice flat.

Bad news, Timony thought.

Adan was her . . . something. Ex? Formerly known as her fiancé? The man she expected to marry, but who had seemed quite happy to find an excuse not to?

Like everything else in her life, the relationship went south about a year ago, when she was caught buying doses of Boost—a lab-created amphetamine drug that not only kept you up for forty-eight hours straight but made the whole thing fun as hell—from her childhood best friend, Jose Carriles. Adan was so straight edge that he barely drank coffee. It was almost charming to Timony at first—that this stiff rule follower was turned on by Corin Timony, a perpetual hot mess—but the novelty had started to wear off by that point, and the disaster she'd created for herself only gave him the out he'd probably been craving for months.

A few weeks after she was demoted from her former job at the Bazaar to the one she had now, she found herself paying all the rent on a Texas 2 studio apartment. She'd come to terms with it, or so she told herself. These things happen.

She hadn't called him in well over a month, at least not that she could remember. Each call was just another message on the pile of unanswered "please call me I miss you" recordings that would destroy her self-esteem if she ever listened to them.

And then he died.

Training exercise. Adan was a pilot, and he was scheduled to be the lead on *Mosaic*. It was during preparations for the mission on the lunar surface when his EVA suit blew. By that point, her pain outweighed her regret. She didn't even cry when she heard the news, just sat on her bed for most of the day, memorizing the stains on the wall. Then she went out and got drunk.

Grief was complicated, and never linear.

The real insult was when Carriles swept in to take Adan's empty pilot seat at the last second. It was bad enough that he only got a slap on the wrist for distribution, while Timony's career was ruined for simple possession. Now he was out piloting the greatest mission in human history while Adan was dead and she was stuck at a desk.

But that's the way life works when your mother is a celebrated Martian senator.

"What about Adan?" Timony asked.

Tobin looked around the bar. It had emptied further, and Tadeen was on the other end, cleaning glasses. At least they had privacy.

"I don't think his death was an accident."

The words hung in the air, formless. Timony wasn't even sure how to process them.

Did that mean someone killed Adan? Mr. Straight-Edge-Never-Did-Anything-Wrong Adan? And why now, months later, was Tobin, of all people, coming to her with this? Timing was as important as the message, she knew—and this timing was very suspect.

Sensing her questions, he put up his hand. "There was a report, after he died. That he'd been . . . under the influence of something. Routine safety inspection was also forged.

Someone made all that disappear. I don't know who and I can't even make a guess." He sat back heavily in the chair. "You're a good agent. You saved my life. I know this is a lot. But I felt like you deserved to know. I'm sorry if this . . . I don't know . . ."

He finished his drink and put down the glass.

"So I had Oneida, my assistant, track you down," Tobin said. "I just felt like I needed to tell you this in person."

"Bullshit," Timony said. "I know how the game is played. You didn't come here because you felt like you owed me something. You came here because you wanted something."

Tobin nodded. "I guess I'm just curious about what happened. I wish I knew. But I find the most helpful question to ask in a situation like this, when you don't have a clear answer, is: *Who benefits?*"

"So, what? You want me to find out what happened to Adan? Way to swing by and dump a ton of shit on my—"

"That's not what I said," Tobin said, his tone suddenly stern, scolding. "I thought you'd want to know. That's all. What you do with it, if you do anything, is up to you."

The senator looked at his watch. Timony watched his eyes, could tell he wasn't really looking at anything, just hoping for an easy exit. He placed a fingerprint on the reader near his drink. She heard a slight beep, signaling that his account had been charged. He smiled at Timony softly.

"It's been a long day," he said. "Try to get some rest. Sleep this off. I don't want to hear that you just . . . kept going."

Kept going. She knew what he meant, and hated him for it. Please don't continue to get more fucked up, okay, you helpless grown woman? Timony had heard that tone from too many people, too many times. She'd like to think she'd become numb to it, but the truth was, it just shamed her. Made her feel lesser than, and she wanted to strangle Antwan Tobin right there.

But she couldn't. Because she had to think.

She mumbled something as Tobin leaned in for an awkward hug. She could smell his oily cologne, could feel his five o'clock shadow scraping against her skin. The sensation trailed into something else, an urge to take any kind of closeness she could get in this moment, and she felt ashamed over that, too.

Tobin turned and left the bar. He might have said goodbye. Timony wasn't sure. By the time she reconnected with where she was, though, he was gone. Tadeen had refilled her glass. With the cheap stuff, thankfully. She grabbed it and took a long, thirsty pull.

"One thing went right today," she said, shaking her head.

She polished off the drink and placed the glass on the bar, heard it land, harder than she'd intended. She let her feet reach the floor, gave herself a few extra seconds to find balance, then slowly walked toward the exit. As she walked, she checked her phone one last time; no response from Osman.

Fine.

Corin Timony was used to this—the lonely, drunken half-waltz home. She was used to bracing for the headache and tumult of the morning, coated with liquor and hazy memories.

One thing she wasn't used to? This much subterfuge in one night, and not having a single damn sense of where she stood on any of it.

Who benefits from Adan's death?

What was Tobin trying to tell her?

Her head was too fuzzy to make sense of it.

As she made her way down the block, she passed an O_2 regulator—designed to scrub carbon dioxide from the air and look like a modernist nightmare interpretation of a tree, all harsh angles and garish browns and greens. Normally they softly hummed and cast a faint glow at night, but this one was dark, construction tape wrapped around the trunk.

Whole place is falling apart, she thought to herself.

As Timony walked by the regulator device, she realized she was holding her breath.

She exhaled hard, breathed in, and gazed at the dome above her that looked out onto the blackness of space. Somewhere out there, the *Mosaic* was barreling toward its destination: a habitable planet, a place where humanity could potentially expand to. Earth and New Destiny had reached an inflection point of sorts. Both places were packed beyond capacity with limited options. The small colonies on Mars and Titan were already overloaded, and there were few, if any, hospitable options left to choose from. Humanity needed room to breathe.

But a new planet? A new planet where people could set up shop? It was the next major milestone for the human race. A new beginning. She wondered what they would find there. A new start certainly sounded nice. Maybe she'd hang a shingle.

Or just show up to give Carriles a solid crack in the jaw.

Assuming the ship and its crew were still in one piece. Who even knew at this point?

The longer she stared through the dome, into all that

nothing, the dizzier she felt. There was something about the enormity of it, all that space out there, that made her head spin.

It made her feel alone.

She snapped back when she heard a shuffle and a step behind her. She wasn't so drunk she'd miss being tailed. Was she?

Even though it was off-route, she took a sharp turn at the next corner, allowing her the space to glance behind her, to see if someone was actually following.

The street was empty.

Timony shook her head. She was off. Must've been the booze.

She buried her instincts and kept walking, her shuffle slightly off-balance.

MOSAIC

BRIDGE

"Approaching Esparar's system, Captain," Carriles announced as he tapped a few navigational switches on the *Mosaic*'s flight deck. "Entering the final stages of deceleration."

Carriles took a moment and rubbed his eyes. It'd been a few days since his "spin move"—as Captain Delmar called it—had saved all their asses. But they were all still feeling it. The ship was crawling to its destination—if not literally, then very much figuratively.

But hey, better to limp than not walk at all, Carriles thought.

"Thank you, Lieutenant," Delmar said from behind Carriles's spot on the bridge.

It was a tight space—much more utilitarian than stylish, slightly bigger than the flight deck, and not exactly a conference room. Carriles was up front, Delmar hung back, and a few other rotating crew members came in as needed, manning the science and engineering stations. Those spots were fluid, mostly because you got more work done elsewhere on the ship, without the din of being in the nerve center—but each department had to have face time with the captain, and this was how you did it.

Captain Wythe Delmar lived on the bridge. Lived in the spotlight. And this was his big moment—leading the first-ever deep space expedition beyond the known solar system.

Carriles felt Delmar behind him. He looked up to see Delmar's smiling face.

"We sure as hell lucked out back there, huh?"

It was the first time Delmar had directly acknowledged him in the aftermath. Granted, the days following the spin were a nightmare—anything that wasn't bolted down had turned into a projectile, and while most of the crew had braced, there were still a lot of injuries and broken equipment. A flying wrench damaged the water filtration system, and the mess hall became exactly that—littered with debris after the spin had destroyed a portion of their food supply. They'd be on two meals instead of three until the cook, Izaiah, was done taking inventory.

And all the repair work and triage had to be done by people who'd just had their brains scrambled. *Hard.*

It'd been a tense, stressful few days, which made recognition from the captain now that much sweeter.

"I'll say," Carriles agreed, a dry scoff punctuating the sentence.

Thinking about the praise kept him from thinking about those moments before the spin. The seconds of life ticking down as the shields withered away. The look on his friend Stegman's face when the percentages dropped below twenty-five. Carriles did not want to die on this ship. He wanted to get the credit that would come to him after this mission and do something else. Anything else. Something quiet and lucrative and featuring lots of green grass and a nice glass of bourbon at the end of each day. The security sector sounded nice, he told himself. He never, ever wanted to experience what had just happened again if he could help it.

As if reading his mind, Delmar continued.

"Well, that was some top-notch flying there, kid. We're in your debt. You debrief with Vicks yet?"

Lieutenant Commander Sandra Vicks was, for all intents and purposes, the second-in-command on board. Technically, she was third—because the official *Mosaic* first officer was Tony Wu.

But that was politics.

When the *Mosaic*'s journey was announced, it was also a political moment—a chance to show the worlds a bit of unity and brotherhood. In that spirit, the executive crew of the ship was split—half of the staff were from the United States, the rest from China. In Carriles's limited experience, politics and getting actual work done rarely mixed well, and this was another instance of that. For show, it all looked good. In practice, stuff got siloed frequently, and Delmar—despite being arguably the best space captain ever—wasn't really keen on trusting an executive officer he'd just met. Optics only went so far.

"No, not yet—just been slammed with—" Carriles started.

"You gotta talk to her, okay?" Delmar said, his grip on Carriles's shoulder tightening for a moment. Carriles almost felt like he'd imagined it. "She'll help you process what happened."

Process what happened.

What happened, Carriles thought, is I nearly killed everyone on board and I'm still spinning out from it.

Carriles nodded as Delmar stepped back to his spot at the center of the bridge. Carriles understood an order when he got one, even if it was coated in genuine concern, like a gummy vitamin: meant to taste good and *be* good for you at the same time.

Commander Wu could read the writing on the wall, Carriles knew, and wasn't one to rock the boat. The fissure between the Chinese and American contingents hadn't become more than that, thankfully—an entire ship potentially dying tends to distract from gossip and backstabbing—but as things inched back to relatively normal, and as the *Mosaic* reached its destination, Carriles could feel the divide deepening again. He didn't really want to add to that by going around Wu, but there was little way out of this.

Vicks's role, at least in terms of how Delmar communicated it, was as a "liaison" to the crew, their link to upper management. Some kind of glorified space human resources, Carriles thought. In his case, Delmar wanted him to talk to her so he could unpack his deepest, darkest feelings in the wake of pulling a *Let's spin the ship around* Hail Mary out of his ass. Successful or not, that kind of thing left scars. Carriles wasn't sure he wanted to pick at them yet.

A slight ping on his wrist display reminded him his shift was over. He flicked a few switches and set the *Mosaic* on autopilot until someone arrived to take watch, which would be any minute now. He got up slowly and nodded at Delmar as he walked toward the elevator. The captain gave him a quick finger-gun and wink.

"Don't forget, Carriles," Delmar said. "You gotta unload this stuff."

You gotta unload this stuff.

The words hung over Carriles as he sat on his bunk in his cramped, musty quarters. He hadn't bothered to make the bed and there was something hard underneath the bunched blanket. He pulled out the flask Stegman had shared with him on the flight deck, with a note taped to it.

Nice job keeping us all alive. Me and some of the crew wanted to get you this.

Carriles smiled—a smile that disappeared when he unscrewed the top and sniffed it. More battery acid. But booze was hard to come by, and this was a not-insignificant gift. He was glad to have it, and considered taking a sip, but secured the top and shoved it between the wall and his mattress. For later.

He looked around the small cabin. It had been the site of his first embarrassment on the ship.

Lieutenant Commander Vicks had shown him through the door during his initial tour of the ship, and Carriles had looked around and said, "Little small, isn't it?" She'd given him a hard stare. "I'm sure you're used to finer accommodations," she'd said. "Should I talk to Delmar about turndown service?"

It'd been downhill after that.

Now, every time Carriles interacted with the taciturn Vicks, he felt himself freeze up. She was everything he was not: polished, professional, and direct. She didn't hesitate to call him out—and it unsettled Carriles. If Delmar was the war hero figurehead, Vicks was the engine that kept everything humming.

She was also intimidating as hell.

He picked up his datapad, his fingers dancing across the surface. He should be resting, he thought. Should be unplugging before his meeting with her, so he could be sharp, all smiles and team-player good cheer. But something was eating at him, and had been since before he sent the ship spinning.

How did three systems go all at once?

Things break, Carriles knew that. Once you were out in space, everything was fair game. What we, as humans, actually knew was infinitesimal in comparison to the unknown. It felt cheap to say, but the system failures could all be summed up easily: Shit happens. Things come out of nowhere. We cannot predict everything.

Carriles let out a long sigh and put the datapad down. He hated this feeling, that he was doing something bad. Like being overheard gossiping about a friend. He didn't have to think hard to envision that familiar look of discomfort and disappointment.

But here he was, looking at something he shouldn't have been looking at.

He couldn't banish that itch at the back of his skull. The drive going haywire—he'd buy that. But the alarm and the wire, too? That's three major system failures. And it didn't seem like anyone on the senior staff was all that worried about it.

He picked up the datapad again, tapped a few spots, and it became a viewscreen, blank at first. A low humming sound emanated from the surface, until a man's face appeared. The *Mosaic*'s chief engineer, Tommy Robinson, was haggard, his scraggly beard unkempt. He probably hadn't slept since the spin. Carriles also knew he'd been with Delmar since day one, and was probably the only person on the ship more loyal to Delmar than Vicks. Robinson was in charge of all aspects of the mechanical side of the *Mosaic*. If it didn't run, he was on it.

"What do you need, Jose," he said flatly.

"Commander, it's Carriles," he said.

"I can see you, Lieutenant," he said, an annoyed smile stretching onto his face. "What've you got?"

"Have a quick question about the system failures," he said.

"What about it? Another problem?"

"No, I just want to circle back to what happened a few days ago. I feel like we need a deeper postmortem on the failure, don't you? I don't want to step on—"

Robinson scoffed.

"Lieutenant, I appreciate your concern, but we're on it," he said, his head tilting slightly, as if to say, *Mind your business, pilot boy.* "I've relayed my findings to the captain. He is well aware of any potential issues."

That was interesting. Corporate speak, coming out of a rough-and-tumble mouth like he was reading off a prompter. Of course, Carriles knew he had no standing here. He was just the ship's pilot, and had no oversight when it came to engineering, command decisions, or the like. But he *had* saved the entire ship. He felt like that merited at least a cc on messages involving any findings in relation to the shit-show that almost killed everyone.

But maybe that was just his ego talking.

"Fair enough," Carriles said, swallowing his pride. "If there's anything I can do, or if there's anything you need to loop me in on, I'm around."

Robinson opened his mouth, then paused, as if reconsidering what he was about to say. A moment later, he recalibrated and spoke.

"Carriles, you kicked some serious ass out there, all right?" he said, that smile back again—but empty now. "You saved the ship. No one is forgetting that, and when we get back to New Destiny, I am taking you out for a couple of drinks and the lay of your life. But sometimes things break. We're in fucking outer space, okay? Don't overthink it. There's plenty more to do."

Carriles nodded. At least that sounded a little more like him.

"Copy that."

"Engineering out," Robinson said. Then the datapad screen went blank. Carriles put it down on his nightstand and let his body fall onto his uncomfortable cot. Sleep was out of the question. So was rest. He looked up at the ceiling and let his thoughts wander.

A vision of the ship exploding lingered in his mind's eye.

He picked up the datapad and got to work.

"You did what?"

Vicks's voice, low and monotone, cut through the tiny office. Carriles felt a soft electric shock run through him. He looked over her stark features: the long, straight black hair that framed a pale, almost feline face. The pristine, rigid blue uniform, and the office itself: an immaculate, almost barren space that surrounded them. Everything in its right place.

He waited a moment before speaking, and tried to calculate the risk-reward of what he was about to say. Then he thought, *Fuck it*, and said it anyway.

"I ran a diagnostic—a secondary one," Carriles said methodically, fact-checking each word before it left his mouth. "I wanted to backstop what engineering had done."

Vicks created a steeple with her fingers and rested her chin on it as she looked across the flat expanse of her desk at Carriles, her eyes narrowing.

"I'm assuming you did this with clearance from Robinson?"

"Well, no, I figured he had enough on his plate . . ."

"I see."

Carriles straightened up.

"Look, Lieutenant Commander, I'm not trying to step on anyone's toes—"

"That . . ." she said, leaning back in her chair, "is what people say when they *are* stepping on someone's toes. And while I, and the captain, appreciate due diligence in all its forms, we do have to respect the boundaries that protect each department. Last I checked, you were the ship's pilot, not our chief engineer."

Carriles could feel his face redden. He should just apologize and take the ding. They were too far out, too close to the goal—it would be so much easier to take the path of least resistance and be a good soldier.

But he couldn't shake the feeling that there was a looming, bigger problem, poised to drop into their laps at any moment.

"Well, then maybe you should be talking to your chief engineer," he said. "Three simultaneous system failures are a big deal."

Her eyes widened. "Oh?"

"I mean, don't you agree? Why *didn't* Robinson run a secondary diagnostic? A deeper one that goes beyond the perfunctory?" Carriles said, his words coming out faster than he meant them to, with some heat on them. He was pissed. He had a right to be, he thought. "That's his job. Meanwhile,

I, the ship's lowly pilot, had to go rogue and run a basic secondary diagnostic on a major ship's system failures. You shouldn't be riding me, Vicks. You should be asking the captain why Robinson is just doing less than the basics."

Vicks responded with a humorless smile, then placed her hands, palms down, on the desk before making eye contact with Carriles.

"A few things," she said, her voice almost melodic. "Never speak to me in that tone again. I do outrank you, and this is not a rowboat out for a jaunt on the river. We are on an Interstellar Union ship. The star of the fleet. I serve at the pleasure of the captain, as do you. Second, you are not the chief engineer. You're barely the pilot, and despite your heroics, remember you were not the first choice for this mission. You were a backup, and not even the backup we wanted, but you have friends in high places. Do not forget why you are here. If Robinson said he's done what he's been required to do, and has relayed that information to the captain, that should be more than sufficient. For you, for me, and for anyone else on this ship. Is that understood?"

Carriles nodded.

He'd miscalculated. He'd thought that by running the diagnostic, he'd find something and be able to share the results with Delmar. Instead, someone realized he ran the diagnostic, and Vicks moved up their meeting—not to congratulate him but to chastise him for stepping out of line. He wasn't a hero in her eyes, he was a hotshot annoyance who had done one right thing among a series of stupid mistakes.

Vicks tapped a console to the right of her desk. She scanned it quickly before turning back to Carriles.

"I think you have a lot on your mind," she said. "That's understandable. I want to help you. But I also want you to understand the landscape here. This isn't some backwater runner ship bouncing between Neptune and Pluto. This is the real deal. And that brings with it a lot of eyeballs, a lot of responsibility, and a lot of expectations. You either live up to them . . ."

She tapped another button. Carriles heard the doors behind him hiss open.

". . . or you go somewhere else." She paused, then smiled. "I know who you are. More importantly, I know who your mother is. But please understand—we can make your life very difficult when we get back home."

Somewhere else? Right now, "somewhere else" sounded a little like being shot out of one of the air locks.

Carriles stood up. He opened his mouth to respond but stopped—Vicks's raised hand was a sign that he shouldn't.

"Just continue doing what you do best, Lieutenant Carriles," she said, her smile as empty as the dark space surrounding the *Mosaic*. "I hope you've found this productive. Please keep me posted on how you're doing. I'm here to help."

Carriles nodded and turned around, stepping out into the ship's main walkway. He felt as if his entire body was tingling, as if every movement increased the static around himself and inched him closer to exploding.

He was halfway through his dinner when a yellow plastic plate appeared on the table in front of him. At the center was a small but enticing piece of chocolate cake. He looked up to see Izaiah. The tall, gangly cook, his head a mop of messy dreadlocks, was smiling.

"Nice work with that spin move," he said. "Whole ship owes you more than this."

At this point in the journey, sweets were in short supply. Izaiah must have either hidden it away, or whipped it up from spare ingredients. Either way, Carriles's mouth watered. Lately the menu didn't consist of more than "vegetable rations" or "meat rations." The dehydrated packets tasted okay if you mixed them together, added a shit-ton of hot sauce, and ate them quickly—but that was a fleeting high and, more frequently than not, led to a bad case of the runs.

"Thank you," Carriles said.

Izaiah nodded. "You earned it. Now choke it down before someone sees you and I'm on the hook to make more."

The chef paused—lingering for a moment, as if he wanted to say one more thing. But a moment later he turned away and jogged back into the kitchen area.

Carriles did as he was told, wolfing down the whole thing in a few bites. The mess hall was otherwise empty, and mostly back in working order aside from a broken coffee machine with a hand-scrawled "SOMEONE PLEASE FIX THIS SHIT" sign taped to it. It was an odd hour—too late for lunch but too early for the dinner rush. In any other circumstance, the slice of cake would have been just okay—it tasted more store-bought than freshly baked. But it'd been a while since Carriles had anything with sugar in it, and it tasted like the finest dessert he'd ever eaten.

He knew how most people saw him: a rich, privileged nepo baby who skated through life on the strength of his last name and legacy. That no matter how hard he worked, he must have gotten this far thanks to a favor or nudge.

Carriles thought back to school. Acing his exams,

setting a new record in the piloting simulations. Walking into graduation with his head held high. After the academy superintendent handed him his diploma with a brief nod and, "Good luck out there," Carriles thought he'd shaken the perception. The feeling didn't last long.

As he returned to his seat, a classmate he'd never spoken to turned to face him.

"Good luck? Guy like you doesn't need luck," he said. "You've got it made, bro." All that pride Carriles felt, squashed like a bug under a heel, in less than a sentence.

He was tired of being underestimated. Luck had only taken him so far. He had ability, too.

Carriles was savoring the last mouthful when he heard a voice ask, "This seat taken?"

Carriles looked up from his dish to see Commander Tony Wu standing before him, looking down at the empty seat across from him. Carriles nodded and motioned for the ship's first officer to take the chair.

Carriles was surprised that he hadn't even heard Wu approach. Was he so lost in thought? If so, it was understandable. After all, he was oh-for-two today when it came to interpersonal relationships at work. He was certain he'd pissed off the ship's chief engineer by undermining him and then going around him, then topped that by basically calling him inept in the presence of the first officer in-everything-but-name, Vicks. It was only a matter of time before it all trickled up to Delmar, if it hadn't yet.

"All yours, Commander," Carriles said.

Wu slid into the seat, placing a mostly empty tray in front of him.

"Thanks," he said. "Totally lost track of time and realized I hadn't eaten all day."

"Eating is optional on the *Mosaic*."

Wu laughed. "Isn't that the truth. I try to subsist on coffee and bread simulations, but my stomach doesn't seem to like that. How's by you?"

Carriles shrugged. It was as close to the truth as he could get. "Glad to be alive."

Wu nodded. "Thanks to you, we all are alive," he said, pointing a finger at Carriles. "That was some next-level stuff you came up with. I wouldn't have ever considered that. Glad you did."

Carriles nodded. He felt a smile spread over his face. "Thanks," he said. "I'm not sure where it came from. But between the alarm system and the drive going at once, and then the wire, I dunno, it just felt . . ."

"Too convenient?" Wu interjected.

Carriles looked up from his tray. That was not what he was trying to say, but that word—*convenient*—jumped out at him. Suddenly Wu coming up to his table felt a lot less casual.

"Well, it was certainly . . . problematic."

Wu lowered his voice.

"These ships are built so no integral systems fail at the same time, ideally. One system being down should send an alert to the others—the drive, life support, shields—to basically brace and hold steady. If you lose more than one, god forbid three, you're dead. We were close to that. Something went very, very wrong."

Carriles took a sip of water and nodded. He wasn't going to say anything else. He wanted a better sense of where Wu was coming from.

"I know you ran a diagnostic," Wu said. "A secondary one. I know because Delmar mentioned it at our executive briefing. He wasn't happy. Felt it undermined Robinson, who's been riding along with him since they were in diapers. That jumped out at me. Delmar never gets ruffled like that, especially not in front of others. I went back and checked the systems. As the first officer, I have access to everything Delmar can see except a few top-level things. One of the things I have access to? Diagnostics. Who runs them, when, why, that sort of thing. I saw yours. The one you ran earlier today." He sat back in his chair and folded his arms. "Problem was, I didn't see any others."

Carriles swallowed hard.

"Now, I'm going to ask you this, not only as the first officer aboard this ship and as someone with the authority to command you to tell me but as a human being concerned for the lives of the crew," Wu said, whispering now. "What did that diagnostic say?"

"Can't you see for yourself?" Carriles asked. "You have access. You should be—"

"That's why I'm asking, Jose," Wu said, his words picking up speed. "The diagnostic has been erased. That check you ran? It raised so many alarms that someone went in and deleted it. The only reason I could even find out that you ran it was because Delmar mentioned it. I was able to slide into the archive to find the root file. I could *see* that it was run, but the results were wiped clean. Someone very capable and smart did that. But why? Why doesn't anyone want there to be a paper trail of something so basic, so expected as a secondary diagnostic test? It's what you do after even the most minor incident of this nature. You run a check, then you run a more thorough check, then you run it again. That's why I'm here. I will ask you again—what did the diagnostic say?"

Carriles let out a quick sigh and looked down at his hands, folded on the table in front of him.

"The drive had been depowered for routine maintenance," Carriles said, his voice soft now, too. Even though he was talking to the ship's second-in-command, something told him that Wu was very much out of the loop—and that was a dangerous place to be in. "Which is not supposed to happen unless we're docked or in a stable orbit. Definitely shouldn't happen mid-flight: there are built-in defenses if someone tries to flip that switch while the ship is moving. None of them kicked in. I don't see how it could have happened accidentally."

"You think someone did it manually?" Wu asked.

"I don't see another option. And considering the alarm was turned off, so that maybe we'd miss it . . . it could've been bad."

Wu nodded, as if saying, *Yes, very bad.*

"Maybe I'm wrong," Carriles said. "Maybe I missed something. But I can't help but wonder why I seem to be the only one worried about this."

"I'm worried," Wu replied, a dash of indignation in his voice.

"Look, I didn't mean . . ."

"You think I don't understand what's going on here?" he asked. "I know we're not working with a typical chain of command. But don't think I'm sitting here just waiting to be told what to do."

"Okay then," Carriles said. "What's next?"

"I think we . . ."

The intercom crackled to life. "Lieutenant Carriles, please report to Captain Delmar's quarters immediately."

Carriles's breath caught in his chest. Delmar's voice

was high and tight, a clear undercurrent of annoyance. Wu could feel it too; the grimace on his face said enough.

"I think the more we keep this between us, the better," Wu said, before abruptly getting up and leaving, in the opposite direction Carriles needed to take.

Keep this between us? What the hell was going on?

No time to wonder. It was never good to keep Delmar waiting. Carriles exited the mess hall, headed for midship, a feeling in his gut like he'd just been called to the principal's office.

That feeling got worse when the doors hissed open and he realized he had an escort.

Lieutenant X Shad, the *Mosaic*'s chief security officer, stood there, hands clasped in front of them. Their long hair hung loosely at their shoulders, and they had dark shadows around their eyes and a bold red lip.

And a look on their face like they'd just stepped in something unpleasant.

There were a lot of tough people on board this ship, but Shad was the one who Carriles was most nervous around. Mostly because they never cracked a smile, never joked, never dropped the on-duty attitude. He imagined they slept at attention.

"Wanted to make sure you got there safely," Shad said, holding up the flat of their palm in a *Let's go* gesture.

Funny thing—Carriles suddenly didn't feel so safe.

NEW DESTINY

NEW LONDON

Timony's head throbbed as her eyelids fluttered open. Her skull and mouth felt like they were jammed with cotton. She inched herself up into a sitting position and reached for the cup on her nightstand. It was empty. Figures.

A thought cut through her hangover haze. Tobin's words echoed in her mind.

Who benefits?

Her pounding headache did nothing to stave off the sense of dread bubbling in her stomach, at her inability to answer that question.

It'd been days since the alarm, since Tobin's news about Adan, and she'd hoped that dread would dwindle, but it hadn't. Osman never wrote her back, which was starting to piss her off more than she cared to admit. Maybe Sandwyn had warned him away from her. And she still couldn't bring herself to reach out to Slade.

With no one to talk to, with the week off, without daily trips to the office to keep her in check, there wasn't much to do but contemplate. And drink.

The drinking wasn't helping the contemplating.

Who had benefited? Carriles, for one. He got the coveted pilot's seat. But she knew him. He wouldn't have had a hand in that. Would he?

Adan knew Carriles, too. They'd all spent a lot of time together. When she started dating Adan, he and Carriles became fast friends. Long video game sessions, bragging to each other about their exploits. Timony had considered it a friendly competition between two talented pilots. Could there have been more lurking beneath the surface?

Her mind drifted to an awkward dinner, just a few days before it all crumbled. Before Adan and Timony fell apart, before her demotion. Carriles was trying so damn hard, she recalled. Just laying it on so thick, desperate to not only impress her but Adan as well with his exploits. She had to pry the check out of Carriles's hands. It'd left a weird taste in her mouth. After all, she'd known him since he was a kid. He didn't need to impress her, and—in retrospect—it had been a warning sign of what was to come.

Adan and Carriles's friendship ended abruptly when Carriles—and Timony—got busted. Adan didn't want to be anywhere near that kind of thing. He had to be around it with his girlfriend, but Carriles was another story.

Timony knew Carriles was upset, but any kind of slight he might have felt didn't rise to the level of revenge. Would he have loved to be the first choice for the *Mosaic* gig? Sure. But not enough to kill for it. It just didn't click.

Then who?

Maybe it had been another jealous pilot who thought they'd get the gig? Still, that seemed unlikely. What kind of person would kill just for a promotion?

She shuffled into the bathroom, each step heavy. She leaned over the sink and splashed some water on her face.

Everything ached, but this wasn't new to Timony. She just needed to pop a few pain meds and drink a strong cup of coffee. Then she'd be good.

For what, she wasn't sure. She didn't have any other plans for her imposed time off. She considered her toothbrush, but decided to lie down again instead. She dry-swallowed a few pain pills before moving toward the bed, passing the framed medal she'd gotten from the Interstellar Union for breaking up an interplanetary sex-trafficking ring. She could still remember the impromptu speech she gave upon accepting the award. She remembered how she'd felt—like she could do no wrong. Like she was living the life she'd always wanted for herself. It felt so far away.

She'd spent six months digging through paperwork, communiqués, and surveillance. The kind of grunt work Timony's peers disdained, but she loved. She found her best leads this way, just digging through the dirt and doing the work. She wove a few details together and discovered a personal cause. Kids across the known colonies were going missing under similar circumstances. Usually in districts and regions with minimal to no police presence or government infrastructure. Timony was able to trace the disappearances back to a band of Titan pirates adding another profit stream to their already illicit organization. The investigation ended with her following a tip she thought would lead her to a stash house full of young women being held against their will, but turned out to be a meeting of two dozen men at the top of the operation. With backup too far in the distance, she went in alone. She walked out with a broken rib and nose, and missing at least a pint of blood. But she was also the only one who walked out, and the ring was destroyed in the process. More than a hundred girls saved.

Timony had a lot of wins on her CV, but that one remained her proudest. She'd made a difference. She still got notes from some of the girls she'd saved, now women—thanking her, updating her on the lives they now lived, thanks to her. In her darkest moments, she reread those notes to remind herself that, once upon a time, Corin Timony hadn't been a complete fuckup.

When she first moved into this shithole of an apartment, she'd found the medal among her things. She'd hung it in this spot with a promise to herself: this demotion was temporary. She'd climb back up to where she had been. She had done it once—she was the first in her family to go to college, supporting herself and her drunk of a father who struggled to hold down work after her mom died. She was no stranger to putting in the hours, to working harder than anyone around her to achieve the same thing. She could do this.

Most days, seeing the medal served as a reminder.

But on days like today, it felt like an accusation. A ghost haunting her from a life that was long over. She considered taking it off the wall but decided it wasn't worth the effort.

She flopped onto the bed on her stomach and reached for the holo-display on her bedside table. She brushed the metallic side of it with her fingertip. As much as she wanted to strangle Carriles, she needed someone to talk to. And up until a year ago, he had been the only person she trusted completely aside from Adan. Funny how everything could change so quickly.

Their friendship had felt rock-solid. Even with their differences. Timony had never gotten anything easily, and Carriles had never had to struggle—but still, they connected. He'd been like a brother, starting in grade school, when they bonded on the playground over a shared love for comic books and fruit snacks. The sibling she'd always wanted but never had. That friendship grew and evolved as they did. Carriles was always quick to lend an ear. At the first sign of trouble, he'd show up at Timony's place with a pizza and a six-pack, opening the door for her to rant for hours.

His kindness had never felt contrived, either. Timony never saw an ulterior motive, and knew he didn't have romantic feelings toward her. He was a friend. Which was more than enough. He was there, and Timony appreciated that. Carriles rarely offered insight, because he didn't pretend he knew things he didn't. He just listened.

She pressed the button on the side of the holo-display and swiped through the screens, until she got to Carriles's name. The last message she received from him.

A flickering image of Carriles appeared floating above the viewer, a shot from the sternum up.

"Hey, Corin," he said, before taking a deep breath. "I know things are bad. I know you're beyond upset, okay? I get it. You have every reason to hate me. The way things went down . . . it was bad. I know you always had my back, and I could have . . . I don't know, protected you more? I was nervous—scared, to be honest. They had all this . . . all these details. But I wanted you to know, I swear, I didn't give them your name. I'd never do that. I hope you believe me. Please. I need to know that you do. This really haunts me, because I'm sure there was something else I could've done . . . maybe taken the whole blame myself. I just . . . I had no idea it'd go down like that. I'm just . . . I'm sorry, Corin. Please call me."

He opened his mouth like he wanted to say something else, and then shook his head and turned off the viewer. The image disappeared.

You could have done so much, she thought. *You could've called in a favor. Talked to your mom. Anything. You're one of the most well-connected people on New Destiny. But you did nothing.*

Of all the people who've let me down, I never suspected you'd be one of them.

She looked up at the ceiling and wondered where the *Mosaic* was and if it was safe.

She grabbed her phone. The pills were kicking in and Timony was starting to feel almost normal. Normal enough to look at her screen and think a bit. Maybe there were some interoffice emails with an update on the situation. Or, hell, maybe there was a news item. Some kind of word about what happened. She'd even take another angry screed from Sandwyn if it revealed a bit more about what was going on.

Instead, she found a notification on the main office feed that Osman was dead.

Before she could even process the information, she was calling Slade.

Timony nursed her second cup of coffee, spinning the ceramic mug on its saucer at the flimsy outdoor table, watching the posh crowds of New London filling up the sidewalks, people coming home from work or headed out to dinner.

New London was the nicest neighborhood in New Destiny. Texas 2, where most of the Americans had settled, was a mess of shoddy, unregulated architecture—buildings stacked on buildings, different styles crashing together to give the city a hodgepodge look, giving off a neo vibe, which Timony liked when the crowds weren't at fever pitch.

Neo Odesa was the one place she avoided, aware that walking through it was dangerous if you didn't have Russian blood. The infrastructure there was in the worst shape of the entire colony.

Not long ago, New Destiny had been seen as a rebirth—a chance to start fresh. But now it felt as broken and beaten down as Earth had been.

Humanity's worst habits died hard.

Here on New Destiny, however, the UK thrived on appearances. Their cute little enclave was all clean lines, spotless streets, and handsome pubs that would have felt at home on the streets of actual London—or at least, how London used to be. They'd somehow managed to give this simulacrum a sense of history and ambiance.

But to Timony, even that felt fake. Choreographed and curated—like something out of an amusement park. It was probably just someone's idea of how London should look or feel. Everything artificial. Fashionable. Dry.

Granted, they lived on a moon base, so nearly everything was actually artificial. But the people here were a little too concerned about things that didn't matter.

She glanced at her cup, at the contrast between the white ceramic and the black liquid. She felt a pang of desire for a big splash of whiskey. She didn't know how else to process Osman's death.

She knew this was bad.

Because she could read between the lines.

According to the brief, internal Bazaar missive, Osman was reportedly mugged the same night the distress signal came in. He'd been stabbed and left for dead on the street. Coincidentally, the NDTV surveillance cameras watching the intersection happened to be broken. Osman wasn't clever, but he was a bulldozer. He wasn't an easy target and wouldn't go down without a fight.

The message made the internal, approved narrative clear: wrong place, wrong time. But Timony knew better. She was built to know better.

She remembered Sandwyn's warning to her as they parted a few nights before. She also remembered the piece of paper he'd handed to Osman. He'd heard the wrong thing. Sandwyn was playing chess. Timony could have value at some point. She was a bishop, at least. Maybe a rook. Not worth sacrificing right away. Osman was a pawn.

And even though their connections were brief and fleeting, they'd been nice. A bit of empathy and warmth in a desert of pain and anxiety. Osman had been sweet. And that made Timony angry. He deserved better.

She leaned back and looked at the dome sky. Since it was still "daytime," it was washed with a blue filter and fake sunlight, but the longer she looked, the more she could see the black void of space beyond it.

Leaning back hurt, though, the remnants of a hangover still rattling around in her brain. She brought her attention back to the table, and found Miranda Slade now seated across from her, sipping from a paper coffee cup.

If it had been anyone else, Timony would think she was getting soft. She had great situational awareness, even when her brain was mud. But Slade moved like a cat. Today she was wearing a dark turtleneck and black slacks, her long hair pulled into a tight bun. Her eyes were obscured by aviator glasses. Her makeup was perfectly on point, her nails trimmed but immaculately painted and polished in a dark green.

Timony let out a little laugh. Timony herself wasn't a bombshell, but she wasn't unattractive. Still, when she was an active agent, she made it a point to dress down. Minimal makeup. Plain, nondescript clothing. New Destiny may have had a population of two million people, and anyone who mattered knew exactly who she was—but she figured it was better to blend in than stand out. Slade seemed to take the opposite approach.

"What's so funny?" Slade asked.

"Just wondering why you don't have a name tag that says 'secret agent' on it," Timony said.

Slade threw up a harsh eyebrow. "I like to look nice."

"You look like you're auditioning to play a Bond girl."

"A Bond girl?"

"James Bond? Classic spy movies."

Slade shrugged. "No time for movies."

Timony sighed. "Think of it as homework."

Slade placed her cup of coffee—now empty—on the table. "What is this about?"

"You're the spy, right?" Timony said. "Don't you know?"

To her credit, Slade didn't move. Didn't even flinch. Timony had taught her well. She remembered when the girl was all sloppy hair and big, nervous eyes. Timony had done a good job molding her. Too good a job, apparently.

"Took you long enough to get back to me."

"I got back to you in an hour," she said. "I've been busy."

"With what?"

Slade scoffed. "Please."

Timony sighed. She had a couple of issues on the table in front of her—Osman, Adan, whatever was happening on the *Mosaic*, and whatever was happening at the Bazaar—which could all be related, or unrelated. These things tended to be the latter, but she didn't have enough information to be sure yet.

She took out her phone and clicked on the white noise app, placing it on the table so Slade could see. The app not only killed ambient noise, it jammed any nearby recording devices. This was a private conversation—as much as those existed these days.

"Here's what I know," Timony said, locking in on Slade. "Something happened on the *Mosaic*. There was a distress call that was almost immediately backtracked and then a whole lot of people at the Bazaar lost a whole lot of shit. Osman overheard and now he's dead. I overheard and I'm on mandated leave. Who looks at a guy his size and thinks they can roll him?"

Slade didn't budge.

"You're tired," Timony said. "I can see the bags under your eyes, even through the sunglasses. How many all-nighters have you pulled? You wouldn't be so busy unless there was something big going on. I hear hoofbeats, so I think horses, not zebras. The US and China are embarking on a huge mission to advance the human race. Russia was invited but sat out. The fact that one of the big three took a pass makes me think there's something going on with them—why else would they do that, unless they were running some kind of separate game?"

Timony was fishing a bit. The Interstellar Union was made up of the United States, China, Russia, Iran, the European-African Union, the UK, Japan, Brazil, the Latin American Federation, and Luxembourg.

But the first three controlled the most people, and therefore had the most power.

The rest were all bit players. Usually, if the Bazaar was in a tizzy, it was Russia's doing, and given the current climate, this would make sense.

Slade was a block of stone. Timony wasn't even sure she was breathing.

But this is what Timony needed. She needed to talk it out. Talking it out untangled the disparate pieces tied together in her head.

"What this has to do with the *Mosaic*, I don't know yet. If there is anything to know," Timony said. "Maybe sabotage? We all know President Volkov is a bit of a nut, but doing something to screw up the *Mosaic*'s mission . . . that's a big play, even for him. It's too out in the open. Volkov lives in the gray areas. There'd be major consequences, and I think he's smart enough to know that in the long run, he'd lose. Still, this is what the chessboard looks like to me."

Still nothing from Slade.

"Meanwhile"—Timony took a sip of her coffee—"I get word that my ex-fiancé may not have died in a training exercise. That there were other factors involved . . ."

Slade's eyebrow twitched. There it was. Timony smiled. A tinge of humanity. Slade knew Adan. Had hung out with him. Laughed at his jokes. He wasn't just text on a screen.

". . . that maybe he was high, which, you knew Adan. He wouldn't touch a drug to throw it out." She tapped the table, the picture growing slightly clearer. "Who benefits when the US and China are divided, and China doesn't get equal play on the field? They must've been pretty upset . . ."

"Who told you that?" Slade asked.

It was Timony's turn to scoff. "Please."

Slade picked up her empty cup, took a pretend swig, and put it back on the table. Timony was mildly disappointed. Slade was basically confirming for her that, yes, this was all somehow connected. Sometimes tics said more than actual words. Good spies—the ones who lived long enough to even fantasize about retiring—knew how to subsume those moments. Slade had just fucked up.

Timony thought she'd trained her better than that.

"I'm asking for a favor," Timony said. Slade started to open her mouth, but Timony put her hand up. "Save me the lecture. I get it. I don't give a fuck what China and the Russians are complaining about. But I can't sit around and do nothing. And this thing with Adan—I want to know what happened. It's personal. I want to know why he turned to drugs after dragging my ass across the concrete about them. Where he got them, too. From whom."

"What does it matter?" Slade asked.

Timony shrugged. She didn't have a good answer. She couldn't confront Adan about it. Maybe she could confront Carriles, if he was involved, but even that felt a little empty and unlikely. Maybe she just needed to know what pushed Adan over the edge so she could feel a little less bad about herself.

To maybe get a sense that he regretted what he did to her.

"It just does," Timony said. "It's Adan. I want to know."

"What are you asking me for, specifically?" Slade asked.

"When I got demoted, my security access went with it," Timony said. "I want to borrow your key. Get to any and all files associated with Adan's death."

For a moment, Timony thought that Slade had gone back to statue mode, but then the woman threw her head back and laughed. A low, loud laugh that attracted a few stares from the other patrons. Slade wasn't one for laughing. It was an unsettling thing to hear. With her laugh, she made it very clear how the rest of this conversation would go.

"Okay, okay," Slade said, catching her breath. "Look, I

get it. It sucks. I'm not being funny right now—I know this is weird for you. You trained me and now I'm in your chair. But do you really think I'm going to let you get me fired? Don't you know better by now? Is this some sort of revenge thing? I thought better of you, honestly."

"Wow, c'mon—are you fucking kidding me right now?" Timony asked. "You think I'm doing this to screw with you?"

"Uhh, yeah," Slade said. "I do."

Before Timony could respond, Slade stood up from the table and slung her purse over her shoulder. She picked up the cup and tossed it into a nearby trash can. Her movements were precise and calculated, like everything she did. Not a movement wasted.

"Do you know how excited I was when they paired me with you? *The* Corin Timony? You were the most important person in the room, every damn time. People who I was afraid of were afraid of you. It was inspirational. I knew I was getting the best of the best. You built me. You taught me everything I know. I will always be indebted to you for that. But this ask right here?"

Slade tapped her pointer finger on the table between them, then looked around. There was no one close enough to hear them.

"It's weak," she continued. "It's insulting. It's petty and desperate. You let me down when I found out what happened. You let us all down. But you're still *you*. Deep down, under the drinking and misbehaving, under the *Who gives a fuck* attitude—it's you, Corin. You always worked harder than anyone else. You worked smarter. I always figured it was just a matter of time before you climbed back up. I didn't think you'd try to yank me down at the same time, though. I'm not having that."

Slade turned to leave.

"Hey!" Timony called after her.

Slade paused. Stood there for a moment, like she was going to turn around, like she'd heard a buzzing noise but just couldn't place what it was.

And then she kept walking.

Timony leaned back in her seat. Stared past the blue facsimile of the sky and into the void.

She picked up her coffee, considered it for a few moments, then shrugged. She needed a real drink. She needed to think.

Six vodka sodas later, and Timony had a new plan: fight Slade.

It would accomplish nearly nothing, and probably make her life a whole lot harder, but in this moment, she was sure it'd make her feel better.

Because otherwise, her options were pretty much nil. She didn't know anyone else with the same kind of security clearance that Slade had. At least, no one who was on speaking terms with her. She knew enough about the Bazaar offices to exploit its security flaws, but that was too risky.

Tadeen was bartending at Alamo again, and Timony waved her glass for a refill. She'd abandoned any hope of using him as a distraction, and let him fill her glass and go off to whatever else was more important. She took a sip and let the sting settle, trying to game things out in her head.

Russia's agents were doing something they shouldn't.

Whatever was happening on the *Mosaic* had been worth killing Osman over. Who did the killing was still foggy. But it was clear to Timony that the Bazaar didn't want anyone to suspect anything, either.

And then there was Adan's overdose, and his mistake on the training mission. That part didn't click for Timony. It was too neat, and it didn't hold water for her, someone who knew Adan intimately. Had Adan been killed? If so, by who? Did China see an opportunity to take advantage of a little chaos and try to slot in their own pilot on the *Mosaic*?

And . . .

And.

That's all she had. Maybe. She wasn't sure.

So much for thinking. As much as she wanted to pretend like it did, the vodka wasn't helping. She paid her tab, threw back the last of her drink, and headed for the door. She needed a full night's sleep, and then in the morning a pot of coffee and a disgustingly unhealthy egg sandwich. The caffeine and salt were sure to jump-start what was left of her brain. Sandwyn had said to take the week, and she still had two days left of her mandated vacation.

Even at her worst, Timony was no novice. She understood a suspension when she got one, and it was clear that Slade had reported back about their conversation. It was the right thing to do if you were working by the book, and Slade was in her by-the-book stage. But Timony would make that fact work to her benefit.

In the morning.

As Timony wobbled home, cutting through the cramped streets of Texas 2, she felt a grumble in her stomach. When did she eat last? She should stop in a bodega, get some chips, some ibuprofen, and maybe a beverage. Something with electrolytes, to soften the blow. That'd make the morning a little easier. Timony had it down to a science. Years of drinking taught you the little turnkey things you could do to soften the landing after a rough night. There was no hangover cure, but there were ways to manage.

She was contemplating which direction to take home—it was late, and she wasn't sure which of the bodegas near her was twenty-four hours—when she heard a scrape behind her.

It was subtle. Like a piece of trash being kicked up by the wind.

Except they didn't have wind on New Destiny. At least, not this far from the air recyclers.

She glanced back. She was on a residential block—apartment buildings, the ground floors lined with businesses shuttered for the night. Half of the streetlights were burnt out. But even in the darkness, Timony could see the street was empty.

It didn't feel that way, though.

She turned the corner and walked quickly to the end of the block. It made her head swim, but she knew the layout of this area. If someone was following her, they'd have to come this way—there was no clear path to circle around her or follow alongside her.

She got to the end of the block and watched the corner where she'd just turned. She positioned herself behind a minicar so she could see if someone was following her, but they wouldn't see her. And she felt silly. She was drunker than usual, and probably just hearing things.

Except, a figure turned the corner—male, tall, wearing a long black coat and a fedora pulled tight over his head. He was moving slowly, scanning the block, looking for someone.

Looking for her.

She considered her options. If this guy meant any kind of serious business, she had a small blade in her boot. But she probably also had lost the ability to accurately wield it two vodkas ago. Not that agents were in the habit of attacking each other in the streets of New Destiny, but it was always safer to assume the other guy wanted to kill you.

So, any kind of physical confrontation was out.

To her left was a wide expanse of street. As soon as she stepped into the open, he would see her, and he was close enough that he could probably chase her down. To the right was an apartment building. A row of them, actually, with smaller housing units currently in the process of being built on top of them. She looked at the door closest to her, and while she couldn't be sure, it looked like it wasn't closed all the way. Not surprising; Texas 2 was already going to shit, but that's what happens when you adopt the same kind of anti-regulation attitude that left Earth's Texas underwater.

But if she made it into the building, and was able to secure the door behind her . . .

Fuck it. She dove for the door, leading with her shoulder. The distance was the length of a sidewalk—not very far at all—but as soon as she cleared the safety of the car, she heard the man turn on his feet and pursue her.

The door wasn't all the way closed, which was great, but when she tried to shut it behind her, she found the locking mechanism was broken. Oops. She ran hard to the end of the hall and found the elevator door open. She slid in and hit the button for the top floor, then mashed the door-close button.

Nothing happened.

She could clearly see the door at the front of the

building open. The man strode in, and since he could see her too, he wasn't even hurrying. Timony looked around for an out-of-order sign, something that would give her a hint about what was happening.

His face became a little more clear. She didn't recognize him, which was significant, because she recognized most of the major players on New Destiny, which means the Russians sent someone new (insulting) or serious (scary).

Timony was considering a new set of options when the elevator doors dinged and began to close. She saw the man pick up his pace, but he was too far away to make it. That was a mercy. She was too drunk for the stairs, too drunk to fight, but the building was ten floors, so she'd be safely on the roof before this guy hit the third stairwell, and then get lost in the tangle of construction up there, maybe climb down a fire escape somewhere—

Just as the doors were about to close, they stopped and opened.

He wasn't close enough to grab them, but apparently had been able to hit the button just in time.

The doors opened slowly and Timony faced her pursuer. He outweighed her by fifty pounds at least. His hands were empty but there was a lot of space to hide things in his long black coat. He had a nasty scar across his forehead.

"Ya prosto khochu pogovorit'."

I just want to talk.

Right. Most conversations with Russian assets in empty buildings on quiet streets were punctuated by broken glass and ten-story falls to the concrete.

So Timony responded, "Khuy tebe."

Fuck you.

And she aimed her shoe at the center of the guy's chest.

Or at least, she tried. She slipped a little, her head spinning. She meant to catch him in the sternum with enough force to get him off his feet and onto his back. Instead, she missed low, hitting him more in the stomach. She wanted to create distance, but instead of knocking him back, it made him lean forward. So she improvised and put her knee into his nose. She felt it crunch, and as he crumbled back, she followed, stumbling on unsteady feet and—with all this exertion—struggling to not vomit.

She didn't want to puke on the guy. As much as she didn't mind hurting him, they were both just doing their jobs. Vomiting all over his head seemed like an indignity that went past the bounds of fair play.

The man went down hard, yelling obscenities in Russian. She tried to move around him, but tripped in the process; she wasn't sure if it was over her own feet or if he managed to reach out and grab her ankle, but she went down hard. She threw her foot back and caught him again, then scrambled to her feet and burst out the front door of the building.

The street was still empty. This was not ideal. She needed crowds. People. And she couldn't go home. Not yet. If this guy knew who she was, he knew where she lived.

So, she took off toward Sixth Street, as quick as her drunken feet would carry her. Within minutes she was coming up on the lights and the sound and the revelry of one of the few blocks in Texas 2, and on all of New Destiny, that stayed open all night. Bars and casinos and restaurants, which luckily for her, were hopping.

She weaved her way into the crowd. Once she felt some safety in numbers, she risked a look back, and could see that her new friend was down at the end of the block, entering the crowd, looking for her. He was trying to wipe the blood leaking from his ruined nose, but no one seemed to notice him. He hadn't spotted her yet, and she could probably spend the next hour weaving in and out of restaurants and bars, trying to lose him, but she was tired, drunk, and needed to get someplace safe. Her ankle felt raw and she was worried something might be broken. She was just too wasted to notice.

She didn't know anyone in this neighborhood. No safe houses.

No one except Adan, who had lived down the block, in one of the newer luxury apartments.

Without even really considering it, she headed in that direction.

To their former home.

It had been his, first, until he invited her to move in. A gorgeous unit with clean white surfaces, voice-controlled everything, and auto-dimming windows to keep it dark during the day so she could sleep . . .

A far cry from the shitty studio she was staying in now.

But the best amenity was the security guard they had in the front lobby. Not just some retired cop who'd gone to seed and fell asleep watching movies. The guards they hired looked like they meant business. To people like Timony and her friend, they were purely bush league, but it was better than an empty building. The guy following her wouldn't want to make a move if someone saw his face.

But would her thumbprint still register? He'd had her move out, but did Adan have her purged from the system?

She hustled down the block, into the wider space between the last bar and the rows of apartments, her heart racing. The door was less than fifty feet away, on the corner, and with Tamati on duty. She'd liked Tamati. A big Samoan dude with thick black tribal tats and a major sweet tooth. She would often drop him cupcakes on the way home, which he always housed on the spot and yet never seemed to put on a centimeter of body fat over his rippling muscles.

She was glad to see him on duty, but he was not glad to see her, frowning hard when she reached the door. When she pressed her thumb to the door, it blinked red.

Great. Adan did have her removed. Which, momentarily, made her forget about the fact that someone was coming after her, someone whose nose she'd just broken who was probably looking to return the favor.

Adan hadn't thought she was coming back. He hadn't wanted her back.

Grief was complicated, and never linear.

This was the moment Timony chose to burst into tears, as she yanked fruitlessly at the handle of the front door.

To grieve the loss of her job, her fiancé, and her life.

All because she made some stupid decisions.

She looked up to see Tamati standing on the other side of the glass. He was curious, and a little confused, and after a moment seemed to see the fear in her eyes. He swiped the door open and let her in. Timony didn't allow herself to breathe until the door closed behind her.

She looked through the glass and saw her new friend emerge from a crowd of people. He looked at her, at the building with all its security, at Tamati, and disappeared.

"You all right?" Tamati asked, reaching out to put his hand on her shoulder. Perhaps thinking it might be inappropriate, he quickly pulled it back.

The muscle memory—of just walking into the lobby—sent Timony's mind spiraling. She was back in their apartment, hastily stuffing clothes into a half-empty box. Her hands shaking—from the anger, but also from the nasty hangover she had been battling. Head throbbing. Mouth dry. It had been a long time coming. She'd been packing all week. But the night before had destroyed whatever chance she'd had at staying.

She'd heard Adan's throat clearing behind her. He had to leave. Couldn't do this anymore. Would be back in a few hours. Perfunctory updates—when to messenger the keys. What he'd tell his family. Timony spun around, the motion sending the box crashing to the floor, the sound of dishes crashing as it made contact.

Adan stepped back.

"You're choosing to do this," she'd said, her voice hoarse and ragged. "I want to make this work. I want to be here. But you're giving up on me."

"Corin," Adan said, each word slow and methodical coming out of his stupidly handsome face. She watched his mind hover over each sentence—calculating, but caring. "How can I give up on you if you already have? You're killing yourself. I can't watch you do that anymore."

You're killing yourself.

"Timony?" Tamati asked. "You okay?"

Tamati's question pulled her back to the present, sending her memory of Adan into the ether. But everything she felt remained. The smell of the apartment. The sound of his voice echoing down the hall. The way his eyes would squint when she said something funny.

She felt a deep pain form inside her.

"I am now," Timony said.

It was only mostly a lie.

MOSAIC

LIVING QUARTERS

Shad moved like a robot. Careful, choreographed, methodical. Carriles wondered what they would do if he cut and ran. Probably they'd subdue him instantly and then drag him to see Delmar.

Carriles wondered, too, if what he'd done qualified as insubordination—or worse, treason. He'd gone behind the backs of his superior officers. He was poking his nose into things above his pay grade. Delmar tended to have a fairly lax policy on most things: he respected and appreciated the bounds of ceremony, sure, but knew they were so far from home and risking so much, they needed to feel at ease, too. Still, Carriles had now fucked up in a few significant ways.

"That was some nice work you did," Shad said.

"Excuse me?"

"Saved the entire ship."

"Right, yeah, well . . . I got lucky."

Shad stopped, so hard and fast Carriles nearly walked into them. They turned and fixed him with a hard stare. "You didn't get lucky. You came up with a solution, realized that the risk was worth the reward, and executed it flawlessly. Don't talk yourself down. Not after saving this entire mission."

"It's just—"

Shad punctured the heaviness with a little smirk. "That kind of thing will carry you pretty far. But only so far if you're getting yourself into trouble. You understand me?"

"Yes, I do."

"Good. Now just try to keep being smart like that."

They resumed their march toward Delmar's quarters, and Carriles was trying to divine what Shad meant—did they know about the engineering report? Was he really in that much trouble? Before he could consider how screwed he was, they reached the door to Delmar's room just as Dr. Sarah Liu was leaving.

A member of the Chinese contingent, and the ship's chief medical officer, she was generally no-nonsense, cool under pressure. But now her eyes were puffy, like she'd been crying, or trying not to. She exchanged a brief, uncomfortable glance with Carriles before stalking off down the hall.

That did not bode well.

Shad stopped by the door and gestured for him to enter.

"Good luck," they said.

Carriles nodded a *thanks* and went inside.

Delmar's quarters were downright regal compared to the bunker-like setup Carriles called home. There was a foyer-slash-living-room area and a hallway that led to what Carriles assumed were Delmar's personal quarters. The space was a shrine to Delmar's career—statues, trophies, pictures with dignitaries and celebrities. Carriles spotted Senators Antwan Tobin, Amina Garrett, and Todd Adlerberg—political luminaries on New Destiny, who he recognized from stuffy dinners hosted by his mother, Olga Carriles, which led to heavy-handed, late-night discussions in her study.

The place felt lived-in in a way his home had felt—important things happened here. It was like seeing a museum exhibit after hours. The items that were collected here meant something, had played a part in the world.

A place to sleep. But Carriles wasn't here to admire Delmar's art collection. Delmar was seated on what looked like a very comfortable, long purple couch propped up against the far wall, windows revealing the dark space around the ship. He was dressed casually, a shiny burgundy robe draped around his strong frame, casual slacks and sandals on his legs and feet.

Just one of the guys, Carriles thought.

"Please," Delmar said, gesturing to a wingback chair across from him. "Have a seat."

Carriles sat, hands folded in his lap. Delmar was smiling, and Carriles couldn't tell what kind of smile it was. The man had so many smiles, and even though this one felt somewhat easy, Carriles wondered what was underneath it. He braced himself, waiting for the tirade he assumed was coming.

"Drink?" Delmar asked instead.

The captain nodded toward the table between them, which held a decanter with a deeply rich amber liquid, and two crystal glasses.

One last drink before Shad marches me out of an air lock? Carriles thought.

Delmar didn't wait for an answer. He took the decanter, pulled out the crystal stopper, and took a deep whiff.

"Do you know who Sir Ernest Shackleton was?"

Carriles shook his head.

Delmar nodded as he tipped the decanter over Carriles's glass. "He was an Antarctic explorer. In 1907—so this is going back a ways—he ordered twenty-five cases of Highland malt whisky to take on an expedition to the South Pole." Delmar moved on to his own glass. "He had to abandon the voyage, because he knew to continue would mean the death of his crew. He was only ninety-seven miles from his destination."

Delmar put down the decanter and picked up his glass, swirling it around. "At their base camp, they left behind three crates. These were discovered in 2007. It was still drinkable. They opened up a number of bottles and recreated it, so they could put it on the market, but this . . ."

He took a sip, and his eyes nearly rolled back in his head.

". . . this is one of the original bottles."

"Holy shit," Carriles said.

"Holy shit is right," Delmar said. "It's worth a fortune. Make sure you savor it, though, because you're not getting a second pour."

Carriles picked up the glass. He hadn't had anything other than vodka, or the rotgut that'd been passed around the ship, in years, and he let the woodsy smell soak into his sinuses before he took a sip. It was harsh—oak and vanilla and sharp as a razor but also a little buttery on the finish. It warmed up his whole body and he understood why an adventurer would take this on an expedition to the Antarctic.

"Now, you might be thinking, if Shackleton ultimately failed, why would I bring this on our mission?" Delmar asked. "I know a lot of the folks here tend to be superstitious, and a lot of the time, so am I. But for me, it's a reminder. Shackleton could have pushed on. He could have tried to cover those final ninety-seven miles. But he didn't. He made a tough call to save his people."

Delmar took another sip as Carriles just enjoyed the aftertaste in his mouth. There were a couple of sips left and he wanted to stretch them out.

"I'll be frank with you, Jose," Delmar said, gearing up for something big. He leaned back on the couch, draping one arm over the back, one leg over the other, and cradled the glass of whisky on his knee. He rarely used Carriles's first name—usually defaulting to rank. Carriles didn't know how to feel about it.

"There are a lot of moving parts here," Delmar continued. "Me, I'm just a captain. I just want to lead missions, explore, you know—science. I want to learn. I want to help humanity. But you can't do that without politics. You can't just be a science vessel, wandering space for the better of humanity. That's a fantasy. In the real world, everything is loaded with expectations, and the *Mosaic* is not exempt from that."

Delmar sighed and took another sip, then threw a curious eye at Carriles, who responded by taking another sip as well.

"When the *Mosaic* was chosen to head out here, it was a US mission. This was our idea," Delmar said. "But because we believe in the Interstellar Union, because we want to foster a sense of unity and diplomacy, we talked to the Russians, we talked to our friends in China—and we said, 'Hey, let's make history together.' I believe in that. I want this to be the start of a better world for all of us. But the Russians passed. They don't like to share the spotlight. Fine. The Chinese were amenable, but they had demands.

They wanted cocaptains. Now, you know as well as I do that you can't run a ship with two captains. It's hard enough with just one. We negotiated it down. China gets half the senior staff. That means we have Commander Wu as our first officer. It's . . . look, it's just not ideal. You get that, right?"

Carriles nodded. He had expected to get chewed out for running that engineering report. He had a million questions about what was going on. Instead, he was getting a civics lesson. Granted, he understood it. You don't grow up as the son of a senator without absorbing a lot through osmosis. Carriles just nodded, hoping to see what would happen.

Because something else was nagging at him. Why was Delmar, who had mastered the art of being charming and distant—in a way that predicted a long, successful career in politics—suddenly revealing everything to Carriles?

It didn't add up.

"Not ideal, right," Carriles said. "But I'm still not clear on what it all means, Captain. Sorry."

Delmar waved Carriles off gently, a gesture of understanding and camaraderie.

"Who could expect you to?" he said with a humorless smile. "This is my plight, Carriles. But I like to be up-front with my people, and you're starting to show me you're on the right team. Just stay vigilant, okay? Keep me posted if anything else comes up. Anything else you think is worth a second look. We have to navigate some pretty choppy waters just getting to Esparar. I don't want to drown because someone on my own side is looking to undercut me to please their bosses back home. You understand, right?"

The picture was becoming a little clearer. Delmar was feeling him out. About what, he didn't know. But he seemed to be expecting some kind of answer. Carriles suddenly felt like he was being interrogated.

"Wu spoke to me before I came here," Carriles said, the words leaping out of his mouth before he had time to consider them.

Delmar nodded and smiled. Like he knew, and was waiting for Carriles to offer it up.

"And let me guess, he was asking about that engineering report you pulled?" Delmar asked.

"Captain, I . . ."

Delmar waved the glass like he was shooing away a bit of smoke. "Vicks told me about your conversation. So did Robinson. Neither of them are your biggest fans at the moment."

Carriles's face flushed. "I'm sorry, I just . . ."

"You think I'd be sharing this whisky with you if I was pissed?" he asked. "You're a goddamn hero, Carriles. You saved every soul on this ship. You did something I couldn't. And I get it. Vicks and Robinson, they think their job is to speak for me. Take the load off so I can focus. Most of the time, that's true. But I'm speaking now. Yes, you bit off a little more than you could chew. But honestly, with everything that's been going on . . ." Delmar paused. ". . . if you didn't?"

Delmar put down the glass, leaned forward, and lowered his voice.

"If you didn't, I would have brushed you off as someone who pulled a lucky shot at the last second. Instead, I see someone who is a hell of a lot more clever than I gave him credit for. Someone who actually gives a damn about the importance of this mission. So, consider this drink my apology. I was wrong about you."

Carriles sat back, took another sip. At this point he had no idea what to do.

"You have questions," Delmar said. "And at this juncture, I don't have answers. Not yet. For the safety of everyone aboard this ship, I need to play this one close. But just know that I see what you're doing." He tapped his chest. "I appreciate it. And . . ."

Delmar leaned even closer. Dropped his voice even lower. Some of the camaraderie disappeared from his voice. "And I'd appreciate it if you brought any concerns you had to me, in private. My door is open. Especially if it's related to our friends."

The way he said *friends*, Carriles knew exactly who he meant. He thought of Liu again, walking out of here like she'd just been reprimanded.

Carriles nodded.

He had so many questions. Why had the diagnostics report been wiped? What happened to the wire? And the alarms? What had Delmar been talking about with Liu right before this? Was someone trying to sabotage the mission?

Instead, he said, "Thank you, Captain. I'll keep an eye out, and I won't let you down."

Delmar smiled, patted his knee, and said, "Good man. I hadn't been sure about you up until today. Now I . . ."

There was a buzz of static, and then Vicks came over the comms. "We are about to enter visual range of Esparar."

Delmar threw back the rest of his whisky.

"Well, I guess it's showtime, kid," he said. "Let's go take a big leap for mankind, huh?"

After months of staring at darkness, Carriles's head spun looking at the precious marble suspended in the void before him. Delmar stood beside him, similarly speechless. The view had stopped them a few steps outside of Delmar's quarters.

The planet had been discovered decades ago and was chosen from dozens of other candidates for this mission because the gravity and atmosphere most closely resembled that of Earth, which meant there was a good chance they wouldn't even need space suits down on the surface, depending on the radiation levels. The planet was tidally locked—not rotating, so one side was always in darkness, the other always aglow from the red dwarf it orbited. High cloud cover and atmospheric circulation kept temperatures fairly steady. Habitability was most likely in the twilight band between the perpetual day and night. Plenty of room for a settlement, for humanity to take a baby step into the vastness of the universe.

In the cascade of colors visible through the clouds, Carriles was most encouraged by the deep richness of the blue.

Water.

That life-sustaining thing, there in abundance.

The planet had had another name. Some scientific nomenclature. But before the mission, it was changed to Esparar.

Hope.

"Hell of a thing, huh, Captain?"

Carriles was so lost in the majesty of it he didn't notice that Stegman had appeared at the window alongside him.

"You're damn right it is," Delmar said.

"That's a whole new planet, bro," Carriles said to Stegman. "We're just looking at it with our eyes."

Stegman offered a fist bump. "Thanks to you."

Carriles couldn't help but beam at that, and wonder what they were going to find on the surface. Carriles gave Delmar a slight nod and the two of them shook hands.

"Okay, fellas," Delmar said. "Lots to do."

Delmar left for the bridge. Stegman watched him leave, then turned to Carriles. "What do you think we'll find down there?"

"No idea."

"I hope we find some cool animals. Though given our luck it'll be covered in monster bugs."

Over the last two decades, humanity had discovered radio signals from around the universe—too complicated to decode, but consistent enough that intelligent beings almost certainly produced them. Those signals were too far away to hope for any kind of contact, but maybe, one day. Esparar emitted no such signals, but that didn't rule out the presence of lesser life-forms. There was no way to tell what was down there until they touched down.

"I just want to get there safe," Carriles said. "Then we'll figure it out."

"All right, man, time to work," Stegman said, smacking Carriles's back and heading off down the hall.

Carriles scanned the now-empty hallway for—what, exactly? A tail? Lingering eyes? He wasn't sure. But even in the face of Esparar, he couldn't ignore the sour feeling in his gut that smothered any sense of wonder.

As he walked down the hall toward the flight deck, he couldn't help but feel like nothing had been resolved. Rather, he had even more questions.

Was it the failed diagnostic? Was it Wu's clumsy fishing for info? Or was it Delmar?

Whatever was happening—it seemed like more than

just diplomatic shell games between the American and Chinese crew members, he thought. But those were dangerous enough.

Had someone intentionally sabotaged the ship to slow down their mission? Was Wu just looking out for himself? Was China planning something?

Carriles shook his head. This was all well above his pay grade.

He needed help.

And there they were, alone and out in the middle of nowhere.

NEW DESTINY

THE STATEHOUSE

Timony stood on the sidewalk amid a throng of about a hundred protestors hoisting signs and chanting at the smartly dressed government officials jetting to and from meetings at the Statehouse, home of the Interstellar Union. The protestors chanted in unison with an older woman who seemed to be their point person, hollering into a megaphone.

"EQUAL DISTRIBUTION OF POWER! EVERYONE SHOULD SHARE THE BURDEN!"

The latest cause among the hoi polloi, Timony mused. The solar grids were undergoing major construction, and in order to lighten the energy load, the city was experiencing rolling blackouts. Oddly enough—or not oddly at all, if you knew how things worked—the blackouts only hit lower-income neighborhoods. It was the latest glitch in an ever-increasing series of glitches. As the population of Earth and, in turn, New Destiny, increased, so did the strain on the already-broken systems. Resources were dwindling and people were beginning to panic. It gave the entire moon colony a feeling of electric desperation, and there didn't seem to be a solution Timony could see.

Timony was glad these people were out making noise. It was a just cause—in the past two months, she'd lost three loads of food in her refrigerator when the power cut out in the middle of the night—but it also gave her a little bit of much-needed cloud cover.

The power brokers making their way in and out of the Statehouse tilted their heads away and walked faster. They weren't embarrassed by the unequal distribution of resources; they were upset at being called on their bullshit on the front steps of their castle.

The Statehouse was a beautiful mix of Palladian and neoclassical design, meant to evoke Earth's White House—a decision that royally pissed off nearly every other country in the IU. But the United States hadn't cared. It still boiled down to the same rationale: we have the most bombs, so you should do what we say. Little had changed over the last century. The inside was drab and gray government-issue decor, a stark contrast to the exterior's columns and cornices. Not that it mattered, because the public wasn't allowed inside.

Timony was still surprised at her lack of hangover. Turns out getting braced by a Russian agent was the best kind of cure. She could still taste the adrenaline rush. She was glad for the clarity. She'd need it. This wasn't the smartest plan she'd ever devised, but she didn't see a lot of other options.

She had to see Tobin. She needed more information. She needed access.

But that was complicated. She'd be lucky if someone in his office even answered the phone, and if she called, the Bazaar would flag it immediately. The safest bet was to hope he'd come looking for her again at Alamo, which brought the added bonus of being able to drink while she waited.

No, she had to find Tobin in person. She'd scanned the morning papers, looking for any events that might demand his presence, and found nothing. That didn't mean he wasn't off at a fundraiser or private function, but it seemed more likely that if he was coming by the office, it would be early in the day.

Getting in required security clearance. Which she wasn't going to get, for a whole host of reasons. Lucky for her, her old training never went away.

Security inside the building was decidedly low-tech. There was a main desk with two security guards. On either side of the desk were a series of security gates. Swipe a badge, the metal arms opened, and you stepped inside. Visitors had to sign in, and obviously she couldn't do that. The facial-recognition cameras still might flag her, but by the time word of that worked its way up, she'd be gone.

What she needed was a mark. She scanned the sidewalk, bristling inside the lavender pantsuit she'd bought for special occasions before realizing she never really attended any, and in the time since, it had grown a little tight around the waist.

A mark who looked like her would be ideal. She knew that when a badge was scanned, the person's ID would appear on a screen at the security desk for cross-check. But the two guards sitting at the desk were distracted by the protests, and were watching the doors in case the crowd decided to storm the building.

With the guards so distracted, any badge would do.

She was thankful when she saw Senator Byrne come out of the building.

He didn't clock her. Why would he? The night she had stumbled into a bar to find some kind of IU after-party and made the bad decision to stay he had cornered her within five minutes, first offering to give her a private tour of his office, and then practically begging her to slap him around and stomp on various parts of his body.

He was pretty stompable, she had to admit. With his square jaw, blue eyes, and perfectly parted hair, it was that kind of handsome that made you want to slap him, just to bring him down to earth a little.

She broke away from the crowd and stepped in front of him, offering a coquettish smile. "Hey, you."

Byrne did that politician thing, where he clearly didn't recognize her but twisted his face in a way that made it seem like he did. "Good to see you again," he said, before trying to step around her.

Timony followed his movements, not being aggressive, just impeding his exit. "Funny that I ran into you. I was just thinking about that offer you made."

Byrne's smile morphed into a confused stare as he ran through his memory, trying to figure out what she meant, but getting the sense that whatever it was, it was not a conversation he wanted to have out in public.

"I'm sorry," he said. "I just . . ."

She moved close to him, placing one hand on his chest and leaning up to his ear, the two movements meant to distract him as she pulled the lanyard with his badge from his pocket.

"Oh, you remember. You wanted me to stomp on—" she said.

His eyes went wide as Timony finished whispering in

his ear. As he stepped back, Timony pocketed the badge. Byrne looked around like someone might hear.

"I'm sorry, you must have me mistaken with someone else," he said.

Timony shrugged. "I guess so."

He lingered in the space for a moment, like he was now considering exploring this, before finally nodding and excusing himself. Once he was gone, Timony marched over to the woman with the megaphone. She dropped it mid-chant to give Timony a curious look.

"That's Senator Byrne over there," Timony said. "He's on the public works committee."

She wasn't sure if that was true, but the woman quickly turned in the direction of the retreating senator. "Senator Byrne! We'd like a word, sir!"

The crowd shifted toward Byrne, who glanced over his shoulder with a look of sheer terror on his sweat-glistened face. The movement drew the attention of the guards in the front of the building, who rushed to the door, talking into their comms, probably calling for backup.

Meanwhile, Timony took Byrne's badge out of her pocket and strolled right in through the front door.

It didn't take long for Timony to find Tobin's office—she'd visited the senator a few times over the years and knew it was on the fourth floor, down at the end of the hall. The door was open. She peeked her head inside, where a young woman with tawny skin and wide-set eyes was busying herself with paperwork at a desk.

Despite Timony's efforts to remain quiet, the young

woman looked up immediately and frowned. "Can I help you?"

Timony stepped into the office. "Is the senator in?"

"Not today, no," the woman said, scanning Timony's ill-fitting outfit and rushed makeup job. "The front desk usually informs us when visitors are on their way up. And I don't have any meetings scheduled for this morning."

"How do you know I don't work here?" Timony asked.

The woman gave a smart little smirk in response.

"Look, I just need to follow up with him on a . . . conversation we had the other night. On the q.t. Is there any way I can get in contact with him?"

The woman took a deep breath and leaned back in her chair. "You must be Corin Timony."

"I don't know if it's a good thing or a bad thing that you know that," Timony said. "You're Oneida, his chief of staff?"

"Close the door," the woman said. "Sit."

Timony did as she was told, closing the door softly and crossing the carpet of the bare office to take a seat on the other side of the desk.

"Yes, I'm Oneida," the woman said. "I'm aware of what's going on."

"What do you mean?"

Oneida shrugged.

"When the senator met with you the other night, he told me to put dinner with a friend on the books in case anyone looked, to allay suspicion. We have a policy that I won't do that unless I know who he's really meeting with. He trusts me."

"Plausible deniability is a powerful tool, you know."

"And sometimes it's a trap. But whatever you say to me, you may as well be saying to him."

"Not sure how I feel about that."

"At the moment"—Oneida smiled—"it's the best you got."

Timony leaned forward and clasped her hands together, staring down at the drab-gray carpet. Maybe the best move was to get up and leave. Find some other way to track down Tobin. Try to corner him after a public event. She didn't like coconspirators, especially ones she didn't know.

And while their initial conversation didn't come with a ticking clock, the encounter with the Russian thug had certainly upped the tension for Timony.

"How much do you know?" Timony asked.

"I know about Adan. You didn't sneak into the building because of that. What happened?"

"Last night I was followed by a Russian agent. He wasn't looking for a polite conversation. It could be a coincidence, maybe something else I did that pinged their radar, but given the proximity of my conversation with your boss, I have to assume they're related."

Oneida gave an understanding nod. "That's a smart assumption."

"I need Tobin to give me access to all the files surrounding the *Mosaic* and Adan's death."

Oneida tried to hide it and did a piss-poor job. What started as a little giggle turned into a full-throated laugh.

Between this and Slade, she was real damn tired of people laughing at her.

When Timony didn't respond, Oneida said, "Oh, you're serious."

"I don't have that kind of security clearance anymore. Tobin does. He came to me for a reason, and I'm starting to wonder if that reason is a little deeper than just giving me a friendly heads-up."

"I won't guess at the senator's reasoning," she said. "I may need to know the *who* and the *where*, but I don't always need to know the *why*. You know as well as I do, whatever we access here, it'll get flagged in the Bazaar headquarters. He didn't track you down at a dive bar and have me build him an alibi to then turn around and let the Bazaar know something was up."

Timony leaned back in the chair and sighed. "Fair." She glanced around the office and said, "Shit, you don't record conversations in here, do you?"

"Of course we do," Oneida said. "It's not running."

"Anyone else recording?"

Oneida held up her phone, which showed the white noise app running. "Started it as soon as you walked in, just in case."

"Well, glad to know you're on top of shit," Timony said.

Oneida slid a pad over from the side of the desk and began scribbling on it, then ripped a page off and handed it to Timony. She'd written the address of a bar in New London, SEVEN O'CLOCK SHARP in thick capital letters under it.

"Now I want you to stand up, open the door, yell at me, and storm out."

"What?" Timony asked.

"I can only control what happens in this room, but outside of it, people see things, and they talk," Oneida said. "The bar has a back room. Cut through it and head past the bathrooms. There's a utility closet next to it. Door will be unlocked. If you're not there by 7:05, I bolt."

Timony walked to the door and opened it. Oneida

raised her voice. "I don't want to have to report you, Corin."

"You think you're hot shit, don't you, you stuffy little bitch."

Timony spun on her heels, already halfway out the door before she caught a glimpse of Oneida's expression: shock and surprise.

She'd played it well, then.

Timony knew why. She'd meant every word she said. They key to faking anything was rooting it in the truth. Find a little kernel you believe in and live there. Ride that wave and people will fall for anything.

As she stepped onto the sidewalk, Timony took the paper, looked at it for another moment, and tore it into tiny shreds, before depositing a few scraps into a trash bin at the curb, and the rest down a sewer grate at the end of the block.

ESPARAR ORBIT

MOSAIC LAUNCH BAY

The *Mosaic* had been stationed in Esparar's orbit for the last few hours, running the kinds of scans they couldn't do from a distance, a final check that the surface was safe for human life. Carriles had spent most of that time cradling a childlike sense of wonder at being one of the first human beings to step foot on an alien planet.

That is, until the orders came in.

Delmar would pilot one of the two transport ships. Wu would pilot the other. It made sense to give both the US and China equal footing. But Carriles had fully expected to be on board one of them. He was the ship's pilot, after all. Not just the pilot—the *hero* pilot.

Instead, he was ordered to wait on the *Mosaic*. One second Delmar is feeding him priceless Scotch, and the next he's relegated to babysitting duty.

Carriles ran through the safety checks necessary to make sure the transport ship was operational, the entire time choking down an acidic sense of frustration. He'd had to give Wu a crash refresher course on how to pilot the transport. Granted, the *Mosaic*'s three dropships' onboard piloting systems made it pretty easy, and if something were to happen, Carriles could assume remote control from the *Mosaic*. But Carriles had gone from expecting to be one of the first humans ever to step onto the surface of an alien planet to just watching from the sidelines.

What if something went wrong? What if they had to turn back?

It wasn't just that he wanted to visit Esparar. He wanted to get off the ship. The *Mosaic*, for all its harsh metal surfaces, had come to feel like home over the last few months. He knew it like he knew his childhood bedroom. There was a sudden feeling of unease radiating off the walls of the *Mosaic*. Something was up. And as much as Carriles thought the safest bet was just to ignore it, hit his marks, and not make a fuss, he couldn't help but wonder what was going on.

In part, because if something went wrong out here, they weren't getting home. And in part, because curiosity was a bitch.

Footsteps echoed from the open bay doors at the back of the docking area.

"We're almost ready," Carriles said over his shoulder. "I imagine you've been trained on these at some point and it's pretty simple, but if there's anything specific you want to go over . . ."

Shad sat carefully on the seat next to him. "Not much to review. I've got some experience on these."

Carriles did a double take he feared was a little too exaggerated.

"Where's Wu?" he asked.

"Change of plans," Shad said, clicking through the same

prechecks that Carriles had, demonstrating they had a strong grasp of the ship. "I'm handling this one."

Carriles snuck a peak at his tablet, sitting on the armrest next to him. There were no notifications, which meant there'd been no new issues ordered.

"Okay then," he said.

Shad turned and fixed him with a hard stare. "Problem?"

Don't say a thing, Carriles thought. Leave well enough alone.

That would have been the smart thing.

But there was that curiosity, flaring up again.

"Seems pretty unlikely China would go for this."

Shad remained still as a statue, save for a few targeted blinks, before breaking into a mischievous smile, which seemed out of place on their face. "Ours is not to question why."

"Right, but . . ."

"Carriles," they said. "This isn't the moment. Now, run me through this tin can."

Carriles did, and it became apparent that Shad didn't really need a refresher course. Still, he made sure to cover everything they needed to know, from the heat shields to the thrusters, to the manual control in case something went sideways.

When they were done, Shad gave a tight little nod and said, "Thank you. If I have any questions, I'll let you know."

Must be nice, to have questions and expect them to get answered, Carriles thought. He got up from his seat, grabbed his tablet, and headed into the expansive launch bay, now bustling with activity as the landing teams prepped. He took a moment to walk around the outside of the transport ship, just to make sure nothing seemed off, then did a quick loop of the other one. There he found a small team of men and women loading black plastic crates through the bay doors.

A couple of things stood out.

First and foremost that he didn't recognize any of these people.

The *Mosaic* was a big ship, and they'd been on it for three months now. Everyone mostly stuck to their lanes, in terms of shifts and duties, so there was a decent enough chance that there were some folks floating around he didn't normally cross paths with. But none of these faces were ringing any bells, except for one guy with a thick chest and a shaved head and the kind of harsh stare that could melt steel.

Deane. That was his name. Where did Carriles remember him from?

Four years ago, that was it. There was a riot at the supermax prison station orbiting Titan. Carriles brought in the strike team meant to quell things, and this guy was the team leader. He was wearing the same kind of tactical gear he'd worn for the riot—shiny armor meant to deflect blasts and blades. And those crates. Carriles remembered watching similar crates being opened during the riots, revealing caches of weapons . . .

Too late, Carriles realized he was staring. Deane locked eyes with him, then made an exaggerated move to rub at his face.

"You got a crush on me or something?" he called over.

"No, sorry, just . . ."

"Then don't fucking stare," Deane said, disappearing into the bowels of the transport ship.

Carriles understood the importance of security.

But this was still an awful lot of firepower for an uninhabited planet.

The door to Stegman's spartan quarters slid open and Stegman looked out, bleary-eyed.

"Yeah, man," he said. "What's happening?"

Carriles stepped inside and tapped the button to close the door.

"Something weird is going on."

Stegman paused for a moment before asking, "How so?"

The pause, Carriles thought, said a lot.

"They're prepping for the first excursion," Carriles said. "Wu got bounced from the second transport. Shad is piloting it instead. There's a strike team going with them. I recognize one of them. They're heavy hitters."

Stegman crossed to the drawers built into the wall, stripping off his shirt, searching for a clean one. "Better to have it and not need it, right? Could be dinosaurs down there for all we know."

"We've been on this ship for three months and I don't recall seeing any of these people before."

Stegman pulled on a shirt and turned. "It's a big ship. In the first half of the mission we went, what, three weeks without seeing each other?"

Carriles shook his head. "It doesn't add up. What do you know?"

Stegman shrugged. "Nothing."

"You're lying."

"Would I lie to you?"

But Stegman had built a little too much artificial hurt

into the words. They were meant to throw Carriles off, not for him to accept they were true.

Carriles dropped his voice. "If there's stuff you can't tell me, okay, fine, I get it." He tapped his ear and looked around the room. "But if there's something going on here that the crew isn't aware of, well—that kind of thing doesn't play well in the long run."

Stegman exhaled and dropped his shoulders, then looked up. "Just keep your head on a swivel. Best I can do right now."

"I'm a little pissed you're not being straight with me."

Stegman took a step closer and dropped his voice, but when he did it, he added a little bit of a threatening edge.

"Then you need to understand that if I'm not being fully straight with you, there's something big going on, right? But you also know that I'm not going to let anything bad happen to you in the end, right? Those would be safe things to assume?"

"Yes," Carriles responded, begrudgingly.

"Good," Stegman said, patting Carriles on the shoulder. "Then let's stick with that for now."

Carriles nodded, thought of saying something else, and—finding he couldn't settle on anything—stepped outside the room. As the door closed behind him, he wondered if he should just head back to the bridge to see if he was needed, see if there was any way he could pitch in.

Maybe by doing so, he could figure out what the hell was going on.

NEW DESTINY

LAST CALL

When Timony opened the door of the dive bar, she was smacked in the face by the stench of stale beer and recycled cigarettes. This establishment was a step below her usual last resort, on a desolate outskirt street between New London and Neo Odesa. Aside from the burly bartender, the place was empty.

But that didn't mean no one was watching.

Timony knew that Oneida was taking a risk meeting with her, and probably wanted to mitigate that risk as much as possible. Even a senator's chief of staff probably had some loose sense of spycraft. Plus, the bar seemed to lack working cameras, as did most of the surrounding streets, as far as she could tell. Timony had clocked one that looked like it was functional around the corner on her way in, and managed to stick to its blind spot.

Timony scanned the collection of empty tables and spotted the tiny hallway that led to the bathrooms. She made her way across the bar, not looking at the bartender, and walked past the chairs and pool table. She almost missed the tiny door at the end of the hall. She turned the knob and it opened.

It was cramped and dark. She didn't see Oneida as much as feel her presence. Okay, Timony thought, another point for Oneida. Don't take anything for granted. Anyone can be watching, so act accordingly.

Timony stepped in. "I'm here."

No one responded right away. Had she miscalculated? Had Oneida set her up?

Timony felt muddy—like her senses were glazed over. All Timony really wanted to do at this point was sit in her tiny apartment, shut off the lights, and disappear.

Then Oneida spoke, her words low, with a dash of menace, cutting through the darkness.

"Let's make this quick," she said.

Timony took another step into the dark room. She felt herself bump into something—someone—and stepped back. "You picked this place, remember? Not exactly comfortable."

Timony heard Oneida take in a long breath. A hand grabbed her shoulder. It seemed to be shaking slightly. Oneida was scared.

"I realized, after you left, that this could get me into a shit-ton of trouble. Not just work trouble—but . . ." she paused. Timony's eyes had adjusted to the darkness now. She could make out Oneida's face—the woman was hastily licking her lips. A nervous tic. "But life trouble, too. I know Tobin trusts you, but—"

Timony placed a hand on Oneida's. "Something is wrong. With that ship out there. Down here. I'm not sure what, but I know it's not good. I need to access those records to see just *what* is wrong."

Oneida let out a long sigh. "If I give you what I have, how do I know it won't come back to me?"

Timony leaned forward, her voice low. "All I have is my word. And my reputation."

Oneida scoffed. "Your reputation?"

"Touché," Timony said.

Timony felt something slide into her hand. An envelope.

"His name's Carvajal," she said, watching as Timony slid the envelope into her jacket. "Do not mention me or Tobin. If anyone can get you into those records, it's him."

Timony nodded and started to back out of the cramped space.

"Thanks," she said. "I'll keep you posted."

"Please don't," Oneida said. Timony could see her dry smile even in the darkness. "I'm not involved. Whatever you're digging into is bad. I don't need you to tell me you know that."

Oneida brushed herself off, like the bar had left a layer of dust on her, and moved past Timony—hustling to get out of the door. Timony ducked into the bathroom, to create some distance between the two of them.

Outside the bar, Timony cracked the envelope open. It was bad form to do it so publicly, where anyone could be watching. But Timony didn't care. Didn't have time to care.

On the paper inside was a number—nothing else. She reached into her pocket for her phone but hesitated. The skin on the back of her neck had prickled.

She didn't wheel around. Didn't need to.

It was the same feeling she had the other night. The same feeling that had sent her running to Adan's lobby, while a Russian thug with a broken nose stalked outside.

Her options were limited. Go back in the bar, and maybe

implicate Oneida in the process. Or run and risk getting attacked by someone who was probably looking for revenge.

Timony turned around. She looked down the long, dark alley that wound behind her. A shadow peeked out from behind a large dumpster. Whoever this guy was, he wasn't as sharp as he thought he was.

"You can come out now," Timony said, bracing herself.

She heard the slushing sound of sneakers on concrete before she saw the shape step out. It was the same Russian from last night. Both eyes black, tape over his nose.

"You're consistent, at least," Timony said, backing up a step.

The man stepped forward.

"Who is responsible?" the man asked, his English stiff and stilted. "Who is doing this? You tell me now, we have less problem."

Timony didn't answer. English was ubiquitous on New Destiny; if it was this guy's second language, he was either from Earth, which meant he was a survivor of the crippled, crumbling environment, and therefore tougher than she'd given him credit for. Or he was from one of the more intense Russian enclaves.

Neither option was encouraging for her.

"Doing what, exactly?" Timony asked.

"The ship. Who did that to the ship?" he asked.

"Did what to what ship?" Timony asked, stepping forward. "The *Mosaic*?"

"You know. You know more than me," the man continued with an exasperated sigh. "You can talk now, or I hurt—"

What happened next happened fast.

She didn't hear the shot, but she saw it. Saw it slice

across the Russian's neck, sending him down like a heavy sack of wet clothes.

Timony dropped to the ground and pushed herself up against a minicar, not that it would be of much help. She had no idea where the shot came from. Could be from the roof, and the shooter was just repositioning, or from across the street, and now they were coming around the other side.

Timony held her breath and listened, hoping to hear footfalls or movement, but there was nothing.

The Russian was gone. His body didn't stir.

So, she waited. Diving for the front door would leave her sitting out in the open. At least behind the minicar she had a chance. Right?

But the longer she waited, the more it felt like it was just her and the dead man.

She stood slowly, risking it, and nothing happened. She surveyed the neighborhood, and it was still and silent. She ran over to the Russian, skidding on the ground, the asphalt ripping through her pants and scraping her knees, patting him down for anything that might be useful, and coming back with nothing.

Even weirder was the wound. Blaster burns tended to look gnarly—black, charred. The wound on the Russian's neck was clean, cauterized. What the hell would have done that? Even suppressors made enough of a pop that she should have heard it.

She only knew one thing to be true.

One very, very bad thing.

She was in way over her head, and she didn't know which way was up.

Back at Timony's apartment, the number just rang.

Timony debated trying again. Debated getting out of her empty shower tub. Debated eating something. But nothing made sense anymore. Nothing felt safe.

She got up and moved to the sink, hoping some cold water would wake her up. What came out of the tap was lukewarm and tinted slightly brown. She sighed and turned off the faucet.

Her apartment was pitch-black except for the gleam of her cell phone. She could hear the gurgling of the pipes. It sounded a little like the sounds the Russian had made in his final moments of life.

There was no need for her to stick around. After coming up with nothing on the body, she'd run—through Little Havana, down side streets, and finally back to the tram home. She'd taken the long way back, too. Switching trains. Stopping in stores. She knew she'd been clean. The Russian had been following her, but whoever killed him hadn't been, as far as she could tell.

Timony picked up a few bottles of cheap bodega wine—her hands shaking, to her surprise, as she tapped her phone to pay. Now she was here in the relative safety of her tiny apartment, dialing and redialing the one sliver of a clue Oneida had left her: the number of a man named Carvajal, who Oneida seemed to think could help her get into the Bazaar's security files and get to the bottom of what had happened on the *Mosaic*. And maybe, if she was lucky, help her understand what had happened to Adan in the process.

After her fifteenth attempt, Timony started to flick the phone off. Then she heard it. A jostling sound, followed by a long sigh.

"Yeah?"

"Is this Carvajal?" Timony asked.

The sound of fabric scraping against a microphone.

"Who is this?" the voice asked. "Who gave you this number?"

"I need your help with something," Timony said. "Something sensitive, important, and, well—lucrative. For you."

That last part, Timony could figure out.

The voice was quiet for a few beats.

"How did you get this number?"

"A friend suggested you," Timony said. Not a lie, and it didn't implicate Oneida.

"I've got you here. Corin Timony," he said. "Correct?"

Timony cursed under her breath. She used to be good at this shit. She should have called through a relay.

"I need your help with something," she said, avoiding his question. "I can pay."

A hissing sound from the other side, like a pot about to boil.

"Why should I help you, lady?" Carvajal said, his voice judgmental and almost musical in its delivery. "Your name, it's bad. It's flagged. You're causing trouble. I can't touch that. I don't want to get burned, okay?"

"Flagged?" Timony asked. "What does that even mean?"

"What do you think it means?" Carvajal said. "Whoever gave you my info didn't know enough about you. You're lucky you're alive. Don't contact me again."

Timony started to answer, but the dial tone overshadowed her voice. She stared at the phone screen until it flicked to black. A dead end.

Okay, she thought. *What do I know?*

Had Oneida gone rogue when she passed Carvajal to Timony? Or was Tobin using Oneida as a cutout to get

Timony info he couldn't be seen handling? If the senator was trying to play puppeteer, it'd been a clumsy move. Either way, Tobin, with Oneida or not, had burned a contact and tipped off some bad actors that Timony was sniffing around them. Not ideal, considering Timony was still trying to figure out who they were.

Then there was the case of the dead Russian. Cut down by a weapon that was a few steps past military grade. What could have done that? Who fired it?

She couldn't say for sure. But the murder squared with something else.

Timony wasn't in the mix anymore. She didn't hear things firsthand. But some chunks of intelligence are so strong, they survive—and trickle down slowly from the agents to their assistants and staff. The one persistent bit of intel Timony kept getting reappeared in her mind now, like a puzzle piece clicking into place. Whispers about a black site space station just beyond Pluto, in an uncharted region of dark space, where advanced weaponry was being developed outside the watchful eyes of Interstellar Union inspectors. The US contingent of the Bazaar was worried. Because if the rumors were true, someone was stockpiling ammo that could threaten the entire balance of power. The US only liked that happening when they were driving.

And if the rumors were to be believed, the whole operation was being funded by the Chinese.

The picture was getting clearer in Timony's mind. But what she was seeing wasn't good at all.

ESPARAR ORBIT

MOSAIC
OBSERVATION DECK

Normally, Carriles loved it up here.

The view from the *Mosaic*'s observation deck was breathtaking. A widescreen look at endless space, in the highest definition possible. Carriles hated the outdated term, but if there was ever such a thing, this was his happy place.

Quiet. Peaceful. Sprawling.

The observation deck was the opposite of every other part of the ship, which often felt like a rickety tin can being tossed across a field—loaded with people experiencing every shade of every emotion at the exact same time. No privacy. No room to breathe. Just endless noise and tension.

Sometimes Carriles thought this was why he wanted to be a pilot. He wanted to see this endless space—wanted to experience it firsthand. He'd always been this way. He wasn't a book guy. As technical as piloting was, he wasn't a numbers or equipment guy, either. Lucky for him, that stuff came naturally to him. All he knew was he wanted a ship. He wanted to fly. So he did.

But this felt bittersweet. Because Carriles was doing all the things he loved, except the most important one: flying the ship.

He scanned the control panel in front of him, watched the tiny red blinking dot move slowly toward Esparar's inner orbit. In less than an hour, the *Mosaic* crew—from the US and China—would be landing on the planet. Exploring. And it wouldn't be Carriles who would get them there.

What's a ship's pilot if he doesn't . . . pilot the ship?

"What's the saying?" a voice asked him from behind. "Penny for your thoughts?"

Carriles turned around to find Chief Medical Officer Liu standing behind him, a slight smile on her face. Carriles didn't know Liu well, but what he did know he liked. Though she was probably a few years younger than Carriles, the medic commanded respect—every word she spoke seemingly thought-out and careful. Her track record, too, was impeccable. Even just a few years into active service, Liu had done her time and earned her stripes. She'd been on the front lines during the brief Martian civil wars right out of the academy and had earned every kind of commendation. What she lacked in experience she more than earned in bravery.

"Sorry, Doc, you snuck up on me," Carriles said.

"That implies intent, Lieutenant," Liu said, still smiling. She stepped up to the edge of the deck and looked out onto the wide view of space and Esparar. "It's magnificent, isn't it?"

"Yeah," Carriles said, struggling for words to reflect what he thought—and settling for something akin to a caveman's grunt. "It's . . . it's why I'm here, I think."

Carriles turned to Liu and saw her nod.

"It's amazing to think just a few decades ago we were hell-bent on destroying ourselves—leaving Earth as a giant piece of smoldering rubble. Now we're about to reach a planet outside our system," Liu said, her voice reverent. "It's a testament to human determination."

Carriles smiled. It was a nice sentiment. But Carriles couldn't bask in it. Something was wrong on the *Mosaic*. Something he couldn't yet figure out. Whatever it was didn't want them on the surface of Esparar. He looked at Liu and wondered just how much the ship's chief medical officer knew. And how she'd react if Carriles told her his side.

"Lieutenant, what's on your mind?" the doctor asked.

Carriles clicked his tongue—a delay tactic.

"I don't know how much I should say," he said, turning to face her, the huge sprawl of space behind them like a massive cloak. "But there's something weird going on."

Liu stared at him for what felt like a very long time. Carriles cleared his throat, wondering if he should break the silence. "Why are you digging into this?" she finally asked.

"I told you. Something isn't sitting right."

"No," she said. "Why are *you* digging into this?"

A little flash of anger flared through him. "What, the privileged goof-off son of a Martian senator? Look, no disrespect, but I'm getting a little tired of people reminding me what my place is in the world."

Liu looked down at the ground. She considered her words for a moment before nodding. "I don't mean this to be condescending. But you could just do your job and go home. No worse for wear. Why not just . . . allow that to be? Because the harder you push"—she nodded to the dropships—"the harder they're going to push back."

The memory came on him like a jolt. His senses flooded

by the experience. It'd been a little over two years ago that he'd buried his mom.

It had happened so fast. She'd been such a workaholic, and ignored the belly pain and weight loss until it was too late. It wasn't until she collapsed in the Statehouse that Carriles finally convinced her to see someone.

The news hit like a sledgehammer to his face. The doctors discovered an inoperable case of pancreatic cancer. There was nothing that could be done. They gave his mom a few months to live, if things went well.

Carriles felt his chest tighten at the memory. His mother had always been his rock. Reliable. Strong. Driven. Prone to bouts of anger and emotion, sure, but even those were always based in love. But after that day, she began to fade away. Carriles saw it each time he came to visit her in the hospital: Each time, a little piece of his mother seemed to be gone. Less hair. Lighter. Darkness under her eyes. A scratch in her throat. His mother was becoming a pile of dust eroded by the wind. He'd visit her daily. Sometimes for hours, other times he'd spend the night. Each time, though, it felt like he was seeing less of her. Little things were changing, disappearing. Her eyes were dimming. Her skin was blotched and dry. Her voice hoarse and alien-sounding. She was leaving this plane, and his heart broke each time he recognized it.

She died on a beautiful day. The kind of manufactured weather that almost felt real. But she'd never see it. Never feel the sun on her face or hear the sounds of the city again. She died quietly, whatever that was worth. A long, quiet death. A series of painful losses. A final stretch that someone of his mami's stature did not deserve. Carriles's hand had been woven through hers at the moment she took her last breath, a skeletal shell of the strong powerful woman she'd always been.

He wasn't sure how he had survived. If it hadn't been for Timony—

She'd been there for him from the minute he'd told her about the diagnosis. After his mother passed, Timony had immediately jumped into action to help ease the transition, and rode alongside him every step of the way. Through the arrangements, and then the funeral one sunny October day, and finally closing down Alamo later that night. As they sat at the bar, still decked in black, Timony ordered their final round at last call and said, "Your mom told me something once, and it really stuck with me."

Carriles had been in a haze and mumbled, "What?" through his sixth—maybe seventh?—vodka soda.

"Your mom was a tough lady," Timony said. "She took a lot of shit, but that's because she was one of the good ones. She was respected and admired by everyone. She was in it for the rights reasons. She reached out to me when I was struggling in the academy. I'd asked her how she handled it. She did that thing where she took my hand, and . . ." Timony choked up a little. ". . . and she said, *You can choose to do nothing or you can choose to do something, and it's always better to do something. You'll sleep better at night.*" Timony sat back and smiled. "I loved your mom, Jose. She was like the mom I never had. And what she said that night has been my North Star since. *Do something.* Don't know if I ever told you that."

"No," Carriles said. "You hadn't."

He'd been thankful to hear it. One more thing to know about his mom. But also, the way it differed just slightly from what she would say to him. She would softly stroke his face and say, *You can choose to do nothing, mijo, or you can choose to do something. You are my son, and I believe in you.*

For the last few years, the confidence he felt remembering those words was often blunted and offset by another memory. A vision of the day he was busted for selling Boost—an easy way to earn a little extra money, he'd thought at the time. He'd considered it harmless, but it had turned out to be toxic. It ruined so much, and had shaken him to his core. As much as he'd missed his mother after she passed, he had been glad she didn't live to see that.

Would she have still believed in him, after that?

Would she have forgiven him for not protecting Timony, who she'd also loved?

Carriles snapped back to the present, standing on the observation deck with Liu looking at him expectantly. He realized he'd been thinking so much about what was going on—the failed engines, the tampered wire, Delmar's half-truths, the mysterious weapons—that he hadn't stopped to think about why he couldn't let it go. Curiosity, sure, but Liu was right. It would be so much easier to just let things play out.

But the answer was simple. *Do something.*

It's what his mom would have done.

And it's what Timony would do.

They'd both *do* something. But how could he explain that?

"Because . . ." Carriles started to say, just as the hiss of the deck doors interrupted him. He and Liu pivoted to see Lieutenant Commander Vicks enter the observation deck, her footfalls heavy. Her eyes were on Carriles.

"Good evening," Vicks said, her tone efficient and

empty. "Dr. Liu, I'm happy to see you here. I've been looking for you."

She didn't seem happy, he thought.

"That's odd," Liu said, tilting her head slightly while stepping toward Vicks. "I didn't get a ping on my comms or at my terminal. I—"

"Please accompany me," Vicks said, moving toward the door. "Captain Delmar's orders."

Carriles watched Liu. Her shoulders were bunched, eyes wide. Something was off here, and she could tell, too.

"That's fine," Liu said. "I'll be there shortly. I was just talking to Lieutenant Carriles here, and—"

"No, the captain has asked me to find you immediately," Vicks said, folding her arms behind her back. "There is no time for delay."

What would Timony do?

Carriles stepped forward before he could stop himself.

"Delmar's on the transport ships," he said. "What's so urgent it can't wait until they're back? What's with all the cloak-and-dagger?"

Vicks looked at Carriles, and the beginning of a sneer formed on her angular, pale face.

"Please stand down, Lieutenant," she said, emphasizing Carriles's rank, which was a few rungs below hers. "This does not concern you."

He could feel the anger rising inside his chest. Before he knew what he was doing, the words came tumbling out of his mouth. "It sure as hell does, Vicks," Carriles said, stepping between Vicks and a surprised Liu. "There's something strange going on aboard this ship, and—"

But before Carriles could continue, his vision went black.

NEW DESTINY

DOWNTOWN

"I shouldn't be doing this."

Timony didn't look up from her pork dumplings as the man she knew only by the name of Chen slid into the empty seat next to her at the street-side stall in New Shanghai.

This was an inauspicious start to the conversation. She didn't know if Chen was his last name or his first. He didn't work in the Bazaar offices. If the state of geopolitics on New Destiny—specifically, China, the US, and Russia—were a Venn diagram, the Bazaar was the overlap. But that left large swaths of real estate that the powers couldn't keep tabs on. Chen was part of the shadow game that happened beyond the organization's walls. And in that game, he was her best contact on the Chinese side. The two of them had reached that uneasy détente that develops between spies working for opposing teams, offering just enough information to make meeting valuable, but not so much that either one of them would jeopardize their own interests. It was Cold War spycraft at its finest. You did just enough to prevent little things from turning into big things. No more, no less.

Chen and Timony had met like this before over the years. They communicated through an encrypted message system hidden within a chess app on their phones, and only ever used it to set meeting places. They put nothing else in writing. Timony thought meeting served both of their purposes. She figured Chen felt the same way. Most of the time.

From his posture, and his agitated demeanor, it was clear that this time he preferred to be anywhere else. But he'd shown up.

"You didn't have to come," she said, not looking at Chen.

She could've been talking to herself if her face was picked up by cameras. This was the game. Act like the person next to you was a complete stranger.

The man tending the stall came over, and he and Chen had a brief conversation in Mandarin before the chef retreated to a wok and got to work preparing whatever Chen had ordered. Underneath the din of the cooking equipment, Chen spoke.

"Heard you've had a week."

"From who?"

"C'mon. You called me," he said with a scoff, insulted. "By the time I'm done eating, I'm gone. What's up?"

Timony dove in. Time was limited.

"The *Mosaic* pilot who died. Adan. Wondering if China had a hand in that. Wanted to slot in their own pilot. And weapons. I'm looking for something that could cut through a person like a hot knife through butter."

The chef was quick. By the time Timony was done laying out what she needed, he'd placed a bowl of Mapo tofu and rice in front of Chen. Chen didn't wait for it to cool, just picked up his chopsticks and went to town. Between bites, he said, "We didn't touch your pilot boyfriend. No move from this side to replace him, either. Offensive suggestion." More chewing. "And the weapons thing? That shit's a rumor. A bad one."

Timony took one of her dumplings, dipped it in soy sauce, and gulped down the whole thing in one bite. "You're telling the truth about the first, using it as a smoke screen to lie about the second."

Chen nodded but didn't say anything, just kept horking down his meal. He was almost done.

"There's some bad shit going down," Timony said. "You know how this works. People like you and me do this dance so the people at the top don't go too far outside the tracks. So that we can live to dance tomorrow. I'm asking you directly—give me something. Help me. I've helped you. For old times' sake."

Chen finished the last of his tofu, then placed his finger on the scanner that would pay his bill. He got up and looked at Timony fully for the first time. She tried not to stare at the nasty scar raked down his left cheek. Timony knew he was one of the few people in this game she wouldn't want to square down with. He was dangerous in a way that most people wished they could be.

"If you want to find the cause of your suffering, look within," he said.

"That's some fortune cookie shit right there."

"That," he said, pointing a finger at her, "might be more than a little racist. You're welcome, Timony."

"I didn't mean it like that . . ." she started, but he was already out of earshot, the chimes ringing as the door swung outward.

Timony turned back to the counter and set about

finishing the last of her dumplings. Chen was being cute, but the message was clear.

Maybe she was worrying too much about the opposing teams, and not paying enough attention to her supposed teammates.

Granted, Chen might be trying to throw her off, too. She couldn't discount that.

But she couldn't ignore him, either.

Now here she was, doing the one thing she didn't want to do.

But she didn't have any other choice. Not that she could clearly see.

Timony strode into the lobby of the apartment complex, her sneakers squeaking on the linoleum floor. Besides the footwear, she'd dressed business casual: a loose-fitting blouse and a skirt she could move around in. She held a clipboard to her chest and marched forward with breezy determination.

Spycraft 101: Confidence and a clipboard can get you into a surprising number of places. People tend to think the job was all gadgets and rooftop stakeouts, but really it was mostly vamping. Making it seem like you belonged went a long way.

So she didn't risk a glance at the older man sitting behind the security desk. The clipboard offered an air of officiality, even though the only thing she had attached to it was a pile of take-out menus.

As she passed the desk, Timony smiled, reveling in that rush she always got when something went to plan.

"Miss?"

Timony sighed, reality crashing down.

Clipboards didn't *always* work.

She turned around and surveyed the man behind the desk. Heavyset, bald, with a bushy gray beard. His uniform was neat and tucked in, so he cared about his job, but the softness of his eyes made her think he wasn't the kind of guy who would bludgeon her with his authority.

"Are you here to see someone?" he asked.

"Yes," she said, making sure to tilt her head away from the camera in the corner, so it couldn't get a clear scan of her face. "I'm here to see a tenant about a listing."

The guard frowned, clumsily tapping the tablet in front of him. "I don't see anyone expecting any guests . . ."

Timony leaned over the desk a little, continuing to turn her head away from the camera so she'd be in silhouette, and clocked the man's name tag: Bill.

"So, Bill, listen, I shouldn't be telling you this, but the tenant I'm here to see, they're trying to break their lease. As I'm sure you can understand, this isn't something they want to advertise just yet . . ."

Bill gave her a hard stare. For a moment Timony wondered if she'd picked the wrong angle, and if she was going to have to come up with a new plan for getting inside. But Bill just sadly shook his head.

"I told the landlord, if he didn't take care of that heating issue, this is exactly what would happen." He looked around and offered a conspiratorial smile. "Serves him right. Maybe now he'll fix it. Hell, maybe he'll give the staff here some kind of raise. One bit of advice, though? Maybe next time don't meet with whoever you're meeting with here."

"How else am I going to take pictures of the apartment?"

Timony asked, offering a mischievous smile in return. "Thanks, Bill. Glad you get it."

The guard went back to his tablet and Timony hustled for the elevator, relieved to be away from the camera. No one had come in, and if they'd spotted her the response would have been swift. She was probably clear, for now.

She hopped into the waiting elevator car and hit the button for the third floor. When the door opened, she got out and quickly moved to the left underneath the camera outside the elevator bank. She rifled through her bag and came out with a small magnetic device the size of a quarter. She balanced it on her palm and softly tossed it toward the underside of the camera, where it stuck.

She crossed the hallway to apartment 3A, and placed another magnet toward the top of the doorjamb, where she knew the laser trip was. With that disabled too, she got to work raking the lock. It popped easily and she stepped into the apartment.

Once she was safely inside, she pulled a small remote out of her pocket and hit the button.

The circuits in both of the jammers she placed instantly fried; they'd stay stuck where they were, but both the laser trip and the camera would come back online. And if she was lucky, whoever was monitoring security would write it off as a temporary outage. She could always go back and remove the devices, but they were untraceable to her. Standard Bazaar tech she had swiped from the office years ago. The kind of stuff spies took home, like most people took home boxes of pencils and tape.

The apartment was dark and quiet, but tidy. More like a staged apartment than someplace someone actually lived. She moved through the kitchen–living room combo until she made it to the bedroom, and found the bookshelf, full of the kind of hardcover books that someone would own for display, not for reading. She reached up to the top shelf, to a copy of *Foundation* by Isaac Asimov, and pulled it back.

The bookshelf swung out, revealing a steel door behind it. This one didn't have any security on it, besides the lock; someone probably decided it wasn't worth the added expense. The apartment was a cover, a way to covertly get people in and out of the Bazaar building, right next door. They probably figured that anyone who made it through the initial layers of security was probably fine.

Saved by the bean counters.

Now she just had to make it down to the bowels of the building, to the secondary server system. The main computer terminals didn't have access to the more sensitive information she needed to get her hands on. The Bazaar was an important building, but it wasn't overflowing with staff. If Timony played it right, timed her movements, she'd not only avoid electronic detection, she wouldn't run into any flesh-and-blood obstacles, either.

It should be easy enough: through the door, which opened within seconds to her rake lock pick, through the janitor's closet, into the stairwell, and straight down to the basement. Then through a security cage. The rest, she would figure out.

They'd find out eventually, she was sure. There was going to be fallout.

She didn't care.

Between the Russian's death last night, the revelation that Adan's death might not have been an accident, Osman's death, whatever was going on inside the Bazaar around that mysterious message from the *Mosaic*, and the possibility that all these things were somehow connected, she couldn't just sit around. If you're not moving when the bodies start falling, you're in the line of fire. She'd learned as much over the years. And after Carvajal, who Oneida intimated was an ally, had tipped her off that someone might want her dead, she was finally and truly at the worst point someone in her position could be in: she had no idea who to trust.

She descended the stairs, listening for any doors, and when one opened below her, she waited for the voices to recede and another door to slam before proceeding. At the bottom of the stairs, she checked to make sure the path was clear, then made her way down a long hallway, toward the desk at the end, where the guard on duty was staring intently into a tablet.

She looked at the thumb scanner on the wall. If it registered hers, it'd be flagged. She poked at it a few times with her knuckle and said, "This stupid thing doesn't seem to be working."

The guard sighed, put down his tablet, and walked around his desk, all without looking at her. She braced herself, ready to grab him by the back of his neck, drive his head into the wall, and render him unconscious, then use his thumb to open the door. It wasn't neat, and it wasn't nice, but she was desperate.

Sometimes you know exactly what you need to complete a puzzle. Other times, you just dive in and hope to stumble upon a clue. This was definitely the latter.

But at least she knew where to start.

Or rather, with whom.

The guard leaned down and peered at the panel, and pressed his own finger to the display. It lit up green and the door opened.

"Seems to be working fine," he said, annoyed, before returning to the desk.

Ah, the wonders of social engineering. Timony let out a breath she didn't realize she was holding.

"Thanks. What's your name?"

"Harris," he said, his attention back at the tablet.

"Thanks, Harris."

She made a mental note once this was all done and settled to make sure he got fired. Her gratitude only went so far; that was a major breach of protocol.

The secondary server room was frigid—the low temperature meant to keep the equipment from overheating. Timony's breath bloomed in front of her as she sat at the closest terminal and logged in using Slade's username and password.

Luckily, Slade hadn't changed it.

This was bad. And probably incredibly stupid.

There'd be a notification upstairs that Slade was signing in, which you generally needed advance permission to do. They'd call Slade to see what was up and find out she wasn't here. Timony had five minutes, maybe, before someone came down to see what was going on.

She flipped through the back end until she got to the *Mosaic* files, and was able to branch off that to find the report on Adan's death, and then the autopsy.

Timony had a feeling in her gut that understanding this would start knocking over dominoes.

Or maybe she was just angry and sentimental.

It wasn't an electronic file, it was a scan of a physical piece of paper, which was rare. And it was redacted, heavy black lines blanking out most of the details. She dropped the picture into a photo editor as she checked her watch—three minutes to go—then futzed with the transparency and vibrancy of the image until she could make out the print that was underneath.

Adan had six hundred milligrams of Boost in his system.

Adan, who didn't like to drink coffee after noon.

She was running out of time. She clicked out of the terminal, gathered her things, and headed for the door. Better not go out the same way she came in. She could risk the alarms on the roof, use a drainpipe to climb back to the building next door, then downstairs and out . . .

Timony opened the door and found herself face-to-face with Slade.

"Hey there," Slade said.

Timony's shoulders slumped. She should have known that this was the endgame. But she was getting desperate and desperate meant dumb. That, plus the rust that had collected around her every joint and muscle since she'd been put out to pasture, left her here.

"Come with me," Slade said, before brusquely turning and leading Timony over to the elevator.

Once inside, the two of them rode up in silence before stepping off into the main offices. The place was empty—surprising for this time of day—which made Timony wonder what was going on.

Slade stopped in front of an interrogation room—the same one Timony had been in the other night—and opened the door. She was about to speak when a Klaxon went off and a white strobe light erupted from terminals placed around the walls.

Lockdown.

"Jesus," Timony said. "All this for me?"

But Slade's face was etched with concern. "I was trying to keep this quiet. Get inside."

Timony stepped into the room and Slade slammed the door behind her. She tried the handle, but it was locked. So, Timony sat heavily on a chair, the alarm hammering her eardrums, waiting for whatever came next.

Hopefully, it would get her closer to the truth about Adan and not just disciplined—or worse.

Adan had a habit of leaving his socks on the bathroom floor. He could never find anything in the fridge even when it was right in front of him, and he often forgot to lock the front door at night. But he also carefully measured out everything he ate to track his protein intake and would use the toothpaste tube down to the final glob. He was methodical about what went into his body.

Six hundred milligrams. A regular Boost user couldn't tolerate more than thirty before going into cardiac arrest.

She pictured Adan. His smooth, tan face. His chiseled features. His dark eyes. They twisted in Timony's mind as she imagined the Boost taking over. She watched his expression spasm. His jaw clench. Teeth grind together. She felt, in the split second that she let her imagination wander down the dark alley, everything.

Every jolt of pain.

Every rush of energy.

Then darkness.

Was that what happened, Adan?

Even the most addled junkies stop themselves before this point. There's no way it could have built up, either. Boost cleared the system quickly. Which meant it wasn't done gradually.

Someone had given it to him.

MOSAIC

BRIG

Waking up was like breaking the surface of a dark lake. Carriles gasped for air and blinked, trying to get his bearings. His brain was muddy, his head throbbed—a slow, dull ache. The last thing he remembered . . . what did he remember? A pinch on the side of his neck? Had Vicks dosed him with something?

Whatever it was, his brain still felt like a bowling ball, hard and heavy inside his skull. Whatever she had done had been fast and focused.

Vicks. He felt sheepish now, but he'd always admired the lieutenant commander. Hell, he'd even harbored some kind of crush on the distant, almost robotic senior officer. Part of him wanted to get through to her. To crack that veneer and make her laugh.

God, he was such a mess, he thought.

He blinked again and took stock of where he was: the brig. A small holding cell with a bunk and glass door. Across the way was another identical cell, holding Liu, who perked up when she realized he was awake.

"It was a fast-acting anesthetic," Liu said, her voice muffled after traveling through two sets of glass. "She swiped it from the med bay. You should be fine in a few minutes. Just don't stand up too quick."

He tried to talk but found the words were thick and viscous in his mouth. "What . . . the hell . . ."

"At this point, your guess is as good as mine," Liu said.

The lights were drilling into Carriles's eyes, so he closed them and rubbed his palms against his face, trying to ground himself. After a moment he felt a little more clear and risked sitting up. A wave of nausea came on quickly, then passed.

"You're not hurt, are you?" Carriles asked.

Liu shook her head. "You?"

Carriles stood, giving himself a moment to steady himself on his feet. "Still trying to figure that out. Vicks brought us here?"

"She did," Liu said. "I didn't see anyone else or hear anything helpful. It happened fast."

"What about the landing team on Esparar?"

"No idea," Liu said, motioning toward the glass.

Carriles paced the small room. The brig wasn't meant for long-term incarceration. There was a small sink and toilet bolted into the wall, but as far as he knew neither of the rooms had been occupied during the course of the *Mosaic*'s journey. They were a just-in-case thing, like if someone got a little too rowdy, a glorified drunk tank or time-out. The crew had been vetted and was trusted enough that no one expected they would be necessary.

Vetted and trusted.

That's what Carriles had thought, too.

He banged his fist on the glass and shouted, "Hey,"

hoping someone would hear. Liu shook her head. "Tried that. You were really out before. Either they can't hear us or they don't want to hear us."

"Great," Carriles said, sitting heavily on the bed. "Guess we should just get comfortable."

"I guess so," Liu said.

They sat in silence for some time, Carriles trying to get his wits about him as the sedative wore off. Then something occurred to him.

"Hey, while we're waiting, what were you talking to Delmar about?"

"What do you mean?" Liu asked.

"Earlier, you were in his quarters," Carriles said. "When you came out, you just seemed a little upset."

Liu drew her knees up to her chest, like she wanted to make herself smaller. After a long pause, she said, "I asked a question I shouldn't have asked."

"And what was that?"

She shook her head. "I learned my lesson."

Carriles got up and walked to the glass in an attempt to lower his voice but still be heard. "I don't trust them, either. You can tell me."

She stared at him for a few moments, as if she was trying to figure out if that was true. Finally, she shrugged and said, "I came across a large stash of stat injectors."

"What are those?"

"It's a device that looks like a syringe. It's packed with an antibacterial expandable cotton. If someone gets hurt, like they get shot, you put it into the wound and depress it. It releases the sponges, which expand and stop the bleeding."

"Sounds like a fairly standard medical device," Carriles said.

"It is," Liu said. "For a military operation. We had tons of them. More than we needed. I thought it was a mistake, but also, it made me nervous. Like someone was expecting something bad to happen on this mission. I brought my concerns to Vicks, who brought me to Delmar, who told me that if I shared that information with anyone it would be considered mutiny. And you know what mutiny gets you out here."

Carriles didn't want to say it, but he knew.

Mutiny meant, if you were lucky, you got to test out the brig.

If you weren't, you'd get marched through an air lock.

"So what you're saying is . . . someone expects to get in a firefight," Carriles said, trying to work it out. "Do you think this is hostility between the US and China? Like one side was planning to wipe out the other?"

"I have no idea," Liu said. "All I know is that I'm the chief medical officer, I was in charge of supplying the ship with med supplies, and I had no record of these things being acquisitioned. I found them completely by accident. Remember that case of strep that went through the ship at the end of the first month? I had to go through most of our antibiotics. I was digging through the medical hold looking for more, and stumbled across them."

Carriles suddenly wondered if he was safer in the cell.

But something scratching at the back of his brain said: Probably not.

Almost anyone else on the *Mosaic* would have been stuck in here, forced to sit and wait to be let out. But Carriles knew this ship. Had memorized every corner of it. His strengths were nuts and bolts. Schematics. Flight patterns. Coordinates. If he was into it, he was into all of it.

And Carriles was really into the *Mosaic*.

He had dreamed of the ship—taking it apart and putting it together. He felt as if the *Mosaic*'s blueprints were burned into his brain.

He dropped to the floor, feeling under the bunk for the access panel he knew was set somewhere in the wall. He finally found it, his fingers brushing the screws that held it in place. He patted down his uniform and found his pocketknife, which thankfully Vicks hadn't thought to remove, and set to work on undoing the screws.

"What are you doing?" Liu asked.

"Getting us out of here."

"Are you sure that's a good idea?"

"Maybe not," Carriles said as the first screw gave way. "Let's find out."

The second screw was slightly more out of reach and he had to stretch to get it, and he ruined the tip of his knife in the process, but he didn't care. With the panel off, he leaned down and could just see into the small opening it created, where a series of wires ran. He didn't recognize them all, but he quickly found the one he needed.

Blue.

Blue was for power.

He yanked it, hard, at the last moment realizing that it could kill the power to the room and leave the doors closed, potentially leaving them trapped, but it was too late. It was already free, and the lights clicked off, followed quickly by red emergency lighting.

The cell doors quietly slid open.

Exactly what he was hoping for. A fail-safe, because when you're in space it's not great to leave people trapped when the power goes out.

He hustled into the hallway and went out of Liu's door. She seemed reluctant to come off her cot.

"You can stay here if you feel safer," Carriles said. "But I'm headed to the bridge."

"To do what?"

"To ask Vicks what the hell is going on."

He reached his hand out to her. She lingered for a moment, before grasping it and allowing him to pull her to her feet. The two of them made it out of the holding room, and the next hallway was perfectly lit: pulling the wire, it seemed, had only killed the power to the brig. Carriles hoped it hadn't set off any alarms.

The ship was desolate, their footsteps echoing down the winding corridors that mirrored the *Mosaic*'s sleek design. It felt eerie—the once-bustling vessel now felt lifeless and inert. By the time they reached the bridge, Carriles realized they hadn't come across anyone on their way.

Carriles steeled himself as he opened the door, expecting to find Vicks sitting at the console, tracking the on-planet team. He didn't know what he was going to say, but he'd figure it out.

Instead, he opened the door to find the bridge in a panic.

It was packed with probably everyone who was still left on the ship. There was a loud screeching sound—a transmission from the Esparar team—and then the sound of gunfire.

Delmar's voice came through the static.

"The indigenous species is a little tougher than we thought. Send down the weapons resupply."

Next to him, Liu whispered, "Indigenous?"

Carriles couldn't respond.

He had no idea what to say.

But a lot of things were starting to make sense.

NEW DESTINY

BAZAAR HEADQUARTERS

“You have to disentangle yourself from this, Corin.”

Slade’s words hung between them in the cold, bland room inside the Bazaar. Timony had never heard Slade use her first name like that. It felt weird. Fake. Calculating.

“Disengage from Adan and Osman being murdered?” Timony said, tilting her head slightly, as if to get a clearer view of a strange object. “Are you not hearing what you just said?”

Slade sighed. Timony watched as her former colleague—former student—paced around the room, her eyes on the ground. Timony knew Slade. Knew her better than most anyone. She was a potent mix of by-the-book and just plain talented, the perfect combination for someone looking to climb the ranks and become more than a soldier or middle manager of spycraft.

But this was a side she’d never seen. Slade was conflicted—still processing what was going on—and Timony could see the wheels turning in her mind. She wasn’t sure she liked it.

"Yes, Adan was murdered," Slade said, as if speaking the words to herself for the first time—as if she was also learning this truth as Timony did. "But you have to leave this alone. There's no winning going down this hole, okay? I know you're upset. I know you feel like the Bazaar fucked you over, but you're just getting deeper and deeper into the shit. There are much bigger things happening, and Adan isn't one of them. Just let it go."

"What has *you* spooked?"

"What?" Slade asked, looking up at Timony.

"You're scared," Timony said. "And I have never seen you scared. You're the one who makes other people scared. But something is going on and it has you shaking. What in the world could do that?"

Slade leaned over the long table that stood between her and Timony.

"I don't have answers on Adan," she said. "I wish I did, if only to just get you off my back. All I have are my suspicions, which are worthless without evidence. You know that. You're not that far gone."

Far gone. It was the kind of language they'd used together in the past to describe an agent who'd lost their way. Not a traitor, but someone who'd spiraled so far into a role, into an assignment, that they'd forgotten the mission and who they were. They'd become the cover.

Except Timony didn't have cover. She was just lost.

She didn't like that feeling.

"Tell me your suspicions," Timony said. She felt a weakness in her voice. A slight desperation. "And let me confirm them."

Slade caught the crack in Timony's voice, too. Saw a flash of empathy on Slade's face. It didn't help. It made

Timony feel even lesser, like a broken agent desperate to recapture the glory days. A washed-up prizefighter desperate for one more shot at the champ.

Slade cleared her throat.

"I think it's the Chinese," Slade said, each word dripping out of her mouth slowly. "Adan was a US pilot. It follows that with him gone, they could slot in their own pilot. They weren't counting on your friend Carriles. Honestly, I don't think anyone was. He's the wild card. Somehow, someone got him in there, and it threw everything off."

The opposite of what Chen told her.

He could have been lying. But there was something about Slade's words that felt a little too tidy, so she followed a hunch.

"Don't bullshit me," Timony said. "Adan is part of it. Of all the anomalies related to the *Mosaic*—the distress signal, whatever's going on with the Russians . . . he was the first."

"What does it even matter?" Slade asked. "Dead is dead."

Timony slammed her fist on the table. "I'm not going to sit around and do nothing."

Slade scoffed.

"Guess you haven't changed that much."

Timony looked down. She felt a slight smile forming on her face.

"I'll always be me."

"Then let me finish," Slade said as Timony looked up. "Follow my thought. So, China takes out Adan. In comes Carriles. Problem for everyone. Let's step back to Adan. Who clued China in that Adan had to go? Who had enough intel to be problematic for the US side? Who had a grudge?"

Timony let out a humorless laugh.

There it was. The hammer dropping. Timony was so wrapped up trying to figure out who was involved in Adan's death—and, in turn, everything else, she didn't stop to think that people might be thinking the same thing about her.

"You can't be serious?"

Slade raised an eyebrow as she stepped closer to Timony.

"You'd think the same thing if you were in my shoes. What's the old line from Sherlock Holmes?"

"*If you eliminate the impossible, no matter how improbable*, or whatever? That's the truth."

"Right," Slade said.

"You think just because I got demoted I would betray everything I'd worked toward—immediately? Just scorch my entire life over some grudges?" Timony asked. "Look, this business is messy. We make tough choices every damn day. But our fallback is we're doing the right thing, the right way. Our side is making the tough choices to survive. That's not something you just shrug off because you're sad. You know me better than that."

Slade shrugged. Timony had made her point.

"The Russians don't know what's going on either," Timony said. She was handing over a treat, a little nugget for Slade to chew on. But it was just out of reach. It was a show of goodwill, but it was also something else. Timony needed to get out, and this was her ticket.

Slade stepped closer. "What happened?"

"I was being followed by a Russian agent," Timony said. "That agent was murdered right before my eyes. Whoever he was, he wanted to know what I knew about the *Mosaic*. He knew something was fucked on that ship—knew something bad was happening. And he basically confirmed that the Russians had no idea what to do. Politically, this is bad for them. China and the US are steering this ship, literally and figuratively. The Russians are flailing a bit. I think they boxed themselves out of something important, or at least they think so."

Slade crossed her arms. Timony could see her processing the sliver of intel.

"This is bigger than I thought," Slade said.

"You think?"

Slade looked toward the door, out into the office, mulling it over. Finally, it seemed as though something about what Timony had said seemed to get through to her. Something she didn't already know. Sometimes that's all it took: plant the seed of doubt.

"Don't make me regret this," Slade said.

Timony didn't respond. She waited. She knew when to let someone pull themselves along.

"I'm going to forget you were here," Slade said as she looked Timony over, as if to say, *Do you understand?* "But you have to return the favor. You have to keep your eyes and ears open for me. Don't run around half-cocked trying to figure this out on your own, okay? We can work together. You feed me what you know, and I'll work my angles. I can't promise you anything—but if this works out, I can put in a good—"

Before Slade could finish, the room went dark.

"The hell?" Slade said.

"The lights—" Timony said.

"I know the lights are out—"

"No, look under the door," Timony said in a hushed whisper. "The lights are out in the whole office."

Slade cracked the door open as quietly as she could.

And they both caught sight of small moving lights scanning the floor.

"Get down," Slade said, and hit the ground. Timony followed suit. She heard Slade sliding her body closer to Timony. Felt Slade's hand tap her shoulder.

"Listen to that," Slade whispered. "Listen to them talking."

Timony did. What she heard froze her in place.

The men were speaking Russian.

MOSAIC

BRIDGE

Vicks came out of nowhere, lunging for Liu. Carriles pushed the doctor out of Vicks's path and slammed his shoulder into the senior officer's body, stopping her momentum. The stoic woman stumbled back, her dark eyes locked on Carriles and Liu.

"These two are seditionists," Vicks said, her voice raised but calm, not looking away from Carriles. The other bridge crew turned to look at them—but only briefly. Whatever was unfolding in front of them paled to the shock and confusion over what was happening down on Esparar.

Vicks's face twisted in fury and she raised her voice: "They need to be taken in. Immediately."

"What the hell is going on, Vicks?" Carriles asked, taking a half step toward her. He caught sight of Liu on the periphery of his vision. She was watching Vicks as well, braced for another attack. "There's a lot here you haven't told us, and clearly we're all at risk."

Vicks shook her head—almost as much to herself as to Carriles and Liu. She didn't want to say. Couldn't say.

"This is an order," Vicks said, speaking to the entire bridge crew, casting as wide a net as she could. "Take these two to the brig. And this time, someone stays with them and holds them under armed guard."

One of the junior officers, a US contingent member named Penagos, looked up from the science station. "With all due respect, Commander, that's our pilot and chief medic." His voice shook from the act of defiance. "We might need them."

Vicks turned her attention to the recalcitrant officer now, which was just the opening Liu was looking for. The doctor leapt toward Vicks, a hypoport in her hand. The soft hiss of contact as the device connected with Vicks's neck sent a wave of relief through Carriles.

A moment later, Vicks was slumped on the ground.

"Same thing she hit you with," Liu said, hovering over the fallen senior officer. "She'll be out for a few minutes. Long enough to secure her."

Carriles let Liu take care of that as he turned to the rest of the crew.

"You all need to hang tight," he said. "Something strange is going on and we're going to figure it out."

A voice rang out from somewhere in the room. Carriles couldn't be sure who said it, but the words seemed to speak for everyone present: "Will someone please tell us what the *fuck* is going on?"

Everyone looked back and forth between each other, waiting for someone else to answer.

Carriles knew how they all looked at him. Some rich kid who privileged his way into one of the best jobs in the universe. For the past three months, it had been impossible to escape the feeling that none of these people took him very seriously. The spin maneuver had bought him some cred, but he could only push that so far.

Fine. This wasn't the time to worry about his Q rating.

"We're going down to the brig," Carriles said, speaking slowly and clearly, not wanting anyone to misunderstand what was happening. "We're going to talk to Lieutenant Commander Vicks. Together, we'll figure out a plan. For now, sit tight. Keep an eye on the drop teams and keep me and Liu posted on any new developments, all right?"

More nods. A few awkward glances exchanged.

That would have to do.

Liu had lashed Vicks's hands behind her back with a zip tie. The senior officer was teetering on her feet, semiconscious. Carriles and Liu hustled her off the bridge, Vicks hanging between them like she was on the bad end of a bender. When they reached the brig, Liu held up Vicks while Carriles reactivated the chambers. He helped Liu drag Vicks into Liu's old cell. Before stepping out, Liu cut the zip tie and snapped a small vial under Vicks's nose. She backpedaled out of the cell and watched the doors hiss closed behind her.

Vicks's eyes shot open and she shook her head vigorously, like she was trying to get something out of her hair.

"What was that?" Carriles asked the medical officer.

"You need her to be alert, no?" Liu asked.

Carriles smiled. He was starting to like Liu. She didn't mess around.

Vicks stood up in one swift motion. She didn't bang on the glass. She didn't demand to be let out. And luckily, she must not have known the ship as well as Carriles did. She just stood there on the other side of the glass, seething.

"There will be consequences for this," Vicks said, her voice flat and distant.

"Vicks, let's drop all the bullshit, okay?" Carriles said. "What the hell is going on down there? Delmar said there were indigenous people. We were told the planet was uninhabited. Doesn't that seem like a big deal? Because from my perch, you don't seem as surprised as everyone else up there."

Vicks said nothing, her eyes focused on something in the distance. She was shutting down, he thought.

"Here's what I know," Carriles said. "Someone fucked with the ship. We're stocked up on combat medicine and we had a bunch of mercenaries heading down to Esparar. And there are clearly conversations happening behind closed doors that were meant to be kept there. This is starting to feel a lot different than the mission we were sold on."

Vicks began to speak, and then shook her head.

"You don't have to be a part of whatever is happening," Carriles said. "You're a good officer. Your rep is impeccable."

Carriles knew this was a strong move. Play to her ego. Whatever worked.

"Delmar is my commanding officer," Vicks said, still not making eye contact.

Was there a crack in her voice, just there? Carriles thought there might have been.

"That's bullshit," Liu said. Carriles almost jumped at the doctor's surprising interjection. "I know there's a chain of command, but our captain isn't a king—he's a delegate. We serve the Interstellar Union and its bylaws. The second the captain deviates from that, it's up to us to say something. So, do it. Stand up for yourself and say something."

It seemed, to Carriles, that Vicks was about to, when a chime cut through the brig.

"Lieutenant Carriles," Penagos said, his voice hesitant.

"What is it?" Carriles said, tapping a button on the nearest terminal. "How's it going up there?"

"Uh, well, fine, sir—but we have an update that I think you would want to hear, seeing as how you're the senior officer—I guess?" he said.

Carriles waited for Penagos to continue.

"One of our ships is coming back," Penagos said. He sounded stilted, as if confused by the words he was speaking. "Delmar's. It's coming back to the *Mosaic*."

"What about the other one?" Carriles asked, leaning closer to the speaker. "What about the Chinese shuttle?"

"I'm not sure, sir—hold on, we're patching in Captain Delmar. Shall I connect you?"

Carriles's entire body braced. Liu's and Vicks's stares bore into him. This was a pivot point. If he took the captain's call, he was admitting he was in charge—and how he got to be in charge. It was no longer business as usual.

It was a hostage negotiation.

But who had the hostages?

"Yes, patch him through," Carriles said.

A burst of static. Then a muffled voice.

"Carriles? What the fuck is going on up there?" Delmar said, his voice rising with each word. "Where's Vicks? Put her on."

"Vicks is in the brig, sir," Carriles said matter-of-factly. "She attacked your chief medic. She also put me in the brig before that."

A pause on the other end. More static.

"I'm sure Vicks had her reasons," Delmar said, his anger still front and center. "We're coming into the docking bay now. I want you, Vicks, and Liu to meet us here so we can hash out what's going on. Okay, son? We can still fix this. We can still—"

"What happened to that other ship, Captain?" Carriles asked, interrupting Delmar.

"The Chinese?" Delmar asked, knowing the answer. "They're gone. Like I said, I'll share my intel once we've docked, and we can get this—"

Carriles cut the connection.

"What are you doing?" Vicks asked, her cool veneer cracking. She was worried and impressed all at once. No one hung up on Captain Delmar. No one who wanted to keep their jobs.

Or, at this point, their lives.

Carriles ignored Vicks. She was useless to him now. He paged the bridge again.

"Penagos, it's Carriles," he said. "Can you connect me to the docking bay security terminal?"

Penagos hesitated a moment, then spoke.

"Yes sir, but we have a ship about to dock right now," he stammered. "Is there something I can do?"

"I want you to let the ship dock," Carriles said. "But do not, under any circumstances, allow anyone off that shuttle. Understood?"

The long pause from Penagos's side told Carriles that the young officer did not fully understand.

"I know this is fucked up, okay?" Carriles said. "This is less than ideal, right? A lieutenant is asking you to lock the ship's captain on a shuttle. But you have to see that something here is even more fucked up, and we need to figure it out."

Another pause. For a moment, Carriles was certain he'd lost the young crewman.

"Shuttle has landed," Penagos finally said, "and I've activated emergency containment procedures. The doors can only be opened from the outside. I have advised the crew on board."

Before Carriles could thank Penagos, the line was dead.

But it wasn't quiet for long.

"You are in deep shit, Carriles," Delmar said—his voice crashing through the speaker. "You hear me? Your career is over. You have crossed the one line that your last name can't pull you back from. I'm a fair man, and I was happy to bring you aboard this ship, despite the fact that you're basically a goddamn criminal. I took a chance on you, son. It's now one I regret, and I'll have to take it with me to the grave."

Carriles shook his head.

A few days ago, words like that from someone as celebrated as Delmar would have cut him straight to his core.

Today, though?

Delmar was lying. And those lies put lives at risk.

Until he saw the full picture, he would choose to ignore Delmar's illustrious pedestal.

He turned to see Vicks, stone-faced, and Liu, lips pursed in anticipation.

Carriles needed time. He needed to think. And he knew whatever evidence was on this ship—whatever clues existed that could help him figure out just what the hell was going on down at the surface of Esparar—would be destroyed the second Delmar returned. The captain was complicit, and Carriles had to figure out what was happening before things got worse.

"Just a minor inconvenience, Captain," Carriles said. "More soon. Carriles out."

He pushed the red button and ended the call.

Probably, his career.

Perhaps, his life.

NEW DESTINY

BAZAAR HEADQUARTERS

Timony slowed her breathing. If she breathed too deeply, it might give away their position, tucked behind a cubicle on the other side of the office. Slade seemed to be doing the same. The two of them looked at each other, and all the tension and conflict suddenly evaporated.

To two spies, the only thing that mattered was the work.

And surviving long enough to keep doing it.

This was one of the first lessons Timony had imparted to Slade, and she was glad to see her protégé still remembered.

This wasn't a friendly visit. You don't cut the lights and walk around with flashlights if you're looking for someone to grab lunch with. The Russians stalking through the Bazaar's corridors were most certainly armed, and they probably thought the floor was clear. This was not the moment to startle them.

The other option was to fight fire with fire. But they didn't have much fire. Besides the knife in her boot, Timony was unarmed, and she could tell from the lay of Slade's skin-hugging outfit that the woman wasn't carrying a blaster.

Timony held her hands in fists, palms facing up, and spread out her fingers, communicating her question—*How many?*—in American Sign Language. Timony had insisted that Slade learn ASL, for moments exactly like this.

Slade cocked her ear. Then she alternated holding up three and four fingers.

Okay, three or four. Slade and Timony were outnumbered, but only if the Russians sent their A-team.

Timony briefly wondered what the ASL sign for "I told you so" was, but now was not the time. She spelled out A-P-T with her hand. Slade nodded, and understood: *apartment*.

The Russians were coming in from the other side of the building, which should give Timony and Slade a clear pathway to the apartment—which the Russians shouldn't know about. Only the Americans knew about it: a crack in the veneer of the peace and harmony the Bazaar was supposed to stand for. If these outside agents knew about it, that meant Bazaar intel was being shared outside the org—violating the idea behind what the Bazaar was. That was the macro. The micro was the pathway, and Timony hoped these Russian agents didn't know about it.

The two women dropped to their hands and knees and crawled toward the other side of the office, cutting through the maze of cubicles, the errant beam of a flashlight occasionally dancing around them, but never landing. Timony strained to listen to their conversations—like any good agent, she understood some Russian—but she could only catch stray words. They were talking in hushed whispers. Something about the *Mosaic*. And a murder, a betrayal. She thought she heard a reference to the wire but couldn't be sure.

At the end of a row Slade froze and put her hand up in a closed fist.

Stop.

Timony froze, and heard soft steps on carpet. Slade dropped to the ground with the grace of a cat and rolled into the cubicle next to her. Timony followed her with slightly less grace, but managed to do so without making a sound.

The two women did their best to cram themselves under the desk, which wasn't easy—whoever usually sat there must have been a hoarder, and there were piles of paper threatening to fall over. But they got in far enough that when two pairs of shoes stopped outside the desk, neither seemed suspicious.

There was a decidedly unpleasant smell that accompanied the two pairs of feet, like one of them stepped in something on the way in. Timony ignored the odor and strained to listen to the conversation the two men closest to them were having.

We don't have long.

We can't leave yet. Not until we find what we came for.

Did you see the message from the Mosaic*? They made contact.*

And it went as well as we expected. Better China than us.

Has the girl said anything?

Not yet.

Keep her safe. She works for Tobin. She hears what he hears.

The girl who works for Tobin.

Oneida?

Did the Russians have her?

Fuck.

Did it have anything to do with their meeting the other night?

Timony was playing the odds in her head when one

of the pairs of shoes turned toward them. She held her breath, and glanced over at Slade, who had clamped her hand over her mouth.

They waited. Timony scanned the space for something that might be useful as a weapon, but found nothing but piles of paper. A tightly rolled magazine could work in a pinch, but if one of the Russians had a blaster, she could end up dead before she was halfway done rolling a thick stack of TPS reports.

Because they wouldn't be sneaking around if they were okay with witnesses.

Instead of what she expected—one of the men to peer down and see them—one of them whisper-shouted: "*Fyodor.*"

A voice called out from the other side of the room: "*What*?"

"The window is closing. Let's go."

The feet disappeared.

Timony knew to wait, in case this was a trick to draw them out. Slade knew to do the same. Timony counted in her head, something to distract from the fear roiling in her gut, and when she got to three hundred—five minutes—she waved for Slade to move out.

The lights flickered back on just as they exited the cubicle, still on their hands and knees, and they stayed that way until they got to the janitor's closet. They slipped in quickly, then through the false wall. When they got through and into the apartment next door, Slade breathed so deeply that Timony wondered if she was holding her breath that entire time.

The two of them sprawled out on the floor, exhausted from the mental stress. Timony stared at the popcorn ceiling, willing her heart to get down to a normal speed.

Finally, Slade said, "What the fuck was that smell?"

"Dog shit, maybe."

"Yeah," Slade said. "How much of that did you catch?"

"You mean outside of the conversation that happened right next to us? Not much."

"Something about a girl who works for Tobin . . ."

"Oneida. His chief of staff," Timony said.

"What do you think they want with her?"

Timony considered telling her about her meeting with Oneida, but despite the shared peril and the momentary laying down of arms, she still didn't trust Slade completely. "Not sure. But if they've taken the chief of staff of a sitting senator, that is a really bad sign."

"And that thing about the *Mosaic* . . . making contact?"

"Yeah. That is . . ."

"Yeah," Slade said.

Making contact could mean a lot of things in the spy world, but when it came to people on a spaceship checking out a planet in a different solar system, it took on a very different meaning. The enormity of what they were dealing with sat firmly on Timony's chest.

"What's the play?" Slade asked.

Timony raised an eyebrow. This felt good. Comfortable. Just two spies doing their thing. She rolled onto her side and caught Slade's eye. Gone was the steely reserve the woman had displayed in the past two days, replaced by that wide-eyed wonder that had painted Slade's face on her first day on the job.

She'd looked so innocent in a frumpy white sweater and no makeup, and her hair had been a little less kempt. Sandwyn had led her over to Timony's desk, said, "New recruit," and then departed, like he was disposing of an annoying party guest. Timony didn't even bother to contain the eye roll. She had enough on her plate, and the last thing she wanted was someone she had to teach to tie their shoes.

But the girl just stood there, wide-eyed and slack-jawed, until Timony asked, "Do I have something on my face?"

"You're her," she had said.

"I'm who?"

"Corin Timony. I think half the case studies at the academy were about you."

The swell of pride pushed away any feelings of frustration, and over the coming weeks and months Timony soon learned that the girl was a quick study. As Slade's skills grew, so did her confidence. She began to carry herself and dress differently. Soon Timony understood: Slade didn't want to be as good as her mentor. She wanted to be better. And despite Timony's competitiveness, this didn't bother her. She wanted the girl to succeed. She needed her to be better, because that made Timony better, too.

Timony sometimes wondered if that's what it felt like to be a parent.

Now she saw that same wide-eyed girl in that moment, on the floor of the apartment. Felt that same swell of pride.

She didn't want to respond: *Fuck if I know.*

"Remember what I used to say?" Timony asked.

"Always know when happy hour starts?"

Timony laughed, and Slade did, too.

"Pick the next right action, however small it is, and do that," Slade said, reciting from memory. "The next step after that will reveal itself."

"Nice work," Timony said. "So the next step is: We cool our jets here for another twenty minutes in case they have someone watching the building. We want to make sure they're gone and no one is connecting us to this. Then we figure out the next step after that."

Slade nodded, stood, and offered her hand to Timony.

Timony took it and allowed Slade to pull her to standing.

She felt good—better than she had in a long time—now that someone was willing to put their trust in her.

She hoped she wouldn't blow it.

MOSAIC

DOCKING BAY

Carriles strode into the docking bay, his heart smashing against the inside of his chest. He thought about what Delmar had said: that he'd crossed a line his political cronies and friends couldn't save him from. Not just professionally; Carriles's life was on the line.

As Carriles approached the docked ship, Penagos turned from the security terminal and nearly threw a salute up, but then nervously put his hand back down. The young, wiry redhead was covered in a sheen of sweat.

"I don't feel good about this," Penagos said.

"You shouldn't, Lieutenant," Carriles said. "You can go if you want some plausible deniability. Tell them I had a weapon or something."

Penagos glanced at the ship and then looked back at Carriles, then slowly shook his head. "I didn't sign up for an invasion. Delmar lied to us. So, in for a penny, you know?"

"Sure."

Carriles wished he did have a weapon. Something to give him some added layer of security. He had pulled

Vicks's blaster off her, but had handed it to Liu in case Vicks found a way out of the brig.

"So," Carriles said, regarding the security terminal. "Doors are locked?"

"They might be able to override on the inside, but it'll take time," Penagos said. "As for now, no one's getting off." He pointed to a red button. "This will open up communications. One other thing." Penagos clicked a few buttons and called up a biomonitor. "We sent down two teams of fifteen. So there should be thirty people between those ships. Right now we're counting fourteen. All the American crew, minus Shad."

Carriles nodded, and rubbed his finger over the button, considering his next steps, before pressing down.

"Captain?" Carriles asked.

Demlar's voice sprung from the console. "Carriles, is that you? Open these goddamn doors right now."

"Not yet," he said. "First tell me what happened. Where's the rest of the mission? Where's Shad?"

Silence. Carriles wondered if he had to keep pressing the button to communicate, when Delmar's voice came through again. "We encountered hostiles. Shad didn't make it."

Carriles's breath caught in his chest. "What do you mean, hostiles? Like, aliens?"

"Yes, Carriles. Aliens. We thought we were landing near a natural structure. It wasn't natural. It had been built. And almost immediately, we took fire."

"What did they look like?"

"What does it matter what they look like?"

Carriles laughed. "You made first contact with aliens, Captain. Can you blame me for being a little curious?"

Delmar sighed. "We didn't get a good look. We took cover and retreated."

"And you left half the crew behind."

Another pause. "At this point, there are things we shouldn't be discussing over the comms."

Carriles felt a presence next to him and turned to find Liu. She nodded quickly, and Carriles trusted the woman had done her due diligence to make sure Vicks was secured in the brig. She was still carrying the blaster, which was comforting.

"If you want out, it's best for you to tell us exactly what's going on."

It was a lie—Carriles didn't have a game plan for what he'd do if Delmar refused, but he also didn't want Delmar to know that.

"If you want to continue this conversation," Delmar said, "it needs to be the two of us."

Carriles pressed the button to stop communication and looked over at Penagos. "They can't hear this in the control room," the lieutenant said.

"Do you want us to leave?" Liu asked.

"No," Carriles said. "I feel like I'm going to end up needing witnesses."

"Or coconspirators," Penagos muttered.

"I guess we'll see which it is." Carriles hit the button. "Go ahead, Captain. It's just us."

Another long pause. "You know I can see you from the ship's window, right?"

Damn it. Okay.

"I mean, the rest of the crew can't hear, but I need Penagos to keep things calm, and Liu clearly knows more than she should, so at this point, you may as well tell us the truth."

"You want the truth? Fine." Delmar said. "Before the indigenous people attacked us, the Chinese turned on us."

"I don't believe it," Liu whispered.

"They were led by Wu," Delmar said. "It was before we were engaged. Yes, I had relegated him to a backup position, but that's because I suspected something was going on. Still, given the politics, I couldn't deny him the chance to be the second person to step foot on Esparar. That was the deal we made with the Chinese. But as soon as we got there the Chinese contingent held us at gunpoint. That's when we were attacked. And oddly enough, it didn't look like any of them were taking fire. I think the two sides were colluding."

"There's no way that's true," Liu said.

"Sorry?" Delmar asked.

Liu had offered it under her breath, like maybe Delmar wouldn't hear, but as soon as he acknowledged what she'd said, her eyes shot open. She gave a little shrug of her shoulders. "You're telling me you made first contact with an alien species and they were working with China the whole time?"

"Oh, if you only knew the truth . . ."

Penagos poked Carriles in the ribs. "Jose?"

"What truth?" Carriles asked, ignoring the lieutenant.

"You know what?" Delmar asked. "I'm done talking."

Penagos smacked Carriles lightly on the shoulder and pointed down at the biomonitors. "I think that's why he's done talking."

"What am I looking at?" Carriles asked.

Penagos whispered into Carriles's ear. "There were fourteen on board a minute ago. Now it's down to thirteen."

Shit. Carriles turned off the comms. "Could anyone have gotten off?"

Penagos put his hands on his hips and looked at the

ship, considered the options, then snapped his fingers. "Goldsmith."

"He's a comms guy. What about him?"

"He's also a scarecrow," Penagos said. "Someone as skinny as him could have wriggled through the landing gear. It wouldn't feel good, but it would be possible."

Shit, shit. "Okay. Where would he go? Can he override the doors? Get them open?"

"Not from anywhere else on the ship," Penagos said, patting the console. "Can only do it from here."

"Then where would he go?" Carriles asked, looking around like the answer might appear to him.

Liu held up her sidearm. "Weapons. He's probably going to get something to overpower us."

There was a weapons locker in the docking bay, but it was right next to where they were standing; that wouldn't be his destination. He'd have to go down to storage. But once he got there, he could get something a hell of a lot more powerful than a blaster.

"I'm going after him," Carriles said. "You two stay and watch the ships."

Penagos nodded.

Liu offered Carriles the sidearm, but he waved it off. "You keep it. In case he comes back armed and you need to defend yourself."

"And if he's armed by the time you find him?"

"Then I'm dead either way," Carriles said, before breaking into a run.

Carriles pushed out of the docking bay and into the corridor, heading for engineering. He could cut through an access hatch that would shave a few minutes off the trip. Another perk of knowing the ship better than anyone. He might get lucky, might outrun Goldsmith. Get to the weapons cache first.

What did Delmar mean, *If you only knew the truth*?

Carriles made it through the access hatch and down a ladder into the next service corridor, which led into the kitchen.

Then he stopped in his tracks.

Goldsmith was there. His feet were dangling in the air, his skinny limbs desperately seeking purchase.

And he was being held aloft by Izaiah, the cook.

Izaiah, the soft-spoken chef who was even smaller than Carriles, was holding Goldsmith in the air without showing any signs of strain or effort.

Carriles opened his mouth, to say . . . what? He could barely process what he was seeing.

Goldsmith made a choking sound, and then there was a crack. He threw his head back and screamed, and his body went limp. Izaiah cocked his head, almost confused by what was happening. And then it seemed like the color of Goldsmith's skin was changing.

From pink to gray, then darker, and finally black, then sloughing off, like a piece of paper set aflame. His body crumbled to dust, his uniform going limp, until it was like Izaiah hadn't been holding anyone at all. Just some dirty laundry.

Izaiah lowered his hand, turned, and saw Carriles standing in the doorway. "I guess we have some things to talk about."

Carriles didn't know what was more unnerving—the way Goldsmith had disintegrated, or the flat affect of Izaiah's voice, like he was recounting the day's menu.

"Yeah," Carriles said, his voice thick, his head spinning. "Lot going on today."

NEW DESTINY

LITTLE HAVANA

There was a small stretch of New Destiny called Little Havana. It was a blink-and-you'll-miss-it piece of real estate. A few blocks, tops. Mostly commercial with a few tenement-like buildings on the fringe. But it was also what Timony liked to call a blind spot. On the border of the American and Russian sections, it didn't fall into either but touched both. It was a good place to get lost.

The name, of course, came from the cuisine. Decent Cuban food was hard to find anywhere on New Destiny, but your best chance was here. Not the gourmet shit you'd get at a resort or a hotel, but the good stuff. Flavorful and plentiful. No fusion dishes. Just hole-in-the-wall spots with lots of options and few questions.

But it was also a hotbed for people trying to skirt the law.

Illegal gambling. Some prostitution. Any drug you could name, and probably a few so new you couldn't. Needless to say, it wasn't along Timony's usual route home. But it was a good default when looking for answers without the luxury of time to make a plan.

"Any leads?" Slade said into her earpiece. She was a few blocks away from Timony, heading into a tiny joint named Victor's Café.

"Nothing yet," Timony said. She'd stepped into an alley to discreetly look at her phone display, which revealed a basic map of the area. She could see two glowing blue dots—one was her, the other was Slade.

She needed a third.

She needed Illyana.

"What's this woman got to do with your dead Russian stalker again?" Slade asked, then muttered an order for black coffee to whoever was working the counter.

"Illyana knows everyone," Timony said, stepping back into the flow of traffic, pulling her hood over her head. "Madams tend to know the people in power in the neighborhoods they serve. She likes to stay off the grid, but I have a tag on her phone. What's happening on your end?"

"Waiting for our boy Carvajal," Slade said. "He was hesitant at first. Still doubt he'll show."

"Keep me posted," Timony said, before disconnecting.

In the hours following the Russians slinking into the Bazaar, Slade and Timony wandered New Destiny, together for stretches, apart for most, but always in contact by earpiece.

Brainstorming, plotting.

They knew some things: The Russians had Oneida. She couldn't get in touch with Tobin. Something major—perhaps a first contact—had happened out in space. But it was all being kept under wraps. Finding aliens was the kind of thing that would dominate any news cycle, the kind of story that would spread in seconds. But they didn't see a story anywhere. There was a reason for that. A reason they had yet to understand.

The list of people they could trust was short, and consisted of the two of them.

The plan was simple: find another person they might be able to trust who could potentially help them—namely, Tobin. Tobin had power. He had contacts. But they didn't know where he was. Until they could find him, they needed more information. And while Little Havana was a great place for drugs or sex or a backroom bolita game, the most valuable asset available for sale, by far, was intel.

Slade set up a meeting with Carvajal. She was going into it fresh, asking for help trying to decipher some black-market bank transactions, so hopefully he wouldn't be spooked—at least not until Slade could brace him to dig deeper on the incident with Adan, see what else it would lead to. At this point, Slade didn't trust that she'd be safe, looking for that information by herself.

Something was still scratching at the back of Timony's head. Why had Oneida sent her after the least helpful hacker on New Destiny? He had every right to be cagey, but the speed at which he declined to even entertain her ask made her think something else was going on there.

But she needed to know more to be sure.

While Slade dealt with Carvajal, Timony needed to figure out what was going on with the Russians. Enter Illyana.

Any good spy has a buffet of sources. Contacts in various pockets and industries they can call on when trying to piece something together. The asks could range from *Is this legit?* To *Can you risk your life here?* Timony didn't like asking for the latter, but she knew this ask might fall into that bucket.

Illyana made a good life for herself and her women on

the fringes of New Destiny society. She ran a high-end service that catered to the powerful and wealthy. And Timony knew that the powerful and wealthy tended to talk while naked. Either boasting or bragging beforehand, or looking for a shoulder to cry on after the fact.

Politicians loved pillow talk. They just tended to do it with women who were not their wives.

But finding Illyana shouldn't have been this hard. The madam floated between three brothels, but Timony couldn't find her at any of them. Phone tracking was a last resort. In addition to working contacts on a basic human level, Timony was also paranoid as fuck, so she tagged all her sources. Some fun little code remotely transmitted to her phone, and boom: location services available 24-7. Illyana would have to get a new phone and wipe her cloud backup to shake it. Which was unlike the technophobic madam.

But given the lack of a third dot on her screen, maybe she had.

Or else the phone was just off.

Illyana had helped Timony a few years back—she'd been integral in averting a bombing during a diplomatic summit. She overheard a few alarming details when one of her girls reported back about a cheap john who refused to tip. The intel had helped Timony and Slade find the terrorists before they could do any real damage, and the summit went off without a hitch.

Since then, Illyana had remained an integral source, and if anyone knew what the Russians were stewing over, it'd be her.

Timony's earpiece came on. She heard Slade talking—polite hellos. She heard another voice—male, nasally, and a little high-pitched.

Carvajal.

Slade was patching Timony in for a second set of ears. Good call.

"Thanks for meeting me," Slade said. But the words were garbled, the reception spotty. Static exploded in Timony's ears. She tried to keep moving, to find a better spot to stand, but the static only got thicker.

Then it clicked for Timony.

That was the reason Carvajal was cagey. He wasn't just a tech wizard—he was a hacker. And hackers used signal blockers.

"You call, I answer," Carvajal said. "Always happy to help the Bazaar. You tend to be good with the petty cash."

More static. Timony missed Slade's response completely, like the woman was speaking underwater, from a thousand miles below.

This was definitely more than just bad reception. She turned around and started walking toward Victor's Café. Her pace picked up, her body reacting before her mind.

"—need to get into some servers . . ." Slade said before cutting out again.

Timony jabbed her earpiece further in, knowing it wouldn't help, but needing to distract herself from the feeling of dread growing like a soap bubble in her stomach.

"—pretty risky to do that, big ask," Carvajal said. "Hope you came with a nice, thick envelope—"

More static. Timony cursed under her breath.

Then her phone pinged. She looked at the display. Another dot.

Illyana.

Really bad timing, Timony thought. She watched as the

red dot inched away from her and Slade's respective blue dots. Wherever Illyana was going, she was moving fast.

Timony took a deep breath. She had to decide. Follow Illyana or stick around to back up Slade.

"—take care of you, don't worry," Slade said, the audio clearer now.

"Come with me," Carvajal said, his voice low, almost impossible to track.

Timony watched Illyana's red dot speed down *Calle Ochenta*. She turned and followed.

Slade was a big girl, Timony thought. She can take care of herself.

Then why did Timony feel like she was bailing on her friend?

She closed the gap on Illyana fast, finally seeing her in the distance. She was walking at a good clip—looking around and moving briskly, as if she didn't want to be noticed but needed to put some distance between her and something. Someone.

Timony took a few long strides forward and reached out her hand and grabbed Illyana's shoulder. The woman turned around to face her.

It wasn't Illyana.

"Yes?" the woman asked in heavily accented English.

"Who are you?" Timony asked.

The woman backed up a few steps.

"You tell me," she said, clearly struggling to find the right words. "You touch my shoulder."

"Where's Illyana?" Timony asked.

"Who?"

From behind, the blonde woman could have been anyone—could have easily been Illyana. But this woman was slightly older. Her face fuller. She grabbed the woman by the collar of her dress and patted her down, coming out with a phone. She couldn't be sure if it was Illyana's—all phones essentially looked alike—but Timony knew the make and model was far more expensive than this woman could afford, from the state of her shabby dress and beaten shoes.

"Who gave you this?" Timony asked.

"I don't . . ."

Timony leaned in closer and dropped her voice to a growl. "I'm gonna give you one more chance—who gave you this?"

The woman paused, her face turning, as if searching for help that wouldn't come. She finally spoke, "A skinny man. He gave me one hundred dollars. Said to just carry it around the neighborhood . . ."

Timony let the woman go. For a split second, she considered interrogating the woman for more information, but it was pretty clear this woman was a bystander, not a player. Anything she gleaned from the shakedown wouldn't be worth the time spent on it.

Timony looked at her own phone display. She saw Slade's blue dot. Unmoving. She tapped her earpiece. More static.

Then she realized what was happening and cursed under her breath.

She barely saw the fist that came sailing at her head.

Timony ducked back, the woman barely brushing her nose. Timony dropped into a squat and hammered her fist into the woman's liver, furious at herself for brushing this woman off, the low moan escaping the woman's mouth not enough to make up for Timony's mistake. She'd been sloppy. She was too scattered. Her concern for Slade was distracting her.

Was she okay?

Timony ignored the Klaxon blaring in her head, telling her to run. She had to deal with what was in front of her. The woman stumbled back and grabbed Timony's outstretched arm and sent a solid chop into her elbow, which shot a wave of pain up through it. Timony pulled back, stumbling a few paces away from Fake Illyana. She put her hands up in a fighting stance.

"You want to do it that way, we can do it that way," Timony said.

The woman answered by pulling out a blaster.

Time slowed down. The muscle memory kicked in fast, as if Timony had never let the rust settle. As if she hadn't been put on the sidelines, as if she hadn't drunk herself stupid. She also knew this was a setup, something to keep her distracted, and she needed to end this quick. Whoever was behind this didn't want her where Timony knew she needed to be.

Slade.

The static in her ear was gone. The connection was dead.

Timony's heart beat faster, pounding inside her.

The woman lowered the blaster, starting to aim, but Timony dove forward before the woman could get a bead on her. She stepped around the woman, clamping the woman's blaster hand, shoving it to the side. But as the woman's arm moved, she fired—filling the air with a deep sizzling sound and the smell of burnt hair. Timony could feel the heat of the gun through her clothes, a burning sensation at her side. She'd been grazed, at the very least. But there wasn't time to think about it. Timony twisted the woman's wrist, hard, causing her to drop the blaster.

Before the pain of it could distract her, Timony sent her palm forward, slamming into the woman's jaw. The crack she heard—followed by the low grunt of pain—told her she'd nailed it. As the woman toppled forward, Timony moved in, sending a knee into the woman's midsection before shoving her down on the ground.

She caught sight of the blaster on the ground, a few inches from the woman's midsection. Timony kicked it away. The clattering echoed down the empty alley. Timony stood over the woman, who was moaning—a long, growl-like sound, like a wounded animal—her hands covering her mouth, which was coated with blood. Timony sent a kick into her midsection.

"Who sent you?"

Moaning.

Another kick, sharper—toes hitting ribs. More moaning.

Timony crouched down. It'd been about a minute since she lost Slade's audio.

"Who sent you?" Timony hissed, her mouth close to the woman's face.

The woman, her face bloodied and bruised, turned toward Timony. She was smiling. Timony felt her entire body grow cold.

"You have no idea?" the woman said, her teeth coated with blood, a painful-looking gap where a tooth once resided. "Did you think you could stop this all by yourself, Timony?"

Timony grabbed the woman's shirt and shook her, watched as she laughed—her head bobbing back, an evil, maniacal glee echoing down the vacant street.

"Who are you?" Timony asked again, hoping the repetition could change the result. But wasn't that the definition of insanity?

Then static. A jumble of sounds in her earpiece.

"—the fuck off me. Who the hell—"

Slade.

Shit.

Timony let the woman drop, her strange, low laugh still rising up as Timony turned and ran back the way she came. She knew this was a bad idea. She knew that leaving the woman behind meant Timony would be losing any intel she could get out of her.

But she also knew Slade was in trouble.

"—ere's your friend now?"

Jostling. Grunts. A crashing sound.

A scream of pain. A familiar voice.

Then silence.

Timony's head was buzzing. Her every footfall felt like she was running through molasses. She couldn't get there fast enough. The silence in her earpiece seemed to echo into itself.

The seven blocks between her and where she'd left Slade felt like light-years.

Timony finally saw the crumbling yellow facade, rounding the corner and dashing through the door. Her shoes skidded on the coffee shop's linoleum floor. She knew what had happened before she looked down.

Before her knees hit the floor next to Slade's body.

Before her fingers touched her neck and didn't find a pulse.

Before she saw the bloodied footprints leading to a back stairwell.

"No, no, no, not now . . ." Timony said, running her hand over Slade's jacket, trying to figure out what had happened. Her fingers found it. The wet, sticky wound in the middle of her chest—masked by the black clothing Slade always favored. Timony looked at her hand. Blood coated her fingers.

Slade's ID badge was lying on the ground next to her. Probably whoever did this had rifled through her pockets and didn't take it; they could be tracked if they did. Timony stuck the badge in her pocket and stood up.

She looked down at her friend. Saw the emptiness in Slade's now-dead eyes. Timony thought she'd heard footsteps—fast, frantic, and getting further away. But she couldn't move. Couldn't think. She just sat on the floor next to Slade. Next to this woman she'd loved—this friend she'd trained from the beginning.

Next to this agent who, now that she wasn't alive to hear her say it, Timony was certain was her better.

She felt the darkness of her hands—covering her eyes, hiding Slade's broken and dead body from her vision. Just for a second. Just for a fleeting moment.

The void. She just needed the darkness. She needed to fade to black.

MOSAIC

KITCHEN

Carriles watched as the ash that had once been Goldsmith was swept away on the breeze of the air recyclers. Tried not to notice as it disappeared into the vent. He brushed aside the thought that, within a few hours, they'd be breathing him in.

There were more disconcerting things to worry about in this moment.

Carriles's eyes moved up to meet the cook's gaze. Izaiah did not seem the least bit distressed, which worried Carriles. A man had just died in his hands and Izaiah had a look on his face like he was brushing his teeth. Carriles suddenly felt a wave of regret over not taking Liu's sidearm.

"I didn't do that," Izaiah said, but his voice suddenly sounded different. Lower. Vibrating, in a way that didn't seem human. "I suspect a suicide pill."

"Why the hell would he need a suicide pill?"

"Probably everyone who went down to the surface had one ready to go," Izaiah said. "Just in case they got captured. Just guessing. They didn't exactly know what they were in for." He put his hands on his hips. "It's possible I was a little . . . aggressive, picking him up the way I did."

"Speaking of," Carriles said, trying to hold himself in place, knowing that if he stepped back he'd reveal just how scared he was. "How the hell did you do that?"

"He was going to attack you," the cook said, looking down at the dwindling pile of ash. "I couldn't allow that."

"I mean, I appreciate it, but . . . why me?"

Izaiah seemed to smirk, but the expression was so fleeting that Carriles thought he might have imagined it.

"You seem to be my best shot at saving this situation."

The cook spun around and started to walk down the hall. Carriles, unsure of what else to do, followed.

"Saving the situation?" Carriles asked. "Do you know what's going on down on Esparar?"

Izaiah stiffened, but didn't slow down.

"Because if you do, it would sure come in handy to have some clarity," Carriles said. He was struggling to keep up. The cook was fast.

"Those people down there? The ones that your captain claims attacked him?" the cook asked. "They're my people. And they would have never attacked anyone unprovoked."

Carriles clamped his mouth closed to keep his jaw from dropping.

"Wait, you're from Esparar?"

Izaiah nodded.

Carriles's head spun.

Before, the "indigenous" people Delmar said he battled on the surface had been theoretical. They could have even been a contrivance on the captain's part to further his own cause, whatever that was.

But here was an actual person from another world

standing in front of Carriles. Jose needed a minute to process that.

And to figure out how he'd gotten on this ship.

Izaiah raised a hand, as if he'd heard Carriles's thoughts, and understood that the pilot was reeling.

"I am not a threat to you," the cook said.

Did he hear my thoughts? Carriles wondered. Was that even possible?

Carriles watched Izaiah—almost heard him grappling with what to say next, brow furrowed and arms crossed. The two men looked at each other. Izaiah pursed his lips before he spoke.

"I guess I should start at the beginning," Izaiah said.

"Please do."

Carriles took a deep breath, bracing his mind and body for whatever Izaiah would reveal. And how it might affect his fate.

"A few years ago, your world picked up our communications," the cook said—the words coming out slowly, methodically. "We did not know. For years thereafter, Earth spied on us, and other members of our collective. We are part of an interstellar organization called the Mutual, an alliance of planets that spans galaxies. We promote the one truth—knowledge. We share ideas. We share technology. We live to serve each other and foster peace, focused on moving the galaxy into the future, without disease, bloodshed, famine, or hate."

Izaiah paused and scanned Carriles's expression before continuing.

"Finally, in time, we realized we were being watched," Izaiah continued. "And your leaders were able to reach out. First they asked for membership in the Mutual. When we didn't respond, they demanded it. We denied them. They proved us right with their response. Humans are too violent. Destructive. Driven to hate and jealousy. You are not ready to be a part of the Mutual."

"Let me guess," Carriles said. "We didn't take it too well when you said *no*?"

Izaiah let out a dry laugh.

"An understatement," he said. "They demanded that we help them. Those demands quickly turned into threats. But we would not be swayed. Once the Mutual agrees on something, it takes much to change its mind. Humans were deemed too primitive and violent. Perhaps, in time, Earth can reapply. But for now, we have moved on. While we are idealistic, we are not fools."

Izaiah looked down the hall, as if staring out into space, toward his home world.

"Esparar is the name you gave it. But our home is called Reos. No one there wants for anything. Everyone is cared for, at no expense. There is no hunger. Everyone has a home. Everyone is embraced and loved as they are and as they wish to be," he said. "Very much *unlike* your planet, Carriles. A place full of hate and recriminations. A place built on fear and the accumulation of money and possessions. A sad state."

"All right, all right, I get it—" Carriles said, moving his chin toward the cook.

Izaiah chuckled. "My home world is not without its faults, mind you. But we've made great progress since our civil war—since we almost destroyed ourselves two centuries ago. We'd hoped to see Earth and its siblings make that same progress," he said. "But we also learned your history, and we expected you might take some kind of action against us, based on what we'd learned. We pride ourselves on always being prepared. With that in mind, we needed people embedded in your society, to keep an eye on you."

"So you learned how to cook? I mean, do you just happen to look human?"

Izaiah grimaced, as if remembering something unpleasant. "Our features resemble those of your kind. With minor procedures, I was able to pass for human," Izaiah said. Carriles noticed a flicker of discomfort as Izaiah lingered over the word *procedures*. He guessed the transition hadn't been as painless as Izaiah suggested. "I was sent into deep cover, along with another agent. We made our way to New Destiny. Our intelligence had learned that your captain, Delmar, was quite the food lover. Foodie? That's the term. It was simple to create a false background in the culinary field. Next thing I knew, I was here."

"There's two of you?" Carriles asked.

"Yes," Izaiah said. "But we have never met. Two were sent, to cast a wider net. I was assigned to this mission, and another was assigned to your Interstellar Union. To prevent what was coming."

Carriles swallowed hard.

"What is that?"

Izaiah's voice got even lower, a hushed growl.

"We soon learned that, frustrated over being rebuffed, a few powerful members of your government colluded to mount an assault on Reos—the closest member planet of the Mutual to Earth," Izaiah said. "They had targeted a key research and mining facility near our capital. By attacking it, they'd gain access to advanced technology and weapons."

Carriles sighed.

"Earth hubris is a helluva drug," he said.

Izaiah nodded, but Carriles could tell the cook didn't fully understand.

There was an awkward pause. Carriles could sense there was more the cook wasn't sharing. "You don't seem that worried," Carriles said.

"I'm not," Izaiah said. "Your people are making a foolish play. One that will backfire."

"In what way?" Carriles asked.

Izaiah shook his head slightly before focusing on something on Carriles's chest. He reached out his hand and Carriles flinched, but Izaiah just nodded. He looked down and watched as Izaiah brushed a small fleck of dust off his navy-blue uniform.

"Goldsmith," Izaiah said.

Carriles shuddered.

"Earth wasn't a threat," Izaiah said. "Now you are."

Another pause. Carriles felt the hairs on his arm stand on end.

"How do we stop this?" Carriles asked.

"It might be too late." Izaiah shrugged.

Carriles sat heavily on a bench bolted to the wall, his head in his hands. His stomach dipped, like he was looking over the precipice of a long and inevitable drop.

Then it hit him. What he had to do.

Carriles said a silent prayer and turned to head to the brig.

NEW DESTINY

CRANOR TOWERS

Timony finished the dregs in her third cup of coffee, still not taking her eyes off the luxury apartment building across the street from her.

Cranor Towers. Expensive. Conveniently located. The height of New Destiny luxury.

Tobin lived here.

And she was pretty sure he was inside.

She'd ditched her phone down an air recycling vent and bought a burner. Not an easy thing to do, but she knew a shop where she could pay triple the price and the owner would erase the camera footage and forget to log the sale. She was a little hesitant to get rid of her phone—she couldn't remember the last time she backed up her contacts and photos—but her suspicions were quickly confirmed. Twice she watched as Bazaar agents cruised by her in unmarked cars. She recognized them right off.

And they were probably looking for her.

No doubt they'd found Slade's body by now. It was easy enough to draw a line to Timony, which meant she would be right at the top on the list of suspects. A motive was a fluid, easy thing to manufacture.

For all she knew, she was the Bazaar's prime suspect.

Even though the dome was slowly drifting into the "evening" phase, the hat and sunglasses she purchased, and the alcove of the little coffee shop where she'd set up shop pretending to read a battered old paperback she found in a box in an alley, provided her just enough cover.

It wouldn't last long.

But she needed to be sure. She'd called Tobin's office, pretending to be a doctor needing to give him test results. The woman filling in for Oneida said he wasn't in, and suggested calling his cell. Timony pretended to have it entered wrong, but the woman wouldn't budge, yet promised to pass along the message.

The lack of a return call meant Tobin was out somewhere busy, or was holed up and staying off the grid.

Timony bet on the latter.

The question was: How to get inside the building?

The answer finally came to her in the form of a woman in a gray uniform, delivering packages. The woman stopped her truck in front of the building, entered with a few boxes, and came out about ten minutes later. The security guard at the front desk barely looked at her.

Bingo.

The truck had stopped twice previously on the block, so Timony bet it would stop again. When it did, further down the block, she dashed over, made sure no one was looking, and climbed onto the back. It was stuffed with boxes, so she slid into an alcove and waited.

When the delivery woman returned, she went about her business, shuffling in the back, music blasting so loud in her earbuds Timony could make out the words of the song. It was easy enough to get behind her and get an arm around her neck.

"I will not hurt you," Timony rasped in her ear. "I need your uniform."

The woman paused. A demand to strip was unsettling no matter the context, but she seemed confused it was coming from a woman.

"I will be back to let you go," Timony said. "Twenty minutes. Do the smart thing. Cooperate."

The woman nodded slowly, then stripped down to her underwear, passing the clothes to Timony. Timony pulled off her own clothes and put the uniform on. It was a little snug, but it would do.

"What's your name?" Timony asked as she lashed the woman's hands and feet.

"Marie."

"I'm sorry about this, Marie."

"I'm probably going to lose my job, you know."

"Well, this is a big deal, too. I'm sorry."

Timony pulled the truck around a corner and into a quiet alley, grabbed a package, and locked the truck up tight. Then she made her way back to the building. She stepped into the lobby and the security guard barely glanced up, before doing a double take. "Where's Marie?" he asked.

Shit. This was probably a regular route for her. That's why the guard didn't pay attention to her.

"A delivery she was supposed to make got sorted onto my truck," Timony said, holding up the box. "They made a big deal about it, said I had to get it over right away or someone's head was going to roll."

"Who's it for?" the guard asked, narrowing his eyes.

She looked at the label and pretended to sound it out. "Tobin?"

The guard stared at her for another moment before shaking his head. "Shit, yeah, he's a big deal."

The guard motioned for Timony to hand him the package.

"I can just take it up," she said.

The guard shook his head gently. "Nah, he's not allowing deliveries," he said, disdain sneaking into his voice. "Too busy to deal with the riffraff, I guess."

Timony saw an in. Shared disdain for the powerful. She could work with that. Because it was true.

"He won't even know I was there," she said with a sly smile. "I'll leave it at the door. I bet you're busy enough without having to cater to everyone's special instructions, right?"

The guard gave Timony a knowing sigh.

"Ain't that the truth. All right, he's in the penthouse." He waved toward the elevator. "If he asks, you walked by me without asking, okay?"

"Sure thing," Timony said. "Thanks."

She walked calmly toward the elevator and hit the button for the top floor.

The elevator opened onto a hallway with an ornate door at the end. No cameras here. Good. Probably so Tobin could do whatever he wanted without worrying about watchful eyes. She made her way to the door and gently pressed the button, heard the chime on the other side, and stepped out of the way of the peephole.

A voice from the other side. "Yes?"

Tobin.

"Delivery," she said.

"Leave it outside."

"Can't do that. Need a signature."

Timony thought she heard a sigh, and then the sound of a door unlocking. It opened, revealing Tobin, his face heavy from lack of sleep, hair disheveled, in a bathrobe and pants and slippers. He looked annoyed, but his entire expression changed when he recognized her.

"Timony," he said, eyebrows raised. "Sandwyn is looking for you. Figured you'd be on a freighter to Europa by now."

"I don't run that easily, Tobin."

"You should probably come in, then," he said.

Timony stepped through the threshold, into a grand entryway—spiral staircase leading to a second floor, an ornate chandelier. Marble everywhere. Not a naturally occurring rock on the moon. How the hell did they even get it up here? The weight alone made it hugely impractical.

Oh, to be rich and powerful . . .

Tobin didn't seem interested in pleasantries. His whole body was caved in on itself. He didn't beckon her, just walked through a darkened hallway, and Timony followed, past a series of closed doors, to one that was open: a study, full of books and paintings and a comfortable couch. He sat heavily and pointed at the chair across from him.

Timony sat and gave Tobin the opportunity to say something, but he didn't. He just reached over to the decanter on the table and poured himself a fat dose of whiskey. It looked old, and when it came to whiskey, old meant good. He looked around for a free glass, couldn't find one, shrugged, and held the decanter toward her.

She could smell it from here. Oaky and sharp.

She wanted to dull the pain.

That feeling that'd been swirling in her gut ever since she felt the lack of pulse in Slade's neck.

But this whole mess was too big. Too deep. She needed a clear head.

"Not today," she said.

Tobin looked surprised. She didn't like how surprised he looked.

"You heard about Slade," she said.

Tobin took a large gulp from his glass, placed it back down, and said, "Yes."

"And Esparar. The *Mosaic*. We made contact?"

Tobin nodded.

"With what?"

"We don't know. As you're well aware, we can only communicate over the wire. Anything else would take months to transmit, with the distance they're at. We've been asking questions and getting nothing in return."

"So they could all be dead?"

"We don't know."

"Okay, then tell me what you do know."

Tobin took another sip from his glass, placed it down hard on a nearby side table, and fixed her with a tight stare. "No, Timony, you tell me what you know. I have to say, things don't look good—you're in even deeper shit than you were the last time I saw you. The Bazaar thinks you killed Slade. So I'm going to make you an offer."

"What's that?" Timony asked.

Tobin smiled. "A little bit of rope. And it's up to you, in this moment, whether you hang yourself or pull yourself up."

She'd never seen this side of Tobin before. He was scared. She cursed herself because she only just noticed the bulge underneath his bathrobe. Either he was happy to see her—unlikely—or he was carrying some kind of weapon.

He suspected her, too.

So she told him. The meeting with Oneida. The dead Russian. The infiltration of the Bazaar. Getting away. Slade getting killed. Recounting it felt good; it helped to ground her, to remind her that what happened had happened to *her*, and not someone else. Tobin listened intently, and by the time she was done, his body had relaxed, and some of the friendly vibe had returned to his disposition.

"I believe you," he said.

"Your turn," Timony said, folding her arms and sitting back in the chair.

He nodded. Then he stood and walked over to the floor-to-ceiling windows on the other side of the study, looking out over the sprawl of New Destiny.

"There's a whole other world out there, Timony. One that existed only in stories until now. Alien races. An organization with limitless technology and power. With their help, we could fix things here. We could grow and expand human society. Make things better."

Even knowing the *Mosaic* had made contact with something, Tobin's words were a lot to take in. She supposed she had expected some sort of primitive species, violent and troublesome. This felt a lot bigger than that.

"We first made contact with this society years ago," Tobin said. "It's called the Mutual. A coalition of races that shares technology and resources. We asked to join and they rejected us. As you can imagine, that didn't sit too well with a lot of people."

Tobin paused.

"We couldn't get into some alien country club?" Timony asked.

"It's not about that," Tobin said. "Look around. Surely you've noticed. Infrastructure crumbling. Supplies running low. Rationing. We're just a few decades behind Earth itself. New Destiny is falling apart."

She had noticed, of course. "How much time do we have?" Timony asked.

Tobin shrugged.

"Until what? Pick your poison: Complete collapse? Massive system failure? Or a slow, gradual decline?" Tobin said. "It's all on the table. I'd say we can keep running like this for another decade. Maybe less."

"The IU told them this? The Mutual? And they declined?" Timony asked. "How bad was it?"

"Bad," Tobin said. "We made our case. Said we were hanging on by our fingertips. That anything they could do to help us would be appreciated. And still, they told us no. So the decision was made among a few members of the government to . . . make our case with a little more force. That was always the point of the *Mosaic*'s mission. It's not an expedition. The plan was for the US and China to obtain resources that would keep humanity alive."

"That's two."

Tobin turned, a curious look on his face. "Hmm?"

"The US and China. That's two. There's a triumvirate at the top. Where did Russia land on this?"

Tobin nodded, turning back to the window. "The plan didn't sit well with a few people, including myself. I've been protesting it since the beginning. I'm part of the so-called Gang of Six. Senators who get a peek at all major confidential information. I made it clear: the Interstellar Union should have been engaging in diplomacy. Russia took issue with the plan too, but somehow I doubt their intentions were as pure as mine. I'm not sure what they're planning." He bowed his head. "And now they have Oneida."

"Why?"

"I'm not entirely sure," he said. "Maybe to get to me. To manipulate me in some way, get me to help them. But I haven't been contacted. I don't think I know anything they don't already know."

Timony got up and joined him next to the window. She didn't like that this conversation was happening with his back turned. She wanted to look him in the eye.

"How did Adan play into this?" she asked. "I saw the report. He didn't die of an accidental overdose. Someone stuffed him with Boost."

Tobin offered her a little smile. "I think Adan was involved. I'm not sure how."

"Why did you come to me in the first place?" Timony asked.

"Because," Tobin said, "you are the only agent in the Bazaar I believe will get to the truth. They made a huge mistake putting you on the bench. I know you're talented. I needed you. And I'm sorry. I knew you'd dig deeper and uncover the truth if it were personal. I should have been up-front with you from the start."

Timony searched his eyes, hoping to find something she could parse out, but instead, she was met with a real sense of regret.

"What about Jose?" she asked. "You were close to his mom. You both served together forever. If anyone could have pulled the strings to get him on board . . ."

Tobin nodded. "He's a smart kid. He has a good heart. And he respects Delmar but he's not a loyalist. What's happening out there, we can't control. We can't even contribute to the conversation. I thought it might be useful to have someone aboard who wouldn't fall into lockstep. I believe that when push comes to shove, Carriles will do the right thing, even if the right thing is the hard thing."

"Carriles is a drug dealer who skated because his mom is famous," Timony said. "Don't glamorize that prick."

"Yes, and you got jammed up good in that," Tobin said. "Jose dealt you drugs. Did he force you to take them?"

Timony didn't want to answer. She didn't have an answer.

"Yes, he got through it on privilege," Tobin said. "That's how the world works. I'm very sorry to break this news to you. It's very frustrating. Get over it. The fate of our species depends on what's happening over there. I made a call that my gut told me might turn up something good. Because the alternative was they put in someone who would gladly jump after Delmar into the abyss. All I have now is hope, Timony. Hope that the better angels of our nature will prevail. That's why I set you on this path. Because I believe in you, too. You're the only one who can do this. Are you going to let me down?"

Timony tried to respond but the words got caught in her throat.

Tobin took a step toward her and lowered his voice. "Are you going to let me down?"

Maybe he meant it as a threat, but in that moment, that's not how Timony took it. It felt more like the way her dad would encourage her, in that tough-love way of his, which she pretended to hate but in reality she knew had made her into the agent she was.

For better *and* for worse.

But right now, she chose to focus on the better.

"No," she said, her voice small, but then she raised it. "I won't. Where does Sandwyn fit into all of this?"

"Sandwyn?" Tobin's eye twitched. "Why do you ask?"

"Because the night I heard the initial alarm, another Bazaar operative overheard it. Osman. Good guy. Hard worker. He ended up dead. With Adan and Slade—that's three dead bodies."

Tobin sighed, long and slow, before saying, "I believe he's involved in the plan. Him and Delmar go way back. Even though the mission is up there"—he pointed vaguely toward the ceiling—"there's still plenty of work to do down here."

The pieces were being knitted together slowly. Timony wondered if that's why Sandwyn let her live. Maybe he needed someone to take some kind of fall, as a kind of cover, after this whole thing played out. And her reputation was tarnished enough that no matter what she said, no one would believe her. A viable patsy if there ever was one.

"Great," Timony said. "Us against the human race."

"We have spent our entire history destroying ourselves in the pursuit of progress," Tobin said. "It is a characteristic so defining that expecting us to snap out of it overnight is impossible. But there is hope. Small actions can become big ones. Do you trust me, Timony?"

She didn't need to think on that one. "Yes."

"Then find Oneida. That takes the Russian's leverage away, and she might have some intel that can make a difference for us all," he said, before patting her on the arm. "I know you can. And together, maybe we can pull our entire race's ass out of the fire one more time."

Tobin turned back to the window, the conversation over. Timony walked over to the chair and picked up the package, knowing she had to now go and free Marie from the truck. But it was hard to think, hard to move, hard to even breathe, knowing the enormity of the even heavier package that'd just been dropped onto her lap.

~~ESPARAR~~ REOS ORBIT

MOSAIC BRIG

Liu sat back in her seat, her gaze falling into her lap. She was processing what Izaiah had just said—pretty much exactly what he'd already told Carriles. It was a lot to take in. Carriles understood; he was still trying to fully grasp it himself.

Then Liu looked up, a hint of anger on her face. "You sabotaged the ship."

Shit. Carriles hadn't even considered that.

Izaiah stared at her for a moment before nodding. "It was a miscalculation on my part. I was hoping to do enough damage to turn us back to New Destiny. Buy some more time to navigate all that's happening—on this ship and on Reos." He glanced at Carriles. "It was never my intention to harm anyone on board . . . please know that I'm sorry for that, and I appreciate what you did."

Carriles sighed. "You couldn't have just screwed with the food rations?"

Izaiah shrugged. "Things got out of hand."

"Yeah they did," Carriles said. "Is that why you erased the wire logs? So we couldn't communicate?"

Izaiah frowned and slowly shook his head. "I don't have access to the wire. I didn't erase any files. I assumed some kind of alarm would go off, warning everyone of the sabotage. I never intended to destroy the ship."

"But the Klaxon never sounded," Carriles said, as much to himself as the others. "The system failure didn't alert the other systems."

"What do you mean?"

Carriles shook his head and sat back in his seat. "Huh."

If Izaiah was the spark, someone else was to blame for allowing the emergency to grow into a full-blown fire. But who? Who was willing to not only take that risk but also erase any evidence of it happening? At this point, Delmar made the most sense. Maybe he didn't want anyone to know there were problems on the mission. Or perhaps he was doing something else that required the alarms to be off. Whatever. It was a not-right-now problem.

"So, what's the next step?" he asked.

"I think it's obvious," Liu said.

Carriles and Izaiah both turned and looked at her.

"We talk to the Mutual," she said. "You have to have some kind of, I don't know . . . governing body? Representative? Someone we can make an appeal to?"

Izaiah shook his head. "They're not going to look very kindly on this attempt to engage."

"All we're asking," Liu said, "is to make the case that not all humans are so . . . malevolent." She put a hand to her heart and glanced at Carriles. "The two of us, and I'm sure there are other people on board who agree, we'd never have signed on to this mission if we knew the true intent. We came here to fulfill the mission we were sold on: one of discovery and science. Not . . . colonization. You can't lump all humans together because of the actions of a few."

"Are you sure about that?" Izaiah asked. "Because it seems like a pretty common habit among humans. I've read your history books."

Liu rolled her eyes a little. "That doesn't make it all right. All we want to do is try and salvage this mission. The initial mission we all thought we were on. At the very least, we can turn around and go home, no one has to get hurt. But my people, the Chinese side of this, they're still down there. And if they're alive, we have to bring them home."

Carriles shook his head. "We're not politicians. We're grunts. At this point, the only thing that matters is our people. All these games are being played at a level we can't reach. Let us save our people and we'll go. I suspect after this, no one's going to be too keen on coming back."

Carriles wasn't sure he believed that—but in this moment, he needed to.

Izaiah leaned his head back and stared at the ceiling. "I think I can get you an audience. The problem is, I can't contact them easily. Like I said before, our communication methods changed when the human race linked into them. We're currently encoding signals on ultraviolet light."

"Maybe I can cobble something together . . ."

Izaiah put his hand up. "What we need is to get down to the surface."

"Great," Liu said. "Let's just go clear out the dropship, which is full of military personnel. They'll just throw down their weapons."

"Maybe we can appeal to their better natures," Carriles said, seconds before realizing how foolish that sounded.

"Izaiah," Liu said, "what happens next? What do your people do?"

Izaiah shrugged. "Not sure yet. They could vaporize this ship with their equivalent of what you'd have lying around in a junk drawer. But that's not their way. The fact that they haven't means either they're so unthreatened by this that they don't care, or they're planning something."

Liu nodded, "I think I have a plan for getting down to Espar—"

"Reos," Izaiah interrupted.

"Reos?"

"That's the name of our planet."

Liu nodded. "Sorry. I think I know a way to get down to Reos. Follow me."

Carriles got to his feet and joined Izaiah as they followed Liu through the brig—straight to Vicks, who was sitting on the bunk in her cell, elbows on knees, head bowed. She didn't move as Izaiah launched into his explanation, for a third time.

Though Carriles figured she already knew a lot of the larger points at play here.

When Izaiah was finished, Vicks looked up and smiled dryly. "And what do you want from me?"

"We need to get on a ship," Carriles said. "Go down there and convince your people to let us take our survivors and go."

Vicks nodded. "And to do that you need what? To overthrow Delmar?"

Carriles laughed. "You're right. I shouldn't have asked . . ."

"I'll do it."

Carriles looked at her. She was staring back, unblinking. Resolute.

"Are you serious?" he asked. "You'd betray him like that?"

"I knew going into this that it would be a tough mission." She nodded toward Izaiah. "We identified twelve potential invasion sites and settled on this one because it seemed like the least defended. And you"—she nodded at Izaiah—"swatted us away like flies. I know when to fold a losing hand. Not something the captain is always good at, even if he tells that damnable South Pole story every time he's half in the bag. But given the choice between dying and going home, I choose going home." She sighed and sat back, puffing out her chest. "And I don't believe in leaving people behind."

"So you'll help us, even if things go the wrong way and it means spending the rest of your life in a cell?" Carriles asked.

She nodded, not taking her eyes off him. "As you know all too well, our court system has loopholes for people like us. People with connections."

Carriles met her stare and tried to read it.

This could be a trick. She could double-cross them, help Delmar wrestle control of the ship. And then what?

Where would she and Delmar go?

They could try and persuade the crew to reinstate them. Or, more likely, they could run. The two of them alone didn't have the power to stand and fight—no matter how skilled Vicks was in combat. Maybe it was a mistake, but Carriles saw in her a steely resolve and believed she wanted to live more than she wanted to do anything else. In his experience, Vicks was a tactical expert, and the smart play was obvious.

So he reached up and started keying in the passcode to open the door.

"Are you sure about this?" Liu asked.

"Nope," Carriles said, pressing the final number.

The door opened and Vicks stood, stretching her arms over her head and cracking her back. Then her hand snapped out, and she grabbed the blaster at Carriles's hip, taking a few steps back to create a safe distance between them.

"Let's go," she said.

"God damn it," Carriles muttered.

"Do you see my point, at least?" Izaiah asked him.

"Not really the moment for I-told-you-sos," Carriles said.

"To the dropship," Vicks said. "Nice and slow. I'll be right behind you. Anyone does anything silly, I'm a pretty good shot, but in a space this tight, I really don't need to be, do I?"

So Carriles led a slow march through the bowels of the ship to the docking bay, cursing himself for falling for Vicks's ploy. He'd wanted to believe her, which may have been the whole problem in the first place. He genuinely liked and respected Vicks. Her track record. Her demeanor. Figured that he'd die at the hands of someone he had a professional crush on.

They made it to the docking bay, where Penagos lit up when he saw them—until his face dropped when he saw Vicks following behind them with the blaster drawn.

"Stop," she said.

The group did and turned to her, and she waved them over to stand near the panel, out of the way. Then she said to Penagos, "Give me access to the ship."

He nodded, and hit a few buttons on the panel, and the door lowered on the ship. Vicks nodded to Carriles. "See you in a few minutes."

As she disappeared up the ramp, Liu turned to Carriles. "Smooth move."

"Seriously, c'mon, we're doing the best with what we got here," Carriles said.

"What happens now?" Izaiah asked.

"We'll do what we can to protect you. I don't know how much leeway we're going to have here, but maybe . . ."

Before he could finish the thought, Delmar came marching down the plank, followed by Vicks, and then Stegman—both of whom had their blasters drawn on their former captain. At the bottom of the ramp, Vicks yelled to Penagos: "Close the ramp and seal it." Then she turned to Delmar and said, "To the brig, Captain."

"You," Delmar said. "Of all people."

"You're going to get us all killed over some twisted political agenda," she said. "This has been bullshit from the jump."

Delmar glanced over to Carriles. "I won't forget this."

Carriles looked at Vicks. "Seriously?"

She shrugged and smiled. "Had to look real. The best lies are born from truth."

Carriles glanced back at the ship. "And what do we do with the angry mercenaries? What if they find another way out?"

"You can't fit them all in the brig. This ship wasn't built to be a prison," Vicks said. "Have any other ideas?"

Carriles racked his brain—Vicks was right, the brig was too small. And letting them off the ship would create a clear pathway to chaos. Carriles, Liu, Vicks, and Izaiah would be overpowered immediately. Delmar's mercenaries needed to be held somewhere that they couldn't maneuver their way out of.

"Vicks, take the captain down to the brig," Carriles said. "I got this."

She nodded to Stegman and turned her captives toward the hallway, while Carriles got to work on the controls. He enabled the autopilot, fired the engines, and directed the ship over to the air lock, watching as it slowly closed, so the outer door could open.

"Um, what are you doing?" Penagos asked.

"Leaving them outside to cool off. I'm setting a tractor beam so they don't drift off," Carriles said. "They'll be fine. They have life support and rations to last a week. I'm going to kill their onboard piloting system. We'll figure out a long-term fix in the meantime."

"They're not going to be happy."

"They can join the club," Carriles said as the docking bay doors opened, and he nudged the ship outside. When it got to a safe distance, he set the tractor beam so it wouldn't drift.

"Keep an eye on that ship," he said to Penagos.

Stegman shook his head. "This is messed up, man."

Carriles patted him on the shoulder. "I know."

Then Carriles headed for the brig.

Moments later, he joined Liu and Vicks, who were standing outside the cell door, Delmar inside. Hands behind his back, resolute, like he was still piloting the ship. Delmar was furious, and all of that ire seemed directly focused on Carriles.

"You understand the consequence for leading this mutiny is death, correct?" Delmar asked.

Carriles shrugged. "All I know is that this mission is getting some updated commands. We're taking our survivors and going home."

"Can we talk alone?" Delmar asked. "Just you and me, Jose?"

Delmar's tone had softened, to the point where Carriles almost wondered if a conversation might be constructive. He turned and said, "Give us the room, please."

Liu and Vicks lingered. Carriles cleared his throat and did his best imitation of the Delmar he'd once admired.

"Let's get the dropship ready. I'll be out in a moment."

Both of them seemed hesitant to leave, to miss out on something vital, but Carriles just nodded at them, and they left.

Delmar pointed with his chin. "He's one of them, isn't he? The cook?"

"You screwed with the logs, didn't you?"

Delmar shrugged. "Had to control the flow of information."

"What happened down there?"

"I told you," Delmar said. "The Chinese turned on us. I suspect they had struck some kind of side deal with the indigenous race. We escaped."

"Is that what really happened?" Carriles said. "Or did you turn on the Chinese?"

Delmar paused, just long enough for Carriles to suspect he was right.

"You turned on them," he said. "And then you left them down there."

"There's still time to fix this," Delmar said.

"Yes, there is," Carriles said. "We're going to go down there, we're going to apologize on behalf of the human race, we're going to ask for their mercy, we're going to get the people you left behind, and we're going to go home."

"You are such a child . . ." Delmar said. "This isn't a storybook adventure, Carriles."

Carriles wanted to disagree, but hearing Delmar say it, Carriles realized that's exactly what he felt like. An idealistic child. For all he knew they'd get down there and be dead within an instant.

"Here's what's going to happen," Delmar said. "You're going to let me out. I'm going to take control of this ship. For letting me out I'll give you a one-time pass. Call it graciousness for saving our asses out there in dark space. But from this moment forward, you fall in line. No more games. We're going to go down there and complete the mission."

"Which is?"

"There are materials down there," Delmar said, "that our scientists believe will solve New Destiny's power issues. With those under control we could focus our efforts on fixing some of the other problems we have. Imagine what we could do if we weren't so focused on just . . . survival? If we could channel all our abilities and potential on the future—on science and exploration? It could help us build the foundation of a program that'll take us to other habitable planets. To really explore the galaxy around us. Don't you want to be a part of that, Jose?"

"So we just, what, go down and take it?"

"We tried diplomacy. We tried to trade. We appealed to their better nature. And those bastards, sitting up there on their pedestals, treated us like ants. Like we didn't deserve the opportunity to save ourselves. I don't know about you, but I'm not going to sit around and watch the human race wither away and die because of a bunch of elitist aliens who don't want to offer minimal assistance."

Something about what Delmar said was sticking in Carriles's teeth. "What do you mean, wither and die?"

Delmar dropped his head and gazed at the floor. "No one knows this." He shook his head. "Well, not many people know this. New Destiny isn't going to last much longer, at the current rate of expansion. We're not able to harvest and store the solar energy we need. We don't have the resources we need to keep New Destiny going. The only thing we can do right now is just stop. Stop growing. Stop having babies. Stop everything. Because we've hit our capacity. We're not doing this because it sounded fun, Jose. We're doing this because they gave us no other choice."

Carriles took a step back. The whole mission took on a different tone, knowing that the Mutual knew of humanity's impending demise and chose not to help.

If Delmar's story was even true.

But maybe what Izaiah told him wasn't the full truth. Maybe whatever Delmar said wasn't, either.

Maybe the truth, Carriles thought, was somewhere in between.

Carriles needed to see the bigger picture. And the only way to do that was to get down to Reos and hear it for himself. He considered arguing back against Delmar, but knew it would achieve little. Instead, he turned to leave.

Delmar called after him, "Jose? A little advice."

Carriles stopped but didn't look back.

"'Heavy is the head that wears the crown,'" Delmar said. "Do you know where that's from? It's a play, *Henry IV*, by William Shakespeare. Before your time, before mine. It's something I always took to heart. Leadership is hard. Whatever you think about this, you're the leader of this. And the time is going to come when you must make hard decisions. I just hope you have the guts for it."

"Well, I guess," Carriles said, "you can just call me Prince Hal."

Delmar tilted his head, curious.

"Sorry, it's a reference to the play," Carriles said. "Guess you haven't actually read it. It's a good one. I'll see if we have a copy. You can use it to pass the time."

Delmar's face twisted in anger, and Carriles walked away, now with a little spring in his step.

The slight cheer disappeared almost immediately as Carriles made it to the docking bay and he realized what he needed to do.

Stegman was standing with a rifle slung across his chest. Carriles stopped in front of him. If anyone had asked him before the mission started who his closest friend aboard was, Carriles would've said Stegman, without hesitation, but so much had changed since then. He started to move on when Stegman reached out his hand for a fist bump. Carriles looked down at Stegman's hand for a few seconds, then returned the gesture.

He didn't have time for enemies now.

"You sure about this?" Stegman asked.

"As sure as I can be."

Stegman looked around to make sure they were alone, and dropped his voice. "You put the captain in the brig, man. And not just any captain. Captain Wythe Fucking Delmar. That is a big deal."

"Pretty sure his middle name is Christopher," Carriles said.

Stegman gave him a light smirk. The joke hadn't landed.

"I know what I've done," Carriles said. "Don't think I'm taking this lightly. But I think this is the best way to get us all home alive."

Stegman took a deep breath, then nodded.

"You better be right," he said, before turning to go.

Carriles watched him leave, an unsettled feeling lodging in his gut. Then he boarded the backup dropship—it was meant for emergencies and didn't feature many of the standard amenities, but it would have to do. With one dropship sitting on the surface of Reos and another serving as a floating space prison, they had little choice. It was less roomy, less advanced, and not as comfortable to fly—but it was also just big enough to fit any survivors they might find on the surface.

Sitting in the cockpit were Liu, Vicks, and Izaiah.

"All right," Carriles said, taking his seat at the steering gimbal. "Let's go down there and plead for the future of humanity."

As Carriles's fingers danced over the ship's controls and lifted it up and out of the *Mosaic*'s air lock, he couldn't help but think about crowns.

NEW DESTINTY

NEW MOSCOW

Timony walked up to the vintage newspaper stand and nodded at the elderly man standing behind it. He gave her a brief look and went back to restocking the reprinted issues of *Time* and *Life* that covered the small stand's back wall, mixed in with vintage copies of Superman and X-Men comics.

New Destiny was littered with stuff like this—retro set pieces that harkened back to a time before anyone on the moon was even born. Some were better than others. Here, on the fringes of New Moscow, the selection got less desirable.

But Timony wasn't here to catch up on the back half of Nixon's first term in photos.

She scratched her neck. The platinum-blonde wig she had on was itchy as hell, and her eyes were tearing at the green contacts she was wearing. She'd ditched the sunglasses on the way here. They were a bit much, even for her.

The trick to a good disguise was to change enough so

that it passed muster on first glance and didn't call attention to you. Because if it did, you were begging for closer scrutiny. Timony didn't need that. Not only was she wanted by the Bazaar; she was now Tobin's last and best hope at salvaging something.

But she wasn't sure what that *something* was.

She did know that she had to find Oneida, and that the Russians had her.

Normally, that'd be more than enough. Timony was a good tracker. Especially when she was hoofing it on her own turf. But being wanted by the system's leading spy agency complicated matters. Timony had no phone. No computer. No home base. Off the grid wasn't easy—off the grid with no end in sight was near impossible.

She wandered over to the makeshift bookshelf at the far end of the stand. That's where she saw it. The spine was tattered and barely legible. But Timony knew it well. She touched the well-worn paperback softly, like patting a passing dog. Then she grabbed the book and pulled it out. She scanned the cover of *The Constant Gardener*, one of le Carré's later works. The clue was a little on the nose. But then again, Piotr always was. The man behind the stand seemed to come alive as Timony pulled the book out. He made his way over to her and nodded toward her imperceptibly.

"What do you need?" he asked, not looking up as he shuffled a stack of papers near the register, his voice barely above a whisper. "Piotr tells me to talk to you, but I don't want to talk to you. Hurt business. Hurt me, even."

Timony followed suit, opening the book and pretending to read a few paragraphs.

"I just need to know where they have her," she said. "Then I will leave Piotr—and you—alone."

The man cleared his throat.

"My name is Evgeny," the man said, wiping his glasses with his shirt, still not looking at Timony. "Piotr says to help you. Says you are to be trusted. I never meet you. Don't know why you should be trusted. But I do my job. This woman—she is deep in New Moscow. Near embassy, warehouse district."

Timony nodded and put the book back on the shelf. She turned and left without another word.

Evgeny's intel seemed to be on the money. It took Timony about twenty minutes to cut through the New Moscow side streets and make her way to the small warehouse district—a pit stop for goods from Earth or elsewhere in the solar system. Most of the basics could be gotten anywhere on New Destiny, but these warehouses specialized in the comforts of home—or in the Russian residents' idea of what home should be.

It was also a hub for illegal imports, drugs, and weapons. Shipments of wood from Earth, illegally collected from outside the heavily regulated growing operations. Drugs manufactured on Enceladus, one of Saturn's moons—a lawless, crime-ridden place where the only export was vice. In her early days at the Bazaar, Timony remembered her fair share of sting operations on the fringes of the area.

She'd spent most of the early evening walking a careful circuit, staking out a handful of warehouses. Most, if not all, should've been abandoned by dusk. The only ones still being guarded were either mid-shipment or housed things that the owners didn't want the police to find if they dared to walk the streets after sunset.

Timony couldn't help but notice the streetlights. How

many were out. How many were flickering, like they were struggling to draw power. Was that because this was a shitty part of town? Or was New Destiny really falling apart, like Tobin had said?

Had it been happening so slowly she had barely noticed it?

She banished the thought. It wasn't going to help her in this moment.

By nightfall, she'd whittled her options down to one spot. A small, nondescript warehouse. Not really big enough to be a major trade hub, so she figured whatever happened inside was more focused on local goods. Timony read the battered sign that hung above the main doorway: *Kramarov & Sons*.

There wasn't a battalion guarding it, only one man.

That one man said a lot.

He was well-built, armed, and clearly using tech that your standard warehouse security guards could never afford. Slung over his back was the kind of rifle more suited for the military than civilians. This wasn't a rent-a-cop making sure a shipment of furs went undisturbed.

Though relatively tiny in comparison to some of the other buildings on the block, this building was still a warehouse. She made her way toward the opposite side. Buildings have back entrances.

She found the door where she expected it to be. Locked. But that was expected, too. She pulled the small kit out of her back pocket and pointed the tiny needle into the small lock space, then raked it open. A moment later, the door clicked. Timony pulled and was relieved when the door gave way. So far, so good.

The inside of the warehouse was dark, and mostly

empty aside from a small shaft of light coming from the other end—a tiny sliver of yellow underneath what looked like another door to an office.

Timony could hear muffled voices. A man's, low and calm . . . and a woman's.

Oneida?

Timony cursed under her breath. She could have gone home before coming here, and picked up her blaster. She hadn't wanted to get caught carrying it, but suddenly felt naked without it. Not that there'd been much time. Her life now had become a flurry of immediate decisions and gambles, inching her toward whatever her goals were at a given moment.

She stepped toward the light, each movement slow and lithe—her body desperate to not make a sound. She thought of Slade again. Thought of all she'd wanted to say to her. How she was proud of her. How she would miss her. But life didn't work that way, Timony knew. Slade was dead.

Timony was as good as dead, too, unless she made some big moves really fast.

The shuffle of her foot on a patch of dusty concrete shook her from her reverie. She'd been sloppy. Distracted. The sound seemed to echo through the large, high-ceilinged space. Timony froze. The voices on the other side of the door stopped as well.

Then she felt it. The cold steel of something on the back of her head. She wanted to turn around. But she knew that wasn't an option.

Sorry, Tobin. I tried, she thought.

"You used to be good at this, Timony."

Piotr.

"What the hell?" she asked.

"Don't move," he said, his mouth near her ear. "Do not do anything right now, okay?"

Timony didn't.

"You're making a lot of people upset," he said. "Making a lot of people worry, Timony. Not good. Why don't we chat?"

"I thought we were pals—as much as you can be pals in this business," Timony said. Piotr's hand gripped her arm and shoved her forward, toward the door.

She turned to look at him—despite the shaved head and the muscled torso and the golden tooth glistening in the dimly lit space, he had a boyish face. She would have previously called him handsome, but the current circumstances were extinguishing that flame.

"That implies I was on your side to begin with," he said. "Bazaar, US, China, Russia—everyone wants to talk to you. I asked myself: *Piotr, do you want to help your friend or make some money?* I'm sorry to say, but money is better."

Piotr held up the blaster and Timony knew she didn't have many options left. Piotr was an ex-agent of the Neo-Kremlin, on Earth. He'd retired to make his fortune importing weapons from Earth to New Destiny under the cover of space and free trade.

He was also her Chen on the Russian side—someone who understood that peace was better than war. He'd been one of her best sources.

Still, trusting him had been stupid.

But people do stupid things when they're desperate, and Timony was very desperate.

Though she wasn't without options. Or hope.

She pivoted on her heels fast, dropping forward out of the line of fire, and bringing a wide spin kick into Piotr's face, feeling a nice rush as she heard his jaw crack under her boot. He stumbled back, still clinging to his weapon. Timony delivered a sharp chop to his arm and the blaster clattered to the floor. Before she could turn fully back to face him, Piotr hit her with a strong left hook. She managed to dodge most of it, but even a graze from a man Piotr's size was going to leave a mark.

She backtracked a bit—she'd hoped to take him down fast, but that window had closed. Now they were matched up evenly and Timony's back was to whoever was behind the mysterious door. She didn't like those odds.

"You're already dead," Piotr said, fists raised, as he stepped toward her. "The girl will be dead soon, too. And we will get our seat at the table. Even I can be a patriot, Timony."

The words hovered in front of Timony—as if asking to be plucked out of the air.

We will get our seat at the table.

She didn't have time to process it.

She sent her palm out, and the bottom of her hand connected with Piotr's chin. He fell backward, landing hard on his ass—followed by the hollow thump of his skull on concrete.

Then she was kicking him, her steel-toed boot stomping on his face, his chest, his arms. He'd stopped fighting, but Timony hadn't. A deep-seated rage bubbled out from her—a rage tinged with fear and sadness. Visions of Slade, her final moments—the surprise of death. Of Piotr's betrayal of Timony just now. Was he responsible for Slade's death, too? He must have played a part.

She kept kicking. Punching. Pushing herself down on this man. This culmination of everything Timony hated and wanted to destroy. Everything that had gone wrong. Adan. Osman. Slade. Carriles. Her job. Her drinking. Her life.

Before too long, she was pulled out of it by a low sound. It took her a minute to recognize it was a moan. She snapped out of it, saw Piotr's bloodied, broken face, how his body was curling into itself, almost fetal. Monstrous. Broken.

He'd live. She hadn't killed him. But she almost had. The skin of his face was scraped and scratched from the concrete floor. She imagined the myriad broken bones. She didn't feel bad. Not yet. Adrenaline was still pumping inside her like a runaway train.

She spun around and ran toward the door. That was when she heard the scream. Not Oneida, though. No. It was another voice. The kind of scream you heard in a horror movie—shrill and primal, like someone being torn apart by a wild beast.

By the time Timony had thrown the door open, she was prepared for anything.

Anything but what she saw.

As she stepped into the small room, she saw Oneida looming over a man Timony had never seen before. If it was possible, the man was in worse shape than how Timony had left Piotr—quivering in the corner, whimpering and mumbling half-hearted prayers in Russian, his hands in front of his beat-up, purple face.

But that wasn't what surprised Timony.

It was Oneida. She wasn't tied to a chair. She wasn't cowering, or captured. She was standing tall, a sneer on her face—her muscles sharp and defined. Her jaw clenched.

Oneida had kicked the shit out of this dude—with ease.

Oneida turned and Timony met her eyes.

"Guess you didn't need my help," Timony said, looking down at the other broken man.

"You took too long," she said. She straightened up, as if embarrassed, rubbing her palms over her blouse and slacks, dirty from days of imprisonment. "You shouldn't have seen that."

"But I did," Timony said, eyebrows raised. "And I think you need to explain."

"I don't need to do anything," she said. "I want to leave. Now."

The thoughts were slowly knitting together in Timony's head. The woman's complete and utter lack of fear or concern for her predicament. She felt like she'd been caught doing something she shouldn't have. Game recognizes game, Timony thought.

This woman wasn't a buttoned-up government paper pusher.

She was a professional.

Timony took a few steps toward Oneida. "You need to start explaining right now . . ."

It happened so fast Timony barely saw it—Oneida swooping around her, putting her in a choke hold, and lifting her off the floor. She kicked her feet, trying to find the ground, but she wasn't even close. She could barely focus on the oxygen supply in her lungs dwindling as she wondered how this slight woman could display so much strength.

An inhuman amount of strength . . .

Oneida let off the pressure a little and rasped in Timony's ear, not even breathing hard, "We can talk, but you must stay calm. Can you promise to stay calm?"

"Yes," Timony said. A croak escaping from her compressed throat.

Oneida dropped her to the floor and took a few steps back as Timony gasped for air, rubbing her hands around her bruised throat.

"That was . . . that was . . ." Timony said.

She looked up at Oneida. At her wide-set features, the way the color of her skin looked slightly . . . *off* in this light . . .

"What the hell are you?" she asked.

Oneida seemed to consider her words carefully. Then she shrugged. "Not human."

Timony's mind went blank. Of all the information she'd had to process during the last week, this was the most destabilizing. Like something out of the science-fiction paperbacks Carriles used to read. Timony's mind drifted to the covers: Colorful, faded pictures of big-eyed, green aliens. Giant saucers floating in the sky. Laser rifles that looked like spruced-up bazookas. Those had all felt so surreal and nonsensical. They didn't seem so nonsensical right now.

"You're one of them," Timony said, climbing to her feet, realizing the truth as she spoke the words. "One of the Mutual. The Russians knew about you, didn't they?"

Oneida scoffed.

"You really have no idea what's going on, do you?" Oneida asked.

"So, educate me, before Tweedle-Dum and Tweedle-Dumber wake up," Timony said, taking her hand from her tender throat to motion at the man in front of them, who'd fallen into a fitful round of unconsciousness. "Because all I have to work off is what Tobin told me."

"Your disguise sucks, too," Oneida said. "Half the Bazaar is probably on its way here."

"Tell me what's going on."

Timony half expected Oneida to say she was nuts. But then the woman rolled her eyes and sighed.

"First of all, it's not the Mutual—that's not a planet," Oneida said. "Our planet—what you've been calling Esparar—is actually called Reos. Our planet is *part* of the Mutual. In good standing, I might add. Unlike you bunch of pirates."

Timony ignored the barrage of insults. "Tobin told me we asked for help, and you told us to fuck off."

"Not exactly," Oneida said. "We decided that getting mixed up with your race would just lead to death and destruction." She waved her hand around the room. "You have yet to prove us wrong."

"Why did the Russians take you? They didn't contact Tobin to say they had you."

Oneida offered a confused look. "Yes, they did. I heard the call."

"Then Tobin lied to me," Timony said. "Why?"

"Aren't you supposed to be good at this, Timony? The Russians opted out of the mission because they thought they could go to the Mutual and back-door their way in. Argue that they weren't the aggressors—it was the US and China. They wanted to negotiate a seat of power and use that to leverage control of New Destiny and the colonies on Mars and Titan. They don't know who I am. Frankly, neither does Tobin, because I, unlike some people, am good at my job. But the Russians knew I was involved, somehow. Not that any of this matters. It's too late."

Oneida's voice trailed off. Timony swallowed hard.

"Care to elaborate on that?"

Oneida looked at Timony, a pained smirk on her face.

"I need to check in with my contacts back home. Let

them know I'm alive and safe. But I haven't had a chance to—not since this group of morons kidnapped me," she said. "I had to play along, to protect my identity. And my communicator was broken in the scuffle when they first grabbed me. So the Mutual probably thinks I'm dead. Which is bad. I'm supposed to check in every twelve hours."

Timony had trouble getting the words out. "What happens if you miss your check-in?"

Oneida looked at her hands. She finally seemed calm. But it wasn't a peaceful calm—it was one of resignation.

"My guess?" she said. "They've sent a hyperspeed warship to New Destiny."

"To what? Scare us?"

Oneida laughed.

"Scare you? The Mutual doesn't use scare tactics," she said. "The Mutual doesn't play with threats. They try their best to lean toward peace. But if something becomes problematic, they execute, literally and figuratively."

Timony looked around the empty room, as if hoping to find a door or warp zone to another place, far from here.

"Well . . . how do we get a message to them?"

"Don't you see, Timony?" Oneida said. "I have no way of contacting my people and nothing you have here is advanced enough to reach out. Even then, I bet the ship set off for New Destiny a few hours after my last missed contact."

"In other words," Timony said.

Oneida nodded. "We're fucked."

REOS

Carriles felt the slight tug of gravity as their tiny ship landed on the surface of Reos. It gave a shudder as the engine settled down.

Carriles scanned his small detail behind him. Liu. Vicks. Izaiah.

Of the group, Carriles wasn't sure who he trusted. But you play the hand you're dealt, right? Each person had their drawbacks. For all he knew, Izaiah could be setting them all up. Vicks could be playing her own version of a long game with Delmar in the brig. And Liu—well, Carriles did trust her. But there was always a wild card.

Carriles stepped off the ship and onto the arid, tropical landscape. Reos was tidally locked, meaning that, as it orbited its host star, one side was perpetually facing the light, and the other, the darkness of space. Both sides were uninhabitable—either boiling hot or freezing cold. But there was a thin Goldilocks zone, approximately three hundred miles in width, wrapping around the planet like a ring. Earth's scientists had determined that, based on an abundance of factors, there was water, breathable air, and habitable land.

"Wow," Liu said.

She was staring up at the sky, and Carriles followed her gaze, at the subdued rose-tinged twilight. That golden hour before the sun sets on a perfect summer day—something he had only seen on a few visits to Earth. On Reos the sun never rose or set, which meant every day the people who lived here lived in this twilight hour.

He glanced over at Izaiah, and for the first time the cook was smiling a serene smile, letting the warmth of the sun's reaching rays warm his face.

"Good to be home?" Carriles asked him.

"You have no idea," Izaiah said. "Humans . . . are not always fun."

Humidity crept in, a dampness forming on Carriles's back and under his arms. It was pleasant, after three months of being on a spaceship that swung in temperature between icebox and sauna, depending on what section you were in, and perpetually stunk of feet. Carriles felt an urge to ditch this entire mission and find a nice watering hole to disappear for a few years.

"You ready?" Liu asked, snapping Carriles back.

He nodded. "Just wanted to enjoy it for a second," he said, scanning the landscape before them—full of green, sprawling things that looked like palm trees, but fuller, and bushes overflowing with purple berries, all of it spreading for miles. It was unlike anything Carriles had ever seen or experienced.

"Reos is beautiful," Izaiah said as he led them down a wide earthen path. "I've missed it."

"We're not here to sightsee," Vicks said, looking down

at her portable scanner. "We need to find the Chinese contingent of our crew and leave. Immediately."

"Vicks is right. Where do we go?" Carriles asked, turning to the former *Mosaic* chef.

"On the other side of that clearing, there's a building—our equivalent of your Interstellar Union headquarters. I imagine your crew is being held there. But finding them will be the easy part."

"What do you mean?" Liu interjected.

"The Mutual is a peaceful league of planets and races. They strive for understanding and harmony. But they should not be pissed off, as you humans say," Izaiah said, motioning for them to follow him. "And if I had to guess, they are very, very pissed off."

Carriles leaned into Liu and lowered his voice, so as not to be overheard.

"We need to be smart about this," he said. "It's not just about getting Wu and his people back. These Reosians—they can just shoot us out of the sky. We need to leave on good terms."

"I agree," Liu said. "But how do we convince an intergalactic superpower that we represent humanity, as opposed to the meathead warmongers they've been dealing with since we first picked up their comms?"

"I never said it would be easy," Carriles said.

He stopped himself from saying anything else. In front of them was a small concrete enclosure. It'd almost snuck up on them, Carriles realized—tucked into a larger rock formation, the entrance almost hidden by marsh and greenery.

"This is it," Izaiah said, motioning for the group.

Vicks pulled out her blaster, more out of instinct than strategy. Carriles stepped in front of her.

"Are you insane?"

"I believe the term you seek is *pragmatic*," she said with a slight head tilt that screamed: *Get this idiot out of my way.*

"Vicks, these people already think we're animals that need to be put down," Carriles said, motioning toward the entryway. "Do you want to prove them right?"

Vicks met Carriles's gaze, her dark eyes wide and fearless. "I want to get our crew back. I want to make up for our captain's treason. Everything else is secondary," she said.

Carriles watched as she slowly holstered her sidearm—which had the telltale scorch marks around the barrel that meant it had been used often.

"But I see your point, Lieutenant." Vicks's emphasis on Carriles's lower rank was not lost on him.

But trivial in the grand scheme of things. It took all of Carriles's self-control to not let out a long, relieved sigh.

A massive stone wall, flat and smooth as concrete but with a subtle blue iridescence, appeared through the tree line. "There we go," Izaiah said.

"Can you go in first? Friendly face and all that?" Carriles said.

The former chef nodded and walked toward a doorway in the side of the construct, covered in heavy black curtains. Carriles tried to make out the shape of the building but couldn't. It was four stories tall, at least, but he couldn't see either end of it, the way it disappeared into the trees surrounding it. Izaiah pushed through the heavy curtains and Carriles half expected to start hearing blaster fire. Instead, he heard . . . laughter? Loud, boisterous laughter.

Carriles, Liu, and Vicks stepped closer to the opening.

What they saw at the other side stopped them cold.

It was Izaiah, hoisting another man—similar in size, but

this man's skin was a pale gray. His skull was shaped slightly differently than a human's. It was narrower, fuller at the top. His musculature seemed slightly off. It made Carriles wonder about what kind of procedures Izaiah had to go through to appear more human—darkening his skin, reshaping his bone structure. And it made him wonder about how advanced these Reosians were when it came to medical procedures.

Carriles was comforted by the sound of the laughter. It was guttural and freewheeling. The kind of noise a toddler would make, but that people grew out of as society burdens them with things like manners. It was the first friendly sound Carriles had heard in days.

Izaiah turned toward the *Mosaic* crew, his arm draped over his comrade.

"So these are them?" the other man asked, his voice at the same slightly awkward register that Izaiah had taken on when Carriles first learned the truth about him. "These are humans?"

"They are," Izaiah said, introducing each of them in turn. Then he said, "This is Graff. We went through the trials together, many seasons ago. We are like brothers."

"The trials?" Liu asked.

Izaiah nodded excitedly.

"When a Reosian reaches the age of maturity, they are expected to become one with not only knowledge—with science, mathematics—but with the planet itself. The water. The air. The dirt. You spend a month in the wildest corners of the Shacos'byan fields—the tangled jungles, the wild rivers, the jagged cliffs, with nothing. You begin with just your clothes and your mind. Being in the wild is not the test, though. It is the backdrop. The Reos leaders prepare a series of tests—mental and physical—that are thrown at you when you least expect it. Natural threats and mechanical. But bonds are formed with your group. The handful of people who head out into the madness with you. Survival is not guaranteed. But deep bonds are."

"Uh, well, nice to meet you, Graff," Carriles said. He fought the urge to extend a hand to the new man. Maybe handshakes weren't a thing on Reos? "We're here to find our crewmates."

"You mean the people you opened fire on?" Graff said, bemused.

"We did not do that," Vicks said tersely. "The people who did were blindsided by their own captain."

Graff grunted. "Is that how humanity conducts itself, Izaiah? With a knife in the back of their own people?"

Izaiah started to nod, but stopped himself.

"Not all of them, brother," he said solemnly. "These here—they are kind, compassionate. They hope to speak with the Mutual."

Graff crinkled his nose, as if smelling something strange and unpleasant.

"You ask much of me," he said. "But I do know our leaders wish to see you, Izaiah. Perhaps that is your path."

Izaiah nodded.

"He's right," the former chef said, looking at Carriles. "You and your crew can accompany me when I give my report. That will be your chance."

"Chance to what?" Liu asked.

Izaiah chuckled.

"To make it out of here alive."

Carriles had expected to be brought to the Chinese contingent of the crew. Instead, they were shuffled into a blank, round room made of polished stone, on one side of which was a curtain. Izaiah disappeared through it, and while Carriles, Liu, and Vicks waited, Graff watched over them. Carriles had so many questions he didn't know where to start.

"So," Carriles asked, "what do you do for fun on Reos?"

"I like to read," Graff said, after a moment of contemplation.

"Read anything good lately?" he asked, realizing it was a silly question.

But Graff lit up. "*The Martian Chronicles* by Ray Bradbury."

"Hey, I know that one!" Carriles said. "I love Bradbury."

"The Mutual has long known of Earth's existence. We largely ignored you. When you first made contact, many became curious. We began to examine your culture. Some of your books have become quite popular. Bradbury. Asimov. Le Guin."

"Good ones. Have you read any Frank Herbert?"

"I have not," Graff said.

"*Dune*. Give it a shot. One of my favorites. Weird and trippy in the best way."

Graff nodded. "I'll have to procure that one—"

He was cut off by Izaiah coming back through the curtain.

"So can I see my people?" Carriles asked the former cook.

"Our leaders want to hear from you first," Izaiah said.

"We already lost Shad. But if there are any survivors, we owe it to them to bring them home. I want to be sure everyone is accounted for."

Izaiah turned to Graff and nodded toward Liu. "This one is their doctor. Take her to see the crew." To Carriles:

"We did our best to treat them, but she might want to look at them as well. Acceptable?"

"No," Carriles said. "How do I know you're not going to march her into a cell, or over a cliff?"

"You're in no position to make demands . . ." Izaiah started.

"I need to protect my . . ." Carriles said.

Liu raised her voice. "Jose, listen to me." The doctor had a look of grim determination on her face. "It's okay. The only way we're going to get trust is by giving it. I'll check on everyone. You go in there."

"Fine," Carriles said, realizing she was right. Graff took Liu gently by the arm and led her out of the room as Izaiah turned to the curtain.

"Let's go."

"Should we coordinate or something?" Carriles asked Vicks under his breath. "Get our stories straight?"

He thought he saw her smile, but he might have imagined it.

Something about Vicks's expression reminded Carriles of his mother. Years before, when he had to have been a little older than twelve. He still felt the itchiness of the suit he was wearing. The discomfort. They'd been in the Martian Senate chamber, awaiting his mother's swearing-in ceremony. It should've been a memorable day for her. The election had been a hard slog, but now she was here—in these hallowed halls.

Even at twelve, Carriles hated it. The ceremony. The clothing. The quiet. The breathless anticipation. Why not get to work, he thought? Why do this part? He let out a long sigh and almost immediately felt his mother's fingernails dig into his arm—deep enough to let him know she'd heard.

"This is an important moment for me, Jose," she said, her tone muted. "I brought you here so you could witness this. Something many would kill to see."

"It's boring," Carriles said with a pouty shrug. "Why do all this stupid stuff beforehand? This is why the government—"

"Jose, I know you feel like you know everything, but you don't," she continued, her eyes on the dais as another senator-elect was brought up. "Sometimes the ceremony is as important as the work. We need to remind ourselves why we do the things we do. Why we uphold these traditions."

"But why do I need to be here? I could be back home with papi, testing out that hover—"

"Life isn't just about what we want to do, mijo," she said, turning to look at him now, a pained look on her face. "We have responsibilities. And one of the biggest responsibilities in the world is simple: showing up. Being present for the people who need you. It's the difference between the successful man with no friends and the good man who is never lonely. You're so smart, Jose. I love you for that. But don't outsmart yourself. Doing the right thing isn't complicated. Don't overthink it."

Carriles blinked the memory away, pulled back by Vicks—her words echoing through his mind.

"Did you hear me?" she said.

"What?"

"I just said it's okay to be nervous," she said, sounding placid and calm. "But you got this."

They stepped through the black drapes and found themselves outside again, in a massive coliseum-like structure, surrounded by seven tall, gigantic stone towers. The edifice felt ancient and modern at once, the aged stone polished to a fine finish. Atop each of the individual towers,

Carriles could make out smaller figures—they were so high up, Carriles wondered how they got there.

They looked down at Vicks, Izaiah, and Carriles, standing in the center. Each of them were draped in flowing red and green robes. Carriles wasn't sure what each color meant, and it was too late to ask. He felt a slight breeze through the sprawling field.

"Jose Carriles, representative of New Destiny, pilot of the *Mosaic*," a booming voice rang through the chamber, echoing across the pillars. Carriles looked up and saw a female Reosian. He assumed she was female; despite being well-built and stocky like Graff and Izaiah, she had longer hair and softer features. She lifted a large, smooth rock over her head. The other Reosian leaders looked on with deference.

This was the boss, Carriles thought. Of Reos, or the Mutual? He had no idea how the power structure worked.

"You were invited here by our envoy, Izaiah, who has told us about you—your people and your cultures. We have had our own experiences, too. Experiences that have left a bitter taste. A sense of betrayal and distrust. Your people spied on our communications. We engaged with your leaders and found them to be petty and selfish. We told them the human race had much growing to do before being considered for membership. Instead of waiting for the right time, you instead chose the path of deception, subterfuge, and cowardice. The hubris of youth does not even begin to account for how you and your people have failed. How do you respond to this?"

A deep silence followed. Carriles could feel Vicks's and Izaiah's eyes on him. Could feel the stares from above.

How had things gotten so fucked up, he wondered?

That he, a screwup pilot coasting on favors onto the *Mosaic*, was now humanity's advocate?

His mouth went dry and his throat constricted.

Why did this have to come down to him?

But the longer everyone stared, the more he realized he had to say *something*.

"First, thank you for this audience. I know we don't deserve it," Carriles said. A little ass-kissing couldn't hurt, he thought. It'd allow him to vamp for a minute. To get his ducks in a row. "And thank you for preserving the life of our crew members, and for allowing us to defend ourselves despite the actions of our fellow people."

Carriles tried to clear his throat. What he'd give for a glass of water.

"It is true, that our leaders tried to deceive you," Carriles said, looking up into the sky, trying to make eye contact with the woman holding the giant, smooth rock over her head. How was she not tired, doing that? Was she going to throw it at him if he said the wrong thing?

"But the decisions of a handful of people do not represent the whole. It doesn't stand for everyone. There are good people on New Destiny. Children. Innocents. We were told the goals of the *Mosaic* were ones of exploration, not war. Of discovery. Most of us wouldn't have signed on to this mission in the first place if we knew what they were planning to do. It's not what we stand for. It's what the insulated people, the elites, want. I wish we lived in a world where we could trust our leaders, but they're often petty and cruel—unqualified and selfish people who are out for themselves, rather than the good of humanity."

The woman seemed to smirk. "But you choose your leaders, no?"

"It's not so simple . . ."

Carriles rubbed his eyes and suddenly felt very tired.

"I ask that you don't judge us as a whole based on the actions of a few," he said. "Our crewmates are here. We knew we might die the second we touched down, but we couldn't consider leaving them behind. Doesn't that say something?"

The woman, far up in the sky, responded by letting the rock drop. It landed with a sharp crack a few feet in front of Carriles. It was obsidian-looking, thick and smooth and large. Despite its size, it didn't seem to damage the floor.

Carriles tried not to think too much about how close it came to crushing him.

After a beat, Carriles looked up and saw another of the robed people—this one a man, in dark green—raise another rock. His voice was thicker, slower.

"We would love to take your words at face value," the man said, nodding up at his hands. "But what have you or your people done to earn mercy? If anything, we have learned to not trust you based on your actions. How do we know that, by freeing your comrades, you won't immediately turn on us?"

"We are a flawed, broken race," Vicks said, stepping forward, sneaking a glance at Carriles as she spoke. He held his breath.

"We destroyed our home planet through our selfishness and inaction. We have lived to pay the price for our own excess and hubris. Some of us have learned. Many of us have not. We do not claim to be ready for membership, but we would like to at least claim *survival*. We are primitive and violent compared to you. Let us go back and work harder, so that when we do feel we are fit to return, we can do it with our heads held high."

When she was finished, she folded her arms behind her back, resolute. Carriles fought the urge to pat her on the arm.

Not the time.

"You are Vicks," the man said, tilting his head slightly. "You were allied with your captain, Delmar. Izaiah tells us you have betrayed him."

"The ship has decided—"

"You betray a betrayer, no?" the man interjected. "You claim the worst of your kind are opportunistic and craven, yet you yourself turn the knife on your leader's back. Am I wrong?"

Carriles had never seen Vicks stumble before—and it pained him to watch the woman, her sharp, feline features, suddenly frozen and stricken with fear. He had to do something.

"She was conflicted, as we all were," Carriles said. "While our leaders are complex and often corrupt, we as a people believe in decorum and the chain of command. We still retain some confidence in the systems that govern us. Vicks was hesitant to make the choice, but she did, because it was the right thing to do."

"You think this is enough to save humanity?" the Reosian leader asked.

The sound of the words traveled down to Carriles and Vicks slowly, like a feather—shifting back and forth, in no hurry to arrive. Carriles heard Izaiah gasp.

Carriles's stomach dropped. His goal was to get their crew members and go home. What was this turning into?

Before he could respond, the Reosian leader said, "The

topic of humanity has been resolved. We sent another to New Destiny, along with Izaiah, to confirm our beliefs about humanity. She has not been heard from. She is more than likely dead."

Carriles wasn't sure if he imagined or actually heard papers shuffling above. The rock was being held higher now.

"While I am open to the suggestion of preserving the lives of you and your crew based on the testimony of our agent, Izaiah, we are certainly not in the business of preserving humanity."

"What do you mean?" Vicks asked, her tone harsh. Carriles winced.

"What I mean—what the Mutual means, Vicks—is clear," the man said. "Our agent is dead at the hands of your people. This is an act of aggression that merits a response—not in kind, but with force. A response that will resonate beyond your solar system. A message that will last for eons."

Carriles started to open his mouth, started to think of what he could do—anything—to prevent the man from speaking the words he knew were coming.

"That message is simple—some things cannot and will not be tolerated," the man said. "And that message will be delivered now."

He let the rock fall, and it slammed into the first rock before Carriles and Vicks, cracking its egg-like shape in two. The crack sounded across the wide, barren face of the stadium-like structure.

Carriles heard Vicks gasp behind him. He felt Izaiah's hand on his shoulder, tight and comforting. He felt his voice catch in his throat.

Jose Carriles knew they'd lost.

NEW DESTINY

NEW LONDON

Timony peered around the alleyway and put up a hand to stop Oneida in her tracks. They were a couple of blocks from the Bazaar headquarters, and there were a lot of people on the sidewalk—this close, there was a good chance someone would recognize her.

"We can't waste any time," Oneida said.

"Let me do my job," Timony responded.

"Isn't that what got you into trouble?"

Timony wheeled around and stared down Oneida. A real-life alien. She still hadn't fully turned that over in her head. The woman passed well enough for human, though upon closer inspection, she could see there were things that just seemed . . . off. Frankly, if Timony had been more on her game, more in practice, maybe she would have clocked it earlier.

"I'm the one Tobin trusted to find you," Timony said.

Oneida rolled her eyes. "And what a wonderful job you've been doing. You're welcome, by the way, for taking care of your Russian pursuer."

Timony flashed back to the Russian's body, dropped like a heavy sack, felled by an invisible projectile. The wound that soundlessly appeared and instantly cauterized. She'd never seen anything like it, and now she knew why.

Because it wasn't of this world.

And she finally understood why it happened, too.

"You used me as bait, didn't you?" Timony asked. "To draw him out. The whole thing with Carvajal was nonsense, too, wasn't it?"

"I knew you were being followed by the Russian," she said. "He planned to take you in, and not for a friendly chat. I figured killing him would scare them off whatever they were doing."

Timony wheeled around and pushed Oneida up against the wall of the alleyway, putting her forearm across Oneida's chest.

"I'm talking about Carvajal," Timony said, her words sharp, the rage fueling her every word and movement. "You sent me to Carvajal. Made him seem like a lead. But he wasn't. Then Carvajal killed my friend. Slade."

Oneida fixed Timony with a hard stare. Something in Timony's gut told her this was a mistake. She could feel the woman's strength, but also her deference. She was tolerating Timony's outburst, but only for so long.

"I made a mistake," Oneida said. "Carvajal double-crossed me. He was more loyal to the Russians than I thought. I didn't . . . it wasn't supposed to happen that way," Oneida said. "For what it's worth, I'm sorry."

"So instead of scaring them off, you agitated them."

Oneida shook her head. "First, let go of me. Second, you had agitated them enough without any help from me. You two were poking into something too big and too dangerous. It would have gone down like that no matter what."

Timony considered it. Oneida might be lying. But in this moment, it didn't matter.

They had work to do.

She let Oneida go.

"Whatever you hit that Russian with, we could sure use now," Timony said.

"It's out of power," Oneida said.

"Plus, you still got captured."

"I let them capture me. I was hoping I would overhear something. When I realized I wouldn't, I decided to leave. It just happened to coincide with you showing up. And I'm not even sure this is the best plan . . ."

Timony laughed. "What else can we do? The *Mosaic* is light-years away. We have to get a message to them. You have to let your people know you're alive."

"Why?"

Timony had seen a clearing in the sidewalk and was about to lead them out when Oneida's words froze her in her tracks.

"What do you mean, *Why*?" Timony asked. "There's a ship on the way to wipe out New Destiny." She glanced at the dome over them. "If we go, there's a couple of settlements and colonies out there, but they're going to die off because they're dependent on supplies manufactured here. New Destiny is the industrial hub for humanity. It would be the end of the human race. That's why."

Oneida just raised an eyebrow and shrugged. "What makes you worth saving?"

"We, we . . ." Timony started, but her head was beginning to hurt. She didn't have the time or the energy to engage in a philosophical debate about the general worthiness of humanity. "How about you save your own ass, then? You think you'll survive a barrage from some alien warship?"

Oneida shrugged again. "It's better to be alive than it is to be dead, but when I accepted this mission, I had to make peace with the fact that I might not be going home. Your kind doesn't always warm to . . . pretty much anyone who looks the slightest bit different from you. And that's just among your own. If I die in service of the Mutual, that's not a bad death." She offered a smirk. "Anyway, my people believe in a type of reincarnation that would take too long to explain. Ultimately, I'll just end up where I'm supposed to be anyway."

Great. An alien, *and* religious.

Timony straightened her spine and stuck a finger in the woman's face. "There are good people here. There are children. There are people who still have a chance. A chance to . . ." She struggled to find the words. "A chance to be better. We may not be perfect, but we do get a little bit better with each generation. So, if you don't want to do this for me, fine. You don't want to do it for Tobin, okay. But you tell me you can look me in the eye and admit that spending your final moments watching innocent children being atomized is okay with you . . ."

"It would be over so quickly we wouldn't actually see it . . ."

Timony instinctively flattened her hand to smack Oneida, who threw up her hands.

"Okay, okay," Oneida said. "That I will give you. I don't believe someone should be punished before they've had the opportunity to make mistakes. What is that concept in that silly little book you all kill each other over?" She snapped her fingers. "The Bible. Sins of the father."

Timony exhaled. *Fine*, she thought. *I can work with this.*

She glanced at the sidewalk, and, finding it still clear, led Oneida down the block and around the corner to the entrance of the Bazaar. There was a guard posted outside. She ducked behind a newsstand before he could clock her, because he'd surely be looking for her.

They'd be covering the secret apartment entrance, too.

She considered her options, and they were few.

She could go to the guard and explain the situation—that if they didn't get inside humanity was pretty much done for—and likely be met with a look of confusion, the business end of a blaster, and another blank room, where she'd sit and wait for whatever the Mutual had coming for them.

Or she could try and sneak them in, but the only other viable entrance was through the roof, and the Bazaar knew it was a weak point, so it was covered in sensors. Too many for her to contend with, and they'd be nabbed instantly.

The Russians got in, though.

That was weird. Despite the political power they wielded on New Destiny, they weren't exactly team players. They kept a desk at headquarters and some nonsense files—Timony knew because she read them, which is probably what they assumed would happen. Other than coming in for the occasional meeting, they didn't show their faces.

And that infiltration was definitely not a scheduled visit.

What did the one man say? Something about the basement?

Timony thought they had been down there looking for something. But maybe that's how they got in.

She glanced down at the sewer grate on the ground at their feet.

And they had smelled like shit . . .

Ah.

"How strong are you, really?" Timony asked.

Oneida followed Timony's gaze to the grate, then pulled up the side as if she were lifting a piece of cardboard. Timony shuddered a little. The grate would have been too heavy for her to budge. She made a mental note to speak a little more politely to Oneida.

Timony climbed down the access ladder, and Oneida followed, letting the grate drop above their heads with a clang, shrouding them in darkness.

—

The stench was overwhelming.

Timony pulled her shirt up over her nose, but it didn't help much. And worse, the going was slow. A river of sludge ran in a culvert next to them, while they navigated the twists and turns of the maintenance pathway above it. Timony had a good sense of direction and knew they'd be under the Bazaar headquarters soon.

It was a risk. This route could turn out to be nothing. Then they'd have to backtrack, and come up with a new plan, which would cost them time.

But as they walked, Timony came across scuff marks on the walkway that looked like they could be footprints.

"This is a little like that old movie," Oneida said. "*The Shawshank Redemption*."

"Never seen it," Timony said, over her shoulder.

"It's considered a classic Earth movie," Oneida said. "I studied a lot of the films and television you produced in preparation for this." A few moments passed in silence before she said, "You know who I like? David Bowie."

"On that we can agree," Timony said.

Oneida laughed. "How do I know more about your culture than you?"

Timony stopped. "First off, those are deep cuts, from way before I was born. Second, I never had to assimilate to my own culture. The reality of being human is we don't have time to sit around and watch movies all day. For what it's worth, the more you show off how much you know, the less people are going to like you, and the more you're going to look like a plant."

Oneida fell silent, and Timony took it as a small victory. She'd take her shots where she could get them.

At this point, the two of them were probably under the Bazaar building. In the gloom ahead, she could just barely make out an access ladder bolted into the wall. She led them to it and found more scuff marks on the floor. Like a couple of Russian men had stood there, and took turns climbing up, then made it back down in a hurry.

The Bazaar wouldn't think anyone would willingly cross a river of shit.

And of course the Russians figured it would work.

Timony turned to Oneida, who was also pulling her shirt up over her nose. But when the woman saw the look on Timony's face, she dropped it and met her gaze.

"I don't think the office will be fully staffed right now," Timony said. "They're probably out looking for me, and probably don't think I'm crazy enough to come back here. That said, maybe it's packed. I don't know. I do know we might have to fight. Which I will do—it's what I signed up for. I'm not asking for that kind of commitment from you. But what I do need to know right now is: Do you have my back?"

Oneida tilted her head, like Timony was speaking in

a foreign language. Then she looked at the ladder. "You really believe they're worth it, don't you?"

A speech formulated in Timony's head. About why she became a spy, to protect the tenuous balance between average people and the powerful men and women who tried to use them as pawns in a game. That no matter how bleak things got, there were always ways to find joy. That she, too, had decided long ago that putting her life down for the greater good would be the best way she could ever hope to go.

But all those thoughts felt like she'd crafted them as part of another life. They swirled around until they became entangled and Timony suddenly felt nostalgic for the person she used to be.

She settled on the best possible answer she could give at this moment.

"Yes," she said. "I do."

Oneida nodded. "Okay. I got your back."

Timony laughed. "Just like that?"

Oneida nodded. Timony left space for her to respond, but she didn't. Rather, they shared a look of understanding.

Oneida gets it, Timony thought. There are greater goods.

And sometimes that greater good can be as simple as hope.

Timony turned and began to climb, focused on the task at hand. Getting to the wire. Sending a message to the *Mosaic*.

And she was a little surprised to discover that she hoped it would be Carriles on the other end of the line.

REOS

Wu stepped forward, then abruptly stopped a few feet away. Carriles walked toward his crewmate, feeling something almost foreign—relief. Carriles wasn't expecting a hug, though Wu's actions seemed a little odd—until he noticed the faint shimmer in the air between them. Wu saw him notice it and offered a pained smile.

"Don't get too close," Wu said. "It gives off a hell of a shock."

A few of the Chinese contingent sported snug, flesh-colored bands around their limbs. Probably some kind of bandage. Carriles couldn't be positive without a list, but at first glance it didn't seem like there was anyone missing. He assumed Wu would be more upset if there was.

Then Carriles's attention drifted to a figure in the corner, sitting on the floor, folded in on themselves, and he was flooded with relief.

Shad.

As if he had called their name, Shad looked up and met his gaze, their face an emotional ruin. Carriles's feeling of relief quickly dissipated.

Carriles nodded toward them. "Delmar said you were dead."

Shad just dropped their head and resumed staring at the floor.

"They came to our aid, when the Americans began to fire on us," Wu said, dropping his voice. "They're taking the captain's betrayal very hard. We had no idea he was going to do that. To start a war. I knew he was doing something on his own, but I never imagined he'd go that far. Shoot his own crew—"

Carriles glanced over his shoulder at the two guards standing against the far wall. They were humanoid, with pallid gray skin, like Graff. They couldn't pass for human, but the more Reosians Carriles met, the more he could see how Izaiah pulled it off.

He also knew how strong they were, but that wasn't what gave him pause now.

No, it was the rifle-like objects they had tucked into their chests. At least, Carriles assumed they were rifles. Long, smooth tubes that pulsed on one end with a faint blue glow.

Carriles turned back to Wu. "Are they taking care of you?"

Wu nodded. "They treated the wounded. Gave us fruit to eat. Sort of like dragon fruit. Very pretty, nearly flavorless, but it's better than nothing." He craned his neck to look at the guards. "We don't know a damn thing about what's going on. Other than the obvious."

Carriles nodded. "Delmar."

"It was brilliant, really," Wu said, bowing his head. "The way he separated us. I noticed that it was a little weird, then brushed it off, thinking he was just favoring his troops. You know how things get. But then the shots started flying—"

"You knew what the mission was for, then," Carriles said. "Why we were here in the first place."

Wu nodded but didn't respond.

"Well, you should know, the whole thing went pretty sideways," Carriles said.

"The intel we had was that this planet was barely populated," Wu said. "A mining and development facility. And if we took it . . ."

Carriles threw his hands up. "See, that right there is why I just had to stand in front of a council of goddamn aliens, trying to argue in favor of the human race."

"Did it work?"

Carriles paused. "They threw rocks. Not at me. But it didn't seem good."

"For what it's worth, I've been arguing with Delmar for most of this trip that we ought to rethink our plan. Make it a peace mission. Show them we were technologically capable of reaching them, that we were worth their patience." Wu sighed. "And that's when he started to freeze me out. Said I didn't have the stomach for what needed to be done. That's why I reached out to—"

"Let's not worry about assigning blame," Carriles said. "There'll be tribunals for that. If we get back to the ship, and get back home in one piece. And if there's a home to get back to. All of which I am starting to doubt." He glanced over at the guards again, both of whom were staring straight ahead.

Liu, Vicks, and Izaiah were outside waiting.

And he wasn't sure what to do next.

Fighting wasn't an option. If he could break the team out of the cell, they might be able to overpower the two guards. But wasn't that just proving the Mutual's point?

There was no way he could get back to the dropship without being stopped. He doubted the Reosians were just going to let him go.

He needed to give them something. Some sign of faith. Something that would prove humans could be better than what they'd seen.

The realization nearly bowled him over.

It was the last thing he wanted to do. The thought of it made him erupt into sweat. It was a Hail Mary pass, but it was the best hope they had.

You can choose to do nothing, mijo, or you can choose to do something.

Maybe it's what he deserved, after all this time. He'd been so arrogant and entitled. Because he was the son of Olga Carriles, legendary senator of the Interstellar Union. Who could touch him?

Had he really served his penance, getting a slap on the wrist when anyone else would have gone to jail?

Was this how he would make amends?

"I've got an idea," he said to Wu, and turned to the guards.

"Want to share it?"

"I'm going to die," he said.

Wu started to respond, but stopped, a look of concern etched across his face. Carriles's head spun, and he knew if he didn't have the guts to do it now, he wouldn't go through with it.

He turned to the guards and stood in front of them. Neither regarded him. Finally, he said, "Hey." He immediately regretted the harsh tone he took, but both guards looked down in unison, more curious than annoyed.

"I want to speak to your leader. You have a leader, don't you?"

Closer now, Carriles could distinguish them better. One was slightly taller, with broader shoulders, and a face that, in his world, would probably be considered handsome. The other was a stout bruiser with a nose that looked like it'd taken some breaks. They looked back and forth between each other. The taller one asked, "Do humans not understand the meaning of the word *mutual*?"

"We do," Carriles said. "But there's always someone at the top. I want an audience with someone I can look in the eye. Not someone I have to stretch my neck to see."

The guards looked at each other again, confused. Carriles laughed, which only served to confound them further.

"I just realized," he said, trying to deflate the tension, "how the hell do you speak English?"

The shorter guard shrugged. "We learned it. We all did, when we realized you were coming. It was simple enough."

Carriles shook his head. He was both impressed and a little offended, but it helped him better understand this species' general haughtiness.

"I'd like to speak to someone," Carriles said. "Tell them I have something to offer, in return for sparing the human race."

"What's that?" the darker-skinned guard asked.

"My life."

That brought shock to both of their faces. They looked at each other again, until finally the shorter guard shrugged and left the room.

So Carriles stood and waited.

It wasn't long before the guard returned.

"Come with me."

Carriles and the guard exited, to another area, where he found Liu, Vicks, and Izaiah huddled in a corner. They moved toward him, but he waved them off. Explaining all this would take too long, and anyway, he didn't want to puncture his own resolve. He still couldn't believe this was the plan he came up with, and began running through ideas in his head, hoping to come up with something that might be more effective.

But he couldn't.

The guard led him down a short hall to a platform. There was a lit circle on the ground, and Carriles joined the guard inside. The platform whisked them upward through a dark tube, so fast he thought he might vomit, before it came to a fast but delicate stop at another floor. Across the way from them was a door, which opened as they approached.

They stepped into a vast room, open on one end, that looked out over the lush jungle. The guard gestured for Carriles to move forward, and then stepped back, the doors closing behind him.

Carriles could barely register the shape in front of him. He found himself face-to-face with a swirl of thick blue smoke that was hard to look at. Every time he tried to focus on part of it, he would feel an intense sense of distress, and be forced to shift his focus.

A delicate, feminine voice filled the room. "To your right. The glasses."

Carriles found an intricate table—it looked like it was carved from stone—atop of which sat a pair of glasses. All glass, no frames, as if they'd been molded from a single piece. He put them on and looked back at the swirl. In its place he found a humanoid creature with odd, spindly features, like a marionette doll. It moved swiftly and sleekly, almost floating across the room toward him. Dark, almost black eyes, with a mane of white hair.

Carriles tipped the glasses down and peered over them. Smoke.

Looked through the glass again—weird alien.

"Huh," he said.

"My corporeal form exists in a liminal state between dimensions," the figure said. "The glasses will help you focus. I suspect that'll make this easier. I have been sanctioned to speak with you privately. My name is Telio. I know that humans are often confounded by gender. My species doesn't conform to a spectrum like yours, but if it makes you comfortable, I would most closely identify as female. May I get you something to drink?"

She gestured with a long, sticklike hand to what looked like a bar on the other side of the room, which was stacked with oblong bottles holding an array of different colored, shimmering liquids.

"I'm sure this is overwhelming for you," Telio said. "Please feel free to take a moment. Your heart is racing, and your perspiration level is increasing. Allow yourself to recalibrate."

"Thanks, yeah," Carriles said, taking a few deep breaths to center himself. He nodded toward the bar area. "Are those safe for me to drink?"

"Some yes, some no," she said. "I have no desire to poison you. If you would prefer water . . . ?"

"That would be great, thank you."

Telio drifted to the bar and returned with a glass bowl filled with water. Carriles accepted it graciously and offered a little bow. He did not remark on how being served water in a bowl made him feel like a pet. He sipped from it, tentatively, expecting something sparkling and refreshing, something somehow different than what he was used to. Instead, it tasted like tap water.

"Please," she said. "Sit."

Carriles sat on something that looked like a sofa but felt like concrete. He looked up at Telio expectantly, who made a movement he interpreted as an indifferent shrug. "My body does not possess the physiological properties to sit."

"Fair enough," Carriles said. He took another sip and placed the bowl down on the arm of the couch. "So you're not from this planet?"

Telio shook her head. "I am from a planet called Stoe, many galaxies away."

"Long trip?"

"Within your limited concept of time, I would say it took about a day and a half to get here," she said. "I arrived shortly before you did."

"Damn," Carriles said. "What kind of engines are you running?"

Telio paused, and Carriles silently cursed himself. The pilot in him was speaking. Probably better to keep this formal.

Then Telio said, "I do not say this with derision, but it would be difficult for you to understand. I must say, the science team in this facility have studied your gravity engines. They are . . . slightly more advanced than what we thought you could achieve."

"Humans," Carriles said. "Full of surprises."

"So I am told you have come to trade your life for that of your race," Telio said. "I must admit, it was intriguing enough to win you this meeting. Normally, Mutual business is not conducted with any less than a quorum of five."

"Does a Mutual quorum always involve throwing rocks at people?"

Telio's face twisted in what Carriles thought—hoped—was a smile. "No, that is a local custom. But one that we honor."

Carriles took another sip to steel his nerves.

"You're right. I've come to offer you my life. A sacrifice. To let my team go free. And, I suspect, to call off whatever attack you have planned on our home, New Destiny."

Telio turned to the window, looking out over the vista. The orange sun, which had a purplish hue on the edges, lit the sky, offering an incredible kaleidoscopic view. Carriles got up and stood next to her, so he could appreciate it better.

Maybe the last sunset he'd ever see.

Then he remembered that the sun never set here.

"Why?" Telio asked.

"We may not be up to your standards, but the human race is worth saving."

"No," Telio said, turning to look at Carriles. "Why *you*?"

"What do you mean?"

"I mean, human history, from what we've come to know of it, is littered with selfishness. It is the cause of your greatest ailments and your biggest failures. You spoke admirably before the others, and in that moment, I thought, of course this man would argue on behalf of his species. Who wouldn't? But to come here and offer your very life . . ."

"Look, I don't want to die," Carriles said, his throat growing thick. He took a breath to steady himself. "But there are people on New Destiny and spread across the colonies who deserve the chance. If I don't get to see another sunrise . . ." He let the emotion flood his voice, maybe it would help his case, but at this point there was no holding it back either, ". . . as long as *they* do, it will be worth it."

He turned to Telio, who turned to him, the perpetually setting sun lighting their faces.

"Meeting you, seeing all this," he gestured out to the

terrace, "the universe is so much bigger than one person. I've made a lot of mistakes in my life. Hurt people I care about." Timony's face floated to his mind. If only she could see him now. She would never believe it otherwise. "Consider this me paying my debt to them. The amends that I need to make."

Telio nodded and moved further toward the terrace, taking in the view. Carriles didn't follow her, hoping the words were sinking in.

"You are a brave man, Jose Carriles," she said. "Not just to make this offer but to admit your own failings. And to seek to grow from them." She turned to him. "Perhaps there is something to humanity after all."

Carriles took in a sharp breath. He watched Telio, his heart thumping inside him.

"We accept your terms," Telio said with a slight nod.

Carriles felt something crack inside him. The realization that he'd managed to save New Destiny was overwhelmed by his own looming demise. He opened his mouth to speak, but couldn't form any words for a moment. When he did, they sounded like a faint croak.

"So . . . do I have to die?"

Telio made a sound that approximated a laugh. "No, I do not delight in the taking of a life. I will allow you to return to your ship." She raised a hand and gestured toward the sky. "But understand a few things. If another move is made against us by you or your government, we will not hesitate to disintegrate you. It'll happen so swiftly you won't even know it's coming."

The sweat returned to Carriles's skin. There was a new coldness creeping into Telio's voice.

"The *Mosaic* will be allowed to return to your solar

system," she said. "As for the fate of New Destiny, however, that is out of my hands. We had an operative on your planet. She went by the name Oneida. She was placed on the staff of one of your senators. She missed her scheduled check-in. She may be dead. When you kill a member of the Mutual, you are striking a blow against all of us, and we do not take that lightly."

"So, what, I just go home to a barren crater?"

Telio gave another shrug-type movement. "There are colonies on your other planets and moons, and other ships. Humanity will survive, because of the nature of the gift you saw fit to offer. But that doesn't mean humanity can escape punishment."

Carriles processed that for a moment. "I don't want to be disrespectful, but—I thought the Mutual was all about peace, love, and understanding. You just told me you don't delight in taking a life. But destroying my entire race seems almost perfunctory to you."

Telio nodded. "A bit of a paradox, yes. But understand it from our perspective. Humanity conspired to come here, to hurt our people, to take our technology. You, Jose Carriles, did not do that. You have spoken bravely and admirably—though I could argue you expected this outcome. But the fact remains: humans did attempt to harm us. And there is nothing in your history that says to us that if we let this go unpunished, it won't happen again. You may go home with the best of intentions, but what can one man do? Your leaders would likely take what they learned here to plan their next assault. We must protect ourselves. You walked into this room understanding that to protect your people, a sacrifice was required. We feel the same way."

"This isn't a sacrifice. This is an extermination."

"A loss of a few to protect many," Telio said. "Again, something it seems like you understand. Or was I mistaken? Do you not understand?"

Carriles tried to argue and found that he couldn't.

All he could do was say: "I suppose I do."

The words felt sour in his mouth.

"I'm impressed. I didn't expect that kind of bravery from you, Lieutenant," Vicks said as the dropship exited the atmosphere on an intercept course with the *Mosaic*. Carriles was piloting the dropship, a tight squeeze with all the survivors on board. The cockpit was cramped with Vicks, Liu, Izaiah, Wu, and Shad, but it was good to have the chance to debrief his meeting with Telio.

"You were really willing to sacrifice yourself for us?" Liu asked.

"I had to do something," he said. "I didn't let myself think about it long enough to totally appreciate the depth of it."

"So what do we do next?" Wu interjected. "If what you said is true, that they can cover galaxies in days instead of months, there's no hope of us getting back to New Destiny in time to . . . warn them, I guess. Evacuate?"

"We'd never stand a chance against their technology," Carriles said. "And even if we got on the wire and warned them, it would probably be impossible to evacuate the entire city . . ."

The wire.

They couldn't evacuate New Destiny in time. But maybe there was another way. Telio had said Oneida, the Mutual's spy, *may* be dead. But what if she was alive?

Oneida. He knew that name sounded familiar. He felt his mind spinning, sifting through stacks and stacks of memories and vignettes—like a dog chasing a scent.

He remembered a place. A conversation.

With Tobin.

Carriles had slept in that day, serving out the final days of his probation, doing the same thing he did for the whole stretch—watching movies, reading his stack of sci-fi paperbacks, playing video games, and hoping he didn't run into Timony, who had never responded to his barrage of apology messages. That day he had been hours into a spirited *Blood Oath: Next Generation* session when he noticed a handful of calls from an unknown number waiting for him. The first one he listened to was straight to the point: it was Senator Antwan Tobin, asking him to get to his office immediately.

He figured it had to do with his mom. Why else would a senator be calling him? Did Tobin want to start a grant in her name? Ask for Carriles's endorsement during a primary? The latter wouldn't help much, especially under his current circumstances.

Carriles showered and shaved and dressed in his best approximation of a suit, even though it needed to be pressed and cleaned. When he arrived at Tobin's office in the IU building, he found the stocky senator sitting behind his desk, poring over some papers. He motioned for Carriles to sit. He asked if he knew about the *Mosaic* mission, which of course Carriles did. Everyone knew about the *Mosaic* mission. It was the dream gig. History. Like the original moon landing. That mission felt galaxies away from where Carriles was now.

"The pilot, Adan Marks, is dead. Routine stuff—training

mission gone haywire," Tobin said. "I want you to take his place."

Carriles opened his mouth to speak, but no sound came out. He was still mourning Adan's death, and he hadn't any designs on taking his friend's place. He was flattered and terrified in the same moment.

"I know what you're thinking, and please stop it," Tobin said. "People die. You know this. But in Adan's case, it was an equipment malfunction that had absolutely nothing to do with the actual mission. This shit happens. But we can't lose a single day. We need *Mosaic* on its way, on schedule. The ship leaves in four days. Your name isn't exactly in demand, Carriles, but I know you're talented. I know you can step in and pilot this ship like it was the plan from the get-go. I made some calls. The gig is yours. I suggest you take it."

"Thank you, sir," Carriles said, the words jammed up. He wanted to leave it at that, but he couldn't. The question was in the air before he realized it: "But why me?"

Tobin leaned back and smiled. "Because I promised your mother I would watch out for you. Because you have potential. It's high time you lived up to it." Carriles felt his skin prickle, couldn't hide the smile growing on his face, and he was about to say thank you when Tobin called over Carriles's shoulder: "Oneida, he's in. Can you make the call? Let them know we're good?"

Carriles caught the flash of a woman ducking out of the room. She must have drifted in mid-conversation.

His attention snapped back to the controls as he pulled back on the steering gimbal, adjusting his intercept with the *Mosaic*.

"Okay, new plan," Carriles said as the ship drifted into the docking bay. "I know who the Mutual spy is. We get on the wire, see if she's still alive. If she is, we might be able to salvage this."

"And if she's not?" Izaiah asked.

"Let's not worry too much about that."

He realized that, in the hustle to the transport vessel, Shad still hadn't spoken. He turned to them, sitting on a jump seat, their head in their hands, hair hanging limp around their head like a shroud.

"Shad, you good?" Carriles asked.

Shad looked up, their eyes distant and hollow.

"What happened down there?" Carriles asked. "Talk to me."

When Shad didn't respond, Wu leaned over to him. "When Shad saw that Delmar was turning his team on the Chinese, they tried to stop it. Delmar called them a traitor and fired on them . . ."

Carriles nodded. He didn't need it explained any further. Shad—like Chief Engineer Robinson, and Vicks—had ridden along with Delmar for years. They were loyal to the captain. But Shad hadn't had time to mull over their decision, like Vicks had. They had been thrown into the fire and had to act.

Now they were nursing a much deeper wound.

As the ship wove into the docking bay, Liu said, "Something's wrong."

Carriles looked around at the void of space surrounding the ship. Something *was* missing . . .

"Where's the other dropship?" Vicks asked.

Carriles realized he hadn't noticed the other ship as they flew across the void of space. Now, as the doors welcomed their ship, it was too late to do anything. They were already touching down, the bay doors closing behind them.

Carriles leapt from his seat and opened the back hatch of the ship. As the ramp slowly lowered, Carriles saw Stegman on the other side of the ramp—a look on his face that Carriles couldn't place.

It was the kind of look someone had when they were about to let you down.

Carriles watched Stegman slowly shake his head. "I'm sorry, man."

As the ramp hit the ground, the full scene was revealed. Carriles saw the mercenaries they'd tried to strand on the dropship in space gathered behind Stegman, each of them strapped with weaponry and ready for a fight. Standing at the center was Delmar, holding a blaster pointed right at Carriles.

"You and I need to have a little talk, Carriles," the captain said.

Carriles's stomach dropped.

Carriles walked halfway down the ramp and looked at Stegman. "You just doomed humanity. Live with that, for as long as we're alive. Because at this point, it won't be long."

His former friend gave a confused look, but Delmar just smiled, waving the blaster, gesturing for Carriles to march forward.

NEW DESTINY

BAZAAR HEADQUARTERS

It was too quiet.

That was Timony's first thought as she pushed herself up and through the tiny—but just wide enough—grating and into the basement of the Bazaar headquarters. She turned to help Oneida out of the sewer, wondering if the alien was just allowing her to help and didn't actually need the assist.

They both stood carefully. The room was dark, and it took Timony a moment to figure out where they were. The basement level of the Bazaar building was usually where the hard copy files were kept. The documents that needed to exist in some nonelectronic form. Timony had always liked being down here. The smell—at least what it smelled like when your own pants weren't covered in shit—and the quiet were soothing to her.

"Guess they didn't know we were coming," Oneida whispered.

"Or they do, and they want us to come closer," Timony said. "This isn't a highly trafficked area. But where we're headed is."

She motioned for Oneida to follow as she stepped out of the large office. The hallway was equally dark and empty.

Where *was* everyone, she wondered?

They walked past another office—the door ajar and empty as well. Timony held out her arm, signaling for Oneida to wait.

"This is bad," Timony said with a shake of her head. "This could be worse than the place being packed with armed thugs."

She walked into the empty office and sat down in front of a terminal. Oneida hovered behind her. Timony slid out Slade's ID card. Timony's access was long dead, but she was gambling that Slade's credentials hadn't been wiped yet.

"You sure about this?" Oneida asked.

"Slade is gone," Timony said, her voice flat. She had to power through this, or she'd find herself dwelling on what had happened, on her own failings. "But she can still help me."

Oneida opened her mouth to say something, but Timony cut her off.

"Yes, I took her ID badge from her dead body," Timony said, turning to face the screen, avoiding Oneida's eyes. "I'm a spy. We do the hard thing first. We're trained for this."

The soft clacking of keys was the only noise filling the tiny office. Timony, logged in as Slade, did a cursory scan of her incoming messages.

First and foremost, she needed to know where everyone was—and if there was anyone who could get in their way right now. She needed to get in contact with the *Mosaic*.

But what Timony found shook her to her core.

She was jaded. She had lived a life of betrayal and

deception, dancing in the shadows. But this was something else. She felt her entire body tense up as she read the series of encrypted messages shared with Slade. She swallowed hard before ducking into the tracing software. Another perk of the job: she could track any phone number anywhere on New Destiny. Not only was the name she sought in Slade's contacts but it pinged just a few floors above them.

Timony turned off the terminal and grabbed Slade's ID card, nearly knocking over her chair as she stood up.

"That was fast," Oneida said.

"We have to go . . . now," Timony said, at regular volume. She wasn't worried about being overheard now. It didn't matter. They had to move fast. "Follow me."

Their footsteps echoed down the empty hallway as they approached the central elevator, which cut through the entire building. They stepped in and Timony jabbed at the button for the top floor.

"Care to tell me what's going on?" Oneida asked.

"Still processing it," Timony said, looking up at the display, the numbers slowly rising as the elevator shunted them up. "But I also think someone will be ready to tell us soon enough."

The elevator stopped. A light appeared above the push-button display. Timony inserted Slade's card, holding her breath, hoping Sandwyn had been too distracted to remove her permissions. The light went from pale white to green. The doors hissed open, revealing a wide, dark space, lit by a series of viewscreens.

This was one of the Bazaar's data centers, where you could pull up communication taps, check CCTV cameras, and keep an eye on the outside of the facility and the surrounding space. Normally, it was humming with activity, but now it was empty, save for a lone figure.

"Sandwyn, is that you?" the figure called out, stepping forward.

It was Tobin, a grim look on his face.

"Ah. And here we find ourselves."

"You have a lot to answer for," Timony said as she and Oneida stepped off the elevator. "And you're on the clock starting now."

Tobin stepped back, and that's when Timony got a good look at him—a shaft of light cutting across his haggard face. Tobin had looked bad the last time Timony had spoken to him, when she'd still considered him a friend. Almost a mentor. But this was something else. Bloodshot eyes. A glossy, pale pallor to his skin. Clothes rumpled and dirty.

Timony marched forward and, without thinking, slammed her fist into Tobin's midsection. He folded forward fast, a low, guttural groan accompanying the movement. She stepped back as he fell to his knees.

"You ordered Slade to kill me?" she nearly screamed in the empty space.

"What . . . what . . . what do you want from me, Timony?" Tobin asked, struggling to get to his feet.

"I want the truth," Timony hissed. Oneida was close now. "About everything."

Tobin shook his head, like a frustrated elementary school teacher.

"The truth," he said, breathing hard. "You're still an idealist? The only truth is our truth. The story we craft. We're in a war for survival. I tried my best to ensure it."

"Where are the Russians, Tobin?" Timony asked. "Why is this place empty?"

Tobin didn't respond. Just that strange, throaty laugh.

"What are we doing?" Oneida interjected.

Timony raised a hand. "I'm waiting for Tobin to tell us what's going on." She stepped closer, taking some pleasure in Tobin's sharp flinch. She would hit him again. He knew this. "But I'm not going to wait for long."

Tobin didn't reply.

"It's over," Timony said. "If I don't get to the wire and alert the *Mosaic* that Oneida is alive, all hell will rain down on us. It may be happening seconds from now."

Tobin took in a sharp breath as he struggled to his feet.

"You're lying," he said.

"I'm not." Timony shook her head. "The Mutual is on their way to wipe us out. Because of the games that you're playing."

Tobin scoffed, but it felt empty—performative.

"You should be dead, Corin. Not Slade. She was my ace in the hole," Tobin said, spitting out each word with anger. "But you won her over somehow. Convinced her to do the *right* thing instead of the thing we *needed*. They're rarely the same. Idealism gets you nowhere. The real work—the real work of politics and espionage—is about creating the world we need."

Tobin took a long, jagged breath. Timony could feel Oneida standing next to her now.

"And you . . ." Tobin said, motioning to Oneida with his chin. "I should've known the Mutual would have a plant. But my own chief of staff . . ."

"You were going to let me die," Oneida said. "You didn't even try to get me back."

"Because some things are more important," Tobin said.

Timony stepped forward and grabbed Tobin's shirt, pulling him up to her, their faces close.

"Tell me exactly what happened, or you're not leaving this building, understand?" Timony said.

From Tobin's expression, she could tell he believed her. Where there had once been defiance and a snide confidence, there was something else. Fear.

"This mission was never meant to be about brokering peace. I told you that much. It was about resources. But we didn't want to do it with the Chinese or the Russians," Tobin said. "Delmar's crew was supposed to kill the Chinese contingent. Adan and Osman's deaths would be pinned on the Chinese, yours and Oneida's on the Russians. Nice and tidy. Lots of blame to spread around."

"And what, the US finally gets to the top of the dogpile?" Timony asked, still clutching Tobin by the collar. "You got dibs on the resources and everyone else would have to claw for scraps?"

"Exactly."

Timony let Tobin go. The senator took a few steps back.

"This is a coup," Timony said. "What about all that shit you fed me, about me and Carriles being your only hope?"

"I don't think I could've asked for two better marks. My only hope was that you would live up to your *sterling* reputations," Tobin said, nodding to himself. "Carriles is a loser who will listen to whatever Delmar tells him to do. He's too afraid of fading into the background, of being forgotten and ignored. And your wine-soaked brain was ripe for conspiracy theories—about the big, bad Russians doing evil things. It's always nice when you're the star of your own movie, huh? I needed you to agitate the Chinese and distract their field agents while I did my work. Which you did. Then Slade would dispose of you, and everyone would be running around like chickens with their heads cut off.

Instead, you're here. You couldn't even be a patsy right."

"You underestimated us," Timony said, her voice shaking. "Me and Jose. You didn't expect us to figure it out. You deserve to die a thousand, painful deaths."

"And you could kill me, easily," Tobin said, a smile creeping across his face. "That's the power you have. But do not forget who I am. As angry as you are in this moment, I want you to think long and hard about what killing me will do. How many parts of this you don't yet see, that you haven't even considered. Your strength is a harsh, brutal thing. What I have, Corin? That's real power."

He was right.

She hated that he was right.

Before Timony could respond, though, an alarm cut through the building like thunder.

Timony and Oneida stepped past Tobin and glanced at one of the viewscreens, which was now lit up and flashing. It was an Earth satellite feed, showing the moon awash in an orange silhouette, the dome of New Destiny jutting from the surface.

But there was something else. From the left-hand side of the screen, a long shape crept in. Something massive. So large that from the skewed perspective of the camera it appeared bigger than the moon itself. Timony and Oneida watched as the shape came to a stop above New Destiny, hovering over the colony's dome. The shape took up most of the screen now, and Timony had lost any sense of its shape.

"A ship . . ." Timony said.

"That's one of ours. A Mutual warship," Oneida said, staring at the small display. "We only use those for one thing."

Timony started to ask, but Oneida finished her thought first.

"Complete annihilation."

Timony turned, ready to deliver a cutting I-told-you-so to Tobin, but discovered the senator was already gone.

MOSAIC

DOCKING BAY

Carriles didn't have time for this.

That thought flashed through his brain as he looked down the barrel of Captain Wythe Delmar's blaster, pointed directly at him. He could feel the self-satisfied grin on Delmar's face before he saw it.

Everything seemed to be moving in slow motion. Carriles was gutted by Stegman's betrayal. He had expected to dock the shuttle and then bolt to the wire to warn New Destiny, to try for one more Hail Mary pass in what felt like a series of them.

But no. Delmar would not let this end.

Carriles glanced at Vicks for a second. Saw her eyebrow twitch slightly in response. He didn't know this woman well. But he did know one thing—she could fight. So could Wu and Shad. They were trained for this kind of thing. He and Liu could hold their own.

But the mercenaries complicated things.

The docking bay was crowded with people—nearly everyone on the ship. He and his little crew were badly outnumbered.

"It's over," Delmar said. Then he turned to Deane, the mercenary Carriles had recognized—who looked pretty pissed about being stuck on a floating prison for the better part of the day. "Put them down in the brig."

"If they get a little roughed up along the way, I hope you won't hold it against me," Deane said.

"Not at all," Delmar said.

"Wait," Carriles said.

"You're not in charge here, Carriles . . ."

Carriles turned to the gaggle of people around them and raised his voice. "As some of you might know—there's a massive warship headed for New Destiny."

Gasps interrupted Carriles. He gave it a few beats before continuing.

"There's a chance for us. For everyone on this ship, and everyone at New Destiny. We blow it, everyone dies. Every member of your family. Everyone you love. But if I can get to the wire and get in contact with New Destiny, I think there's a way to save us. We can't waste time with this."

"Carriles . . ." Delmar said, raising his voice.

"We have one shot at this. And if Delmar gets his way, everyone dies."

Looks shot through the crowd—anger, fear, confusion. But no one moved. No one said anything.

They were alone in this.

Carriles sighed, his shoulders dropping. It was too much to ask. Too much to ask the crew members here to put their lives on the line, to go against the captain. There was no time.

Then he heard a click. He looked up and found Penagos holding a blaster at Delmar and Deane, his hands shaking slightly. "Captain? I—uh, I hate to do this, but . . . but I think we should hear them out."

"Penagos? Have you lost your mind? Do you want to be tried for treason, too?" Delmar looked around. "Anyone else? There's not enough room in the brig. I'll start kicking people out of the docking bay if I have to."

Carriles saw a fleeting opportunity and took it. He swung his elbow out, connecting with Delmar's blaster and surprising the captain. He sent a fist into the captain's midsection and watched him jerk forward—more in surprise than pain. He heard Deane moaning in surprise and hoped Penagos got a good lick in on the mercenary. As Carriles continued to attack Delmar, the docking bay erupted into chaos, shots firing out, people yelling and grunting.

It distracted him just enough for Delmar to throw himself forward and body check Carriles.

"You little prick . . ." Delmar said.

Delmar tried to reach for the blaster that had landed on the floor, only to realize it was gone. Carriles caught a flash of movement in his peripheral vision, and then saw Shad wrapping an arm around Delmar's neck, yanking him to his feet, and putting a blaster to the side of his head.

"Stop!" the security officer yelled.

The sudden silence was unnerving, Carriles thought. The din was replaced by complete silence.

The skirmish halted for a moment, the room crackling with energy. Carriles looked around. There didn't seem to be any major injuries, but a few people were lying on the ground, mid-struggle.

"You left me there to die," Shad said into Delmar's ear.

"You disobeyed my orders," Delmar said, wincing. "That's treason, Shad."

"Your orders disobeyed everything we stand for," Shad said, before dashing forward.

Carriles picked up the blaster that Delmar dropped. "Let's go."

Carriles felt a shift. Of energy. Of electricity. Of something he couldn't see or touch, but that was there. Delmar's power was gone. The crew was looking to Carriles now.

No pressure.

Carriles looked down and saw Stegman cradling his own head, blood trailing down the side of his face. Someone must have got him good. Carriles considered saying something clever to his former friend, but that felt empty and pointless now. He just didn't have time.

Wu stepped forward, holding a blaster on Deane. Penagos was at his side, doing the same. "Go," Wu said. "We've got them covered."

"Thank you," Carriles said.

He turned and ran, quickly hitting a sprint. He could feel Vicks and Liu keeping pace as the three of them careened down the main shuttle deck, toward the elevators. The two women briefly stopped at a weapons locker to grab blasters, and then caught up.

"What's your plan?" Vicks asked, matching Carriles's speed as they reached the main elevator doors. "How far are we going to take this?"

Carriles shrugged as he stopped and jabbed at the elevator display.

"We know what we need to do. Somehow, someone has to get to the wire and call New Destiny. Hopefully, their spy is alive, and we survive. That's it, I think," Carriles said, his voice harried and exasperated. "I mean, there isn't much further to go, right? Best case, our careers are over.

Worst case, we're dead. We may as well die doing the right thing."

Before Vicks could respond, a low shriek cut through the docking bay behind them.

They all stopped and turned toward the noise in unison.

What they saw would be burned into their collective memory forever.

It was a struggle. Stegman and Wu, their arms locked together, each one groping and reaching for the blaster that Stegman held precariously. Carriles caught sight of Penagos, looking at the struggle while holding his own blaster on Deane and Delmar, trying to keep them back.

Wu must have lost control of the docking bay. He had a deep gash across his face—but everything was moving so fast. By the time Carriles had braced to head back, by the time he took a step in Wu's direction, Stegman had overpowered him.

The two men fought hard, but Stegman had the weapon now, had taken it from Wu. Carriles watched as Stegman swung the hilt of the blaster across Wu's face. Even from across the room, Carriles could hear the weapon connect with bone. The fight should've been over then, but Wu leapt forward, his hands gripping Stegman's throat and clamping down. Vicks aimed her rifle, angling to find a clean shot, but the struggle was too quick, the two men throwing their bodies back and forth.

Carriles saw the abject panic in his old friend's face—a look that said *I am going to die now*. He wanted to believe that Stegman didn't want to kill Wu. That Aaron Stegman wasn't a murderer. But wants don't trump reality, and in that moment, Stegman crossed a line he could never erase.

Carriles screamed as Stegman tilted the blaster up and

sent a bolt into Wu's midsection. Kept screaming as he watched Wu fall, a low thump signaling that the *Mosaic*'s first officer was gone.

Carriles felt Vicks's hands pulling him back as his scream faded. Stegman stood over the body. Then Stegman turned to face them, his eyes wild with rage and hate and fear.

Stegman charged toward them, one hand clutching what looked to be a ripped sleeve from his shirt over his face, blood soaking through it. In his other hand was the blaster. Delmar came in close behind, his expression a blend of confidence and manic embarrassment.

They'd just killed their own crew member, Carriles thought. There was no coming back from this. He shuddered to think what the other crew members were going through on the docking bay, having witnessed Wu's death firsthand. This was spiraling, fast. And it wasn't going to get any easier. And it was all happening as New Destiny inched closer to decimation. A decimation that was guaranteed if they didn't reach the wire soon.

"Give up now, Jose," Stegman said, wobbly on his feet. "Wu is dead. As you can see, we're not fucking around. There's nowhere you can go. The captain has taken the ship back. You five are traitors. We're well within our rights to kill you on sight."

Before Carriles could think of a response, Liu jumped into action. She fired at Stegman, striking the wall next to him, knocking him back into Delmar, causing the two of them to duck around a corner for cover. Liu motioned for Vicks and Carriles to keep going. To get to the wire.

"There are more people coming," Liu said. "I heard them over the comms. Delmar's given the security crew your locations and told them to shoot to kill. You have to keep moving."

"What about you?" Vicks yelled.

"If you win, we'll be okay," Liu said, pointing her blaster at the hallway they'd all just run through, expecting a cadre of security goons to barrel down at any moment. "If not . . . well, it was nice working with you."

Carriles felt Vicks's hand on his shoulder, tugging him back. Carriles spun around and they boarded the elevator. The hissing sound of the closing doors blended with the low hum of blaster fire.

"We're as good as dead," she muttered as the elevator sent them upward, toward the bridge.

"That's one point of view," Carriles said, leaning back on the elevator's far wall. "What would they expect us to do in this moment?"

Vicks tilted her head. Carriles wasn't sure if it was admiration or confusion.

"What would you expect me to do?" Carriles asked.

"I'd expect you to get to the wire," she said, eyes on him—she was intrigued now. That was good.

Carriles felt the elevator shudder slightly. He stepped forward and punched a few buttons. The elevator shuddered again, changing direction.

"Then Delmar would think that, too," Carriles said. "We're going somewhere else."

Vicks raised her other eyebrow.

The *Mosaic*'s engineering area was more chaotic than the rest of the ship—a collection of ladders, walkways, and tunnels, more like a network of sewers and passageways with an overhead collection of paths above it. The elevator took them to the top, and they walked onto one of the main catwalks to the ship's central nervous system.

And Delmar was waiting for them, standing on a metal walkway suspended over the whirring engines. His blaster was gripped tightly in his hand, which lingered at his thigh, but looked ready to whip up and aim directly at Carriles's face.

"Shit," Carriles said under his breath.

"You're smart, Carriles, I'll give you that," Delmar said, stepping toward them, each footfall barely audible over the sounds of the engine array. He held the blaster up with an ease and confidence Carriles knew he'd never have. "No one's caused me as much trouble as you. Hell, even on the other side. Didn't think the biggest pain in my ass on this mission would be part of my own crew. But here we are. I should've flagged you, if we're being honest. The second you started asking those stupid, nosy questions, I should've known. But did you really think I wouldn't be able to find you? This is my goddamn ship."

Carriles nodded.

"You got me, Cap," he said with a shrug. "I thought I'd be able to get away with it. But if you really think the Interstellar Union is going to give you a pass on this . . ."

"What, that collection of spineless sycophants?" Delmar asked. "They'll do what they're told. They've been trained to listen to the loudest voice in the room. It's usually me."

"Why do this, Delmar?" Carriles asked. "Surely you didn't plan this alone."

"Alone? No. It takes brave people willing to untangle the beliefs and traditions weighing us down. I've got Tobin to handle the Senate and Sandwyn to handle the Bazaar," he said. "We kept it tight and focused. We knew that no one else would be willing to make the hard choices necessary to survive. To thrive. It doesn't matter. Once we fulfill the mission, the rest of them will come around."

As Delmar ranted, Carriles clocked the control panel to his left. It was within arm's reach. It was why he'd come here first. It could leave them stranded all the way out here, with no hope of returning home, but it would give him the time he needed to save New Destiny. Or die trying.

He'd have to be quick. He'd have to distract Delmar somehow.

Delmar's expression morphed slowly—from steely confidence to slight hesitation. Despite all of Delmar's bravado, he was certainly not stupid. And Carriles's glib tone had given more away than the pilot had hoped to share.

Delmar pivoted, pointing the sidearm at Vicks. "I'm disappointed in you. I had high hopes for us. With the Chinese contingent gone, you would've finally been my number two, just like it should've always been," Delmar said. "We can still achieve that. Just tell me what's going on. Why are you two down here?"

With Delmar's attention focused on Vicks, Carriles glanced down at the captain's boots, to make sure the gravity function hadn't been turned on—it hadn't. He moved his body slowly to the left, snaking a hand behind his back, toward the control panel . . .

"You're asking the wrong person, Captain," Vicks said flatly. She wasn't lying, Carriles knew. "I've chosen sides, but I'm not tapped into the acting captain's brain."

Acting captain? Did Vicks just make a joke?

"Have you both lost your minds?" Delmar asked. "It's over. The ship is mine again. I will complete the mission assigned to me—I will get what we came for. You will be lucky if you survive the trip back home. Now, let's make this easy, okay? Hand me your weapons and—"

Carriles slid his hand over the fingerprint access point and heard a small, reassuring *ding*, barely audible over the grind of the engines. He was grateful that Wu had done his part.

The plan had come together fast. On the short flight back to the *Mosaic*, he'd laid it out to Wu and Wu alone. Whatever happened next would happen fast. Carriles needed full access to everything on the ship.

Like any good, complicated starship, the *Mosaic* didn't have many simple on or off switches. To turn it off, you'd need to complete an elaborate series of movements and motions that required approval and sign-off from different departments and sections of the crew. Only the captain could override those mundane processes.

Oh, and the first officer.

So Wu had swooped into the system to give Carriles that access.

And now, while Delmar was focused on Vicks, Carriles flipped the now-accessible plastic cover of the kill switch on the control panel.

The switch that would turn off the gravity engine.

It was a safety measure for engineering, in case someone was in danger. Killing it would power down the ship. With it, the life support and their ability to travel. They'd risk drifting off into dark space, and being lost forever. Similar to Delmar's own slow move into his own, personal void—one Carriles didn't think their captain could come back from.

If the switch was hit, all systems would be useless.

Along with the artificial gravity.

As Carriles pressed the button, he put his foot on the

guardrail, pushing up hard, hoping Delmar wasn't quick enough to fire, but bracing himself for the possibility. Rather than fall into the engines, which were now groaning to a halt underneath him, his stomach leapt as he floated toward the ceiling.

Carriles twisted hard so that he was facing Delmar, and watched his plan play out exactly as he'd hoped.

Delmar's face contorted in confusion as he realized what was going on, hovering a few feet in the air now. He swung his blaster toward Carriles, now a floating target. But Vicks had clocked what Carriles was doing too, reaching down to activate the gravity tethers in her boots, and then clomping across the walkway to Delmar.

Delmar heard Vicks approaching. Rather than fire on Carriles, he turned his attention to her.

Too late.

Vicks crashed into her former boss, sending him backward. The sound of the blaster clattering off the railing and down into the twisting tunnels and walkways below gave Carriles a brief jolt of relief. But then he saw Delmar and Vicks, the two of them grappling in midair, both of them struggling for dominance. Carriles looked for something to push off of, so he could launch himself toward them to help her, but there was nothing close by.

He was stuck, left to watch the battle play out.

Helpless.

Helpless as Delmar wrapped his hands around Vicks's throat. As her oxygen was cut off and her face went red. As Delmar opened his mouth in a wordless scream.

As a blade appeared in Vicks's hand.

She swung outward, slicing across Delmar's neck, opening a wide, red gash that streaked globules of dark blood. She managed to pull herself back onto the railing as the captain gasped—a choked, soggy sound—for life, hands clutching his neck. She hastily put a med-strip over the worst of the wound.

Carriles watched, his mouth agape, then bumped into the ceiling and realized he could now move again. He twisted his body around, using his feet to launch himself back toward the control panel. He nearly missed it, but managed to grab a railing to stop his momentum. He slapped the button, reengaging the drive.

Gravity yanked hard and Carriles fell into the railing and tumbled onto the walkway, his body ringing with pain. He looked up to find Vicks and Delmar in a heap on the other side of the catwalk.

"Will he live?" Carriles asked.

"He has a chance," she said. "I'll take him to Liu. Nice work."

"Don't say that just yet," he said. "Life support and gravity will function fine. With all the stress the engine's been through, and our lack of supplies out here, there's a really good chance this ship isn't going anywhere."

Vicks went silent, processing the information. She nodded, then strode over to Carriles, their faces close. "Get to the wire. Now. Don't fuck this up," she said. "This can't be for nothing."

Before Carriles could respond, Vicks dashed to the captain, threw his arm over her shoulder, and dragged him toward the elevators.

Then they were gone.

Carriles looked down at his tunic. Splashes of Delmar's blood had marred the blue cloth. Carriles fought back the urge to throw up.

Instead, he turned around and headed for the communications array terminal.

Where Wu had used his admin access to patch him into the wire terminal.

Those familiar dots and dashes of a message coming through.

Carriles was familiar with how the wire worked—atoms split across space. It twisted his brain into a pretzel to think about, but he didn't need to understand it. He just needed it to work.

Before he could even think about what he would say to whoever was waiting on the other side back on New Destiny, he found a message waiting.

-- --- ... .- .. -.-. --..-- / .--. .-.. . .- ... . / .-. . ... .--. --- -. -.. .-.-.- / - .... / .. ... / -.-. --- .-. .. -. / - .. -- --- -. -.-- .-.-.- / - .... . / -- ..- - ..- .- .-.. / ... .--. -.-- / .. ... / .- .-.. .. ...- . .-.-.- / .... . .-. / -. .- -- . / .. ... / --- -. . .. -.. .- .-.-.- / - .... . .-. . .----. ... / .- / .-- .- .-. ... .--. / .- -... --- ...- . / - .... . / -.-. .. - -.-- .-.-.- / ... --- -- . --- -. . --..-- / .--. .-.. . .- ... . / .-. . ... .--. --- -. -.. .-.-.-

Even though Carriles knew Morse code, a little monitor underneath the feed translated what it was saying.

Mosaic, *please respond. This is Corin Timony. The Mutual spy is alive. Her name is Oneida. There's a warship above the city. Someone, please respond.*

And Carriles was flooded with a strange combination of relief and guilt.

NEW DESTINY

BAZAAR HEADQUARTERS

Timony stared at the terminal, wondering if anyone would see the message she had just sent. The *Mosaic* was light-years away. Even the wire had its limits. If it was broken, if there was an equipment malfunction . . .

She took a moment to check the *Mosaic*'s recorded logs. The last message sent was from yesterday: the ship was approaching Esparar and preparing to go down to the surface. According to the log, it'd been more than a day since *Mosaic* had checked in; they were supposed to do that every six hours.

This was bad.

They could all be dead. Especially if Oneida's people were as vindictive as she made them sound.

"What's going on?" Oneida asked.

"Just wait," Timony said.

As if on cue, a message appeared.

- .. -- --- -. -.-- .-.-.- / .. - .----. ... / .--- --- ... . .-.-.- / - .... .- -. -.- / --. --- -.. .-.-.- / - .... . -.-- / - .... .. -. -.- / - .... . / ... .--. -.-- / .. ... / -.. . .- -.. .-.-.- / - .... . -.-- .----. .-. . / --. --- .. -. --. / - --- / ... .--. .- .-. . / ..- ... / -... ..- - / .-- .. .--. . / --- ..- - / -. . .-- / -.. . ... - .. -. -.-- .-.-.-

Timony. It's Jose. Thank god. They think their spy is dead. They're going to spare us but wipe out New Destiny.

Carriles.

Both the last and the only person she wanted to hear from at this moment.

Timony thought about the last time she saw him. When he'd gotten the assignment to replace Adan. Carriles had carried on, falling upward and forward, the gravity of his own name dragging him along. She was somewhere else. She was in the white-hot center of her grief, and they had been passing each other in the Bazaar lobby. They'd locked eyes, and he'd looked away and down from her, like he was hiding from her gaze . . .

No, Timony thought. This wasn't the time.

"Tell them I'm alive again," Oneida said, reading the screen underneath the code. "Tell them they have to tell Telio I'm alive. Tell them I told them to ask for her specifically."

"Spell that," Timony said.

"T-E-L-I-O."

MOSAIC

ENGINEERING

Carriles held his breath. He wanted to ask Timony if she was okay. Tell her to be safe. If this was the last moment in which he could communicate with her, he wanted to tell her that he was sorry. About Adan. About her career. Everything.

But their personal history meant nothing when put up against the history and future of the human race.

So he waited.

- .... . / ... .--. -.-- .----. ... / -. .- -- . / .. ... / --- -. . .. -.. .- .-.-.- / ... . / ... .- .. -.. / - --- / ..-. .. -. -.. / - . .-.. .. --- .-.-.- / - . .-.. .-.. / - . .-.. .. --- / .... . .-. / -.-. --- -- -- ..- -. .. -.-. .- - --- .-. / -... .-. --- -.- . .-.-.- / -... ..- - / ... .----. ... / ... .- ..-. . .-.-.-

Repeat—the spy's name is Oneida. She said to find Telio. Tell Telio her communicator broke. But she's safe. She's alive.

Carriles's entire body let go of the tension he'd been holding. Here, finally, was something. Something he could work with. But did they have enough time?

He typed into the wire: *How long do we have?*

And he waited.

The response came back quickly.

-- --- ...- . / ..-. .- ... - .-.-.-

Move fast.

Great. Given the chaos on the ship, there was no way he'd make it down to the planet in time. He searched around the communications array, hoping something would come from him. His heart raced and his palms erupted in sweat. He closed his eyes and took a deep breath.

Then he typed out one last message.

Whatever happens next, I just want you to know I'm sorry.

He waited a few seconds for a response. None came. That was okay, he told himself. He'd said his piece—that was all that mattered in this moment. It was a selfish act, in a way—unburdening himself. It only meant something if it was done with the intent to help her, not relieve him.

It only meant something if he could save them all.

He got to work. He had to get a message down to the planet. He had to do that knowing that whatever communication band the Mutual was using was different than the frequency the *Mosaic* used.

The wire would be useless. It depended on shared atoms—a direct line, like two tin cans connected by a string. It was incredibly unlikely the Mutual would be able to access or read the messages they were trading. Communications at closer distances were typically encoded onto electromagnetic waves—specifically, radio waves. Which the Mutual would know. Maybe they had once used the same technology before they moved away from it. What other waves could transmit data?

Wait. Izaiah said something about that.

What was it?

Carriles racked his brain, trying to shake loose the one detail that mattered in the jumble currently occupying his attention.

Then it came to him: ultraviolet light.

Light was the fastest thing in the universe, so yes, a great way to communicate. Carriles clicked through the array in front of him, scanning the cosmic radiation surrounding the ship, narrowing the band until he was scanning the available light. Normal light waves—waves of any kind—should look like a gentle, consistent rise and fall. But the ultraviolet light waves surrounding the ship were jumping in stops and starts.

Carriles changed the frequency of the deep space communicator and was hit with a fierce rattle and buzz from the speaker in front of him. He turned on his comms, took a deep breath, and spoke.

"This is Jose Carriles, acting captain of the *Mosaic*. I need to speak to Telio. Please, the Mutual spy on New Destiny is alive. Oneida is alive. Please come in."

He was met with static in response.

Maybe he was wrong, maybe he needed to try another frequency—

Something hard slammed across the back of his skull. He tumbled from the chair, his head spinning, and rolled away, trying to put some distance between him and whoever hit him. He struggled to his feet and found Stegman, holding his chest. He must have been wearing body armor, and the blaster fire Vicks and Wu pumped into him no doubt broke some ribs. He wasn't happy, but he was standing, holding himself up, his own blaster hanging at his side.

"Let's go," Stegman said.

"Why the hell are you doing this, Aaron? We're friends, dude."

"We were," he said, raising the blaster. "We were friends."

"You understand what's happening here, right?" Carriles asked. "We're going to eradicate the entire human race because of politics. Is that what you want?"

"It's us or them," Stegman said. "They knew we were hanging on by our fingertips. They knew they could help. They chose not to. So we're choosing to survive."

"Is that what Delmar told you?" Carriles asked. "The only thing that happened was we couldn't get into their fancy club, because we were acting like a bunch of drunken assholes. They weren't wrong. The answer isn't to storm the club and take it over. We need to sober up and mind our manners."

"You know what your problem is?" Stegman asked. "What your problem has always been? You're too much of an idealist. You've never had to struggle."

"Yeah? And you're blind. You're following orders without any thought of the consequences. There's a warship sitting over New Destiny right now, ready to wipe the whole place out. Us? We're going to be stuck here. Without New Destiny as a travel and manufacturing point, the rest of the colonies are going to wither and die. The human race will hobble along for a bit, but not much longer. It's a death sentence. That's the reality. And if that's what you want to happen, sure, shoot me and go get your gold star from Delmar. Pretty soon there won't be anyone left to admire it."

Stegman had nearly drawn the blaster to arm's length, but as Carriles spoke, his hand dropped a little. His eyes darted to the side.

"C'mon, man," Carriles said. "I need you to trust me."

A burst of static cut through the communicator, dying down moments later, followed by a voice.

"Carriles? This is Telio. Your message has been received. We wish to speak with Oneida."

Carriles put up his hands. "I need to answer that."

Stegman gripped the gun a little tighter.

"Please," Carriles said. "Your mom is on New Destiny. Your sister. If nothing else, let me just try to save them."

Stegman sighed and dropped his arm, the gun falling from his hand.

Carriles dove for the comms. "Telio. Her communicator is broken and our system of communication is . . . rudimentary. I'm not sure if you can speak to her directly, or only through a relay."

"We are aware of your communication capabilities," Telio said. "It's relatively impressive. Most societies require more time and advanced technology before they can crack quantum communication. We have something that may work, but I will need to come aboard with a team. We have paused the warship, but any lapse in communication, or any threat made to us, will give us reason to eliminate the *Mosaic*, as well as New Destiny and every other human colony in your galaxy."

"I understand," Carriles said. "Get up here and we'll make it work."

Carriles turned to find Stegman shaking his head. "Now you're inviting them to tea . . ."

"Shut up, man," Carriles said. He looked down at the wire, ready to explain the situation, when he found a response from Timony, to his apology.

.. / -.- -. --- .--

I know.

Knowing what he knew about Timony, that short message made his heart swell.

NEW DESTINY

BAZAAR HEADQUARTERS

- .... . / .- - - .- -.-. -.- / .. ... / --- -. / .... --- .-.. -.. .-.-.- / - . .-.. .. --- /
.-- .. .-.. .-.. / -... . / -.-. --- -- .. -. --. / .- -... --- .- .-. -.. .-.-.- / ... .
/ - .... .. -. -.- ... / - .... . .-. . .----. ... / .- / .-- .- -.-- / - --- / -.-. --- --
-- ..- -. .. -.-. .- - . .-.-.- / .-- . .----. .-.. .-.. / -... . / -... .- -.-. -.- / ... .
--- .-. - .-.. -.-- .-.-.-

The attack is on hold. Telio will be coming aboard. She thinks there's a way to communicate. We'll be back shortly.

Timony sat back and sighed.

Okay, that was something.

"What did he mean?" Oneida asked. "When he said he was sorry."

Timony leaned back in the chair. "Carriles is the ship's pilot, and I guess he's running the show now. Not sure how that happened." She gazed around the room. "We've been friends since we were kids. His mom was a bigwig Martian senator. My parents were . . . not so important. We went to school together and we stayed friends. I got into the Bazaar, he got into the pilot academy. But he always frustrated me . . ."

Oneida sat in a chair across from Timony and locked eyes with her.

"Why?"

That was a big *why*. Timony got the sense that Oneida wanted to understand what had happened between them, the way a zoologist studies animal behavior. Curiosity with a dash of empathy.

"Carriles is one of those people who is just naturally talented at whatever he picks up. He could trip over a violin, and by the time he got to his feet, he would know how to play a concerto. He rode on his natural ability and his mom's name and he just . . . floated. I had to break my ass in half just to keep up with him. I had to study harder. Work harder."

Oneida offered a sheepish little grin.

"I have a friend like that," Oneida said. "We love each other, but she resents me for the things I've achieved."

"It's not about resentment. I don't begrudge him for how easy he has it. It just frustrates me that he doesn't seem to *get* how easy it was for him. When I got into the Bazaar, I was competitive. I wanted to be the best. So I went looking for an edge. I got into Boost. It's a drug . . ."

"I'm aware of Boost," Oneida said. "I tried it once. It made me sleepy. Not designed for my physiology, I guess."

"I guess not," Timony said. "Anyway, I was getting my Boost from Carriles. He was dealing as a way to earn a little cash. And because he just thought he was untouchable, and wanted to prove it. And he was, until he got caught with a felony quantity. Anyone else would have been thrown in jail. Not only did he get a pass but he got to stay a pilot."

Timony sighed, tried to center herself.

"Anyway, they traced his contacts and found he was dealing to me. And because I didn't have boundless potential along with a famous mom, I got demoted, with probably no pathway to get back to where I used to be. He skated. I took the brunt of it."

Oneida nodded slowly. "That sounds very hard."

"It was. Even with his mom gone, his name still carried weight. But what made me the angriest is the fact that he could have, I don't know . . . done something. Not just sat back and watched my life fall apart."

"But you made your choice, too."

Timony wanted to defend herself, and realized she couldn't. "Yeah, I did."

"There are limits to power," Oneida said. "And there are consequences to actions. He apologized. Do you accept?"

Timony considered the swell of emotion in her chest, and finally said, "Yes."

"Why?"

Timony laughed. "All humanity is standing on the edge of a cliff. And your people are ready to push us over the side." She shrugged. "It seems petty, in light of that, doesn't it? To hold a grudge?" She folded her hands in her lap. "If I'm going to die in the next hour, I don't want to die feeling the way I've felt for the last year. I want to meet it with a little bit of serenity. I know he never meant to hurt me. I'm forgiving him as much as I'm forgiving myself."

"Hmm," Oneida said.

There was a lot in that *Hmm*, Timony thought. She wasn't sure what, but she liked the way it sounded.

"So now what?" Oneida asked.

"We wait."

Timony got up and moved over to the window looking

out over the streets. When she looked out, she was hit by a sight she hadn't even considered, but made total sense given the situation.

Bedlam. Absolute chaos.

People were running in the streets. Screaming—though Timony couldn't hear them through the double-paned, bulletproof glass. The panic was palpable. Parents ushering their children inside. Mobs forming, stomping down the street. Small fires burning.

That's why the Bazaar offices were empty.

They weren't just looking for Timony. It was all hands on deck out there.

And this would only get worse. Timony watched as someone smashed the front window of a fancy jewelry store. Then saw a group of young men storm in to pick the place clean.

Right.

Everyone was just finding out what she'd already known. She tilted her head, to look up and toward the dome. The vast of space suddenly didn't seem so vast.

Because there was something blocking the view.

Oneida appeared at Timony's shoulder. She gazed out over the chaos in the streets and shook her head. "This is why we made the decision we did."

Timony felt a surge of anger. "So every planet, every society that makes up the Mutual, they're all perfect, huh?"

Oneida paused. "Well, no, I mean—"

"These people are *scared*," Timony said. "For all they know, they're about to die. To be perfectly frank, I'm not even sure I want to be a member of your fancy fucking club at this point, if you lack the ability to just consider what someone else might be feeling."

Oneida drew a long breath. She looked out at the street and shook her head.

"Maybe you're—"

Oneida was cut off by a sharp bang as the door was swung open. Six Bazaar security agents swarmed in, wearing black tactical gear, carrying stun sticks, the blue ends crackling with electricity. They filed into the room, forming a barricade between Timony, Oneida, and the door.

Sandwyn, wearing his own set of tactical gear, sans helmet, strode into the room with a blaster clutched in his right hand.

"Timony—I'm so disappointed in you."

Timony's stomach dropped. Their entrance into the Bazaar had been too easy up until now. She thought maybe she'd just gotten lucky, that everyone was out in the streets, so busy looking for her, or dealing with an alien invasion, that they'd skirted through unnoticed.

But Tobin must have alerted Sandywn.

"What did I tell you, Timony?" Sandwyn asked. "I told you to forget it."

MOSAIC

DOCKING BAY

Carriles met Vicks and Shad in the docking bay. Shad had a rifle slung across their chest. Their face was bloodied, but they were standing. The rest of the area was chaotic. Some people were still alive, tended to by Liu and other crew members.

The firefight that had cost Wu his life hadn't been limited to his brawl with Stegman. The Carriles contingent had to engage with Delmar's group—which included the mercenaries they'd initially snuck aboard to take on the Mutual.

Bodies were strewn around the docking bay. Some crew members. Some mercenaries.

The fallen included Penagos. Carriles didn't need to check to make sure. The man's body was still, motionless, his vacant eyes staring at the ceiling. Carriles closed his eyes, took a breath, and said a quick prayer for his fallen comrade.

But, for now, order had been restored. The remaining mercenaries had been subdued, their hands lashed behind their backs, held at gunpoint. Temperatures, for the moment, were cool.

"How's Delmar?" Carriles asked Vicks.

"He'll live," she said. "But he won't bother us anymore."

Carriles thought he saw Vicks smirk, but when he looked again, her stoic expression returned. Maybe he'd imagined it.

They gazed out at the landing door, which would soon open to allow Telio and a team of whoever she brought on board. He hoped the ship would be able to fit and dock properly. He hoped this whole thing wouldn't go sideways.

He hoped for a lot of things.

"Second thoughts?" he asked.

"No, I don't do that," Vicks said. "I also don't feel like dying. Trust is hard to earn, but easy to lose. Delmar lost mine. I've had a bad feeling about this mission for a while now. It's easy to romanticize it all, as you know. But it's not just about the good in humanity. It's about survival."

"Thanks for having my back," Carriles said.

Vicks laughed. "I don't particularly trust you, either. Not all the way. Not with that last name. At the same time, you were willing to step up. I respect that."

"But?"

"No buts. You can be the face of this all you want." She patted the rifle. "Just don't forget who made it happen for you. And know that my loyalty is to me. And to people who do what they say, and mean it. Understood?"

"Copy that," Carriles said, taking a subtle step away from Vicks.

"Where the hell are they?" Vicks asked.

Carriles checked the screen next to him. "There's definitely a ship out there. Just waiting for some kind of . . ."

Before he could finish, there was a sound behind them, like a steak sizzling on a grill, and the air grew hot. Carriles turned to find Telio's swirling blue mist, along with two Reosian men. From the Reosians' long white cloaks, Carriles guessed they were scientists. At their feet was a heavy black case made from a material that Carriles couldn't be sure was metal or plastic.

"Hello, Carriles," Telio said.

"That's a hell of a magic trick."

"I suspect from a human's point of view, magic is a catch-all term for anything you don't understand."

"We'll try to keep up."

"This quantum communicator of yours," Telio said. "We require access."

Vicks leaned into Carriles, her voice a whisper. "What the hell is that?"

"Just roll with it."

Carriles nodded to Telio and put up his hand, pointing them toward engineering. One of the Reos scientists leaned down and pressed the side of the box, which gently floated a few inches into the air. He and Vicks led them through the ship, the box following, and Carriles thought about how this was probably a whole new set of criminal charges, if things went wrong. Not only did he invite them aboard but he was giving them access to their tech.

He'd worry about that later, he thought.

If there was a later. If things went wrong, he probably wouldn't make it out alive.

Carriles locked eyes with the chief engineer, Tommy Robinson, as they entered the main engineering hall. The room still felt charged. Carriles was still recovering from the last time he'd been in engineering—watching Vicks slice open the captain's throat. He hoped this time would be a little more mellow. But based on the scowl decorating Robinson's face, he couldn't be sure.

"Commander," Carriles said with a nod.

Robinson didn't flinch. He turned to follow the group as they passed through the engine room. Robinson's mechanics stood pressed against the walls, scowling.

"It bears repeating, Carriles, but the way this ship harnesses gravity waves is impressive for a species of your level of knowledge," Telio said.

"I love how every compliment you offer us feels a little backhanded," Carriles said.

"I enjoy your sense of humor. I would like one of my team to remain here and examine the engine. I see that it's currently disengaged."

Robinson stepped forward, his face smeared with grease, his barrel chest pressing out. "First off, I'm not taking orders from a cloud of smoke. Second, I'm not letting them touch my baby. Nonnegotiable."

Carriles held his breath. Robinson was the kind of guy who looked like he got into bar fights as a hobby.

"Robinson, stand down," Carriles said. "We're going to play ball, or no one goes home, because home will be dust."

"You're not in charge."

Carriles took a step toward the burly engineer. He was a head shorter than Robinson, and he knew that in any kind of showdown he'd end up crushed into a ball. But Carriles looked up and fixed Robinson with the best hard stare he could muster. "Right now, I am. And I'm saying they get to look at the engine. You can keep an eye on them, but if you want to act like an idiot and be responsible for the death of the entire human race, I guess that's on you."

Robinson took a deep breath, then offered an even deeper exhale. Then he gave a small nod.

"Gonna be checking their work. And they can't use my tools."

"Montzar," Telio said, and one of the scientists stepped forward. "This seems to be your specialty."

The tall, gangly scientist nodded, and pressed the side of the floating box. A seam appeared in it, and the box split into two equal parts. One side followed Telio, the other followed Montzar.

Carriles gave one final look to Robinson, who seemed incredibly unhappy but willing to collaborate, and then brought Telio and the other scientists to the communications array. Carriles presented it to them, and the remaining Reosian scientist stepped forward and took the box, which now developed another seam in the top and opened again. The third alien began pulling out and setting up equipment around the wire. It looked like smooth panes of glass that, once moved into position, stayed there, floating in proximity to the console.

"What are you doing?" Carriles asked.

"You understand how the wire works?" Telio asked.

"On a rudimentary level," Carriles said. "It's quantum entanglement. Take an atom, split it in two, whatever you do to one side is immediately reflected on the other side."

"Do you understand how exactly they communicate?"

"No," Carriles said. "Frankly, no one does. We just know that it works."

"The universe is so much bigger than you know," Telio said. "And also so much more connected. You saw a little of that, when you discovered that you could ride gravity waves in such a way that let you travel here in months instead of hundreds of years. These two halves of atoms that you use to communicate are connected by an invisible, microscopic wormhole. Right now you can only send messages through cause and effect. We can open that wormhole a bit more, to allow actual data to be transferred."

"And how does that work?" Carriles asked.

"I only understand it on a rudimentary level," Telio replied with amusement. "I just know that it works."

"Well, if it works—"

"Testing," one of the scientists said, leaning into the comms receiver. "Do you hear us?"

NEW DESTINY

BAZAAR HEADQUARTERS

"Do you hear us?"

"What the hell was that?" Sandwyn asked. They all knew how the wire worked; it didn't transmit voice. But there it was, a voice—and a strange one, too. Hollow-sounding. Ethereal. Even through the static, it made Timony think of Oneida's—something about it was just *off.*

"Sandwyn, we really don't have a lot of time here," Timony said. "I need to answer that."

"Who's on the other end?"

"Aliens, I think." She raised her hands and nodded her head toward Oneida. "She's one of them. They have a warship over the city, and we're trying to talk them out of annihilating us. You should let us do that."

"Wait a goddamn minute, Timony," Sandwyn said, exasperated. "First, I—"

"Sandwyn, listen to me and listen to me now: we don't have time to explain this," she said. "Surely you know there's a lot of bad stuff going on. I'm telling you that this is the only way to save us. All of us. You included. You need to trust me."

Another voice from the radio. "Hello? Timony? Are you there?"

Carriles.

"Please," Timony said to Sandwyn.

Sandwyn looked away. Timony couldn't place the look on his face. It looked like he was sad, briefly, but then it dissolved into a resolute blankness. "I used to trust you, Timony. But you lost that trust." He turned to the SWAT team. "Take them, now."

As the first guard approached, Timony turned to Oneida. "Let's make this quick," she said.

Oneida nodded almost imperceptibly before snapping a push kick into the guard's stomach so hard he came fully off his feet and landed with a thud on this back.

Timony knew she only had a moment to capitalize on Oneida's move. She didn't waste any time. The exhaustion that'd been hanging over her like a fog disappeared. She launched herself forward, combat rolling over the downed guard and coming back up with his stun stick. She swung it into the kneecap of the guard closest to her. He fell to his knees, electricity coursing through his body, before collapsing completely.

Timony could hear grunts behind her—hopefully Oneida could handle the rest of the guards—and she focused on Sandwyn, the only one with a blaster.

Sandwyn was old-school Bazaar. Not much older than Timony, but philosophically from an earlier generation. He didn't see good or bad, black or white—he just swam through the gray, an old shark trying to survive. He was locking in on her carefully, trying to get a bead, the blaster following her as she moved. She juked left, throwing off his aim. While he repositioned the blaster,

Timony tossed the stun stick at his hand, hoping to disarm him.

She missed, but the stick connected with Sandwyn's face.

Sloppy, but effective.

Sandwyn screamed, clutching his bloody nose. The blaster fell from his hands and she dove to scoop it up. As she spun around, she sent a kick into the back of Sandwyn's knee. He went down with little fuss.

She placed the blaster to the back of his skull. Sandwyn put his hands up without hesitation.

She leaned down to his ear. "I should kill you for what you did to Osman. Lucky for you, there are more important things to worry about."

She struck him across the head with the depowered stun stick. He fell into a heap on the floor, a low moan escaping his mouth.

That settled, she looked up to see the rest of the SWAT team scattered around the room, Oneida holding one of them up by the throat, then effortlessly throwing his body into the wall. He hit it hard, slid to the floor, and didn't move.

"Can't take you anywhere, huh?" Timony said.

"You wanted this handled fast, right?" Oneida asked.

Carriles's voice was crackling from the console. "Timony? Please answer. Please—"

"I'm here," she said. "How the hell is this happening?"

"Not the most important thing we need to discuss," Carriles said, his static-coated voice erupting from . . . somewhere in the machine. She didn't even know from where.

But Carriles was right. It was a not-right-now problem.

Oneida stepped forward. "This is Oneida. I'm here. I'm safe."

Another voice came through. Human, but not quite. Like it resonated at a slightly different frequency. It made Timony's ears scratch a bit.

"Oneida, this is Telio," the voice said. "You haven't checked in."

"I allowed myself to be captured, hoping to discover some much-needed information," Oneida said. "But in the process my communicator was destroyed."

"Did they hurt you?"

"They tried," Oneida said with a grin. "There's a lot happening here, and I'm still trying to get a good sense of it. The humans acted as expected. A lot of petty squabbling and power plays. Is everyone on Reos safe?"

"Yes," Telio responded. "I'm sanctioned to speak on behalf of the Mutual, but there is a great deal of dissent about what to do next. You being alive is certainly a good sign. But as you can imagine, a great deal has happened that we must also take into consideration."

Oneida nodded, then turned and looked at Timony.

Timony didn't know what to take from that look. She wanted to jump in, to plead their case, but she realized nothing she could do at this point was going to change anyone's mind.

She just had to have some hope.

"One of the humans—a spy, like me," Oneida said. "I'm here with her now. She came to save me. She protected me. Not that I needed it. But there are flowers here, among the weeds."

"Every race has flowers," Telio said. "But when the weeds run too wild, you have to burn them out."

"I know that this isn't my decision to make, but as a member of the Mutual, I also have the right to share my thoughts." She turned and looked at Timony again. "I don't believe we should judge the human race on their worst actors."

"And why is that?" Telio asked.

"Because I've eaten their food," Oneida said. "Some of it is quite good. I've watched their films. I've lived among them. I've seen them at their worst, but I've also seen them at their best. And just now I sat and watched someone take a great deal of pain and anger, and let it go in favor of forgiveness," Oneida said. "I've seen kindness. It makes me feel inclined to show them the same in return. I see that they're capable of it."

Timony fought the urge to get up and throw her arms around Oneida.

"Thank you," Telio said. "As noted, we have much to discuss. We'll send word soon."

The transmission cut out.

Timony stopped fighting the urge. She stood and wrapped Oneida in a tight hug. For a moment, the alien woman stood there, her arms at her side, stiff as a board, before slowly wriggling her arms up and placing them awkwardly around Timony's back.

"Such an awkward custom . . ." Oneida said.

"Oh, shut up, you weirdo," Timony said.

MOSAIC

COMMUNICATIONS BAY

Telio continued to swirl around the vicinity of the wire terminal. Carriles knew this was his chance. The words leapt from his mouth, before the idea was even fully formulated.

"A trial period."

"Excuse me?" Telio asked.

"Give us a trial period. Like probation. Let's open up the channels of communication. Don't make us full-fledged members of the Mutual. Not until we've earned it. But let us earn it. With the right leadership, we can."

Telio seemed to consider his words, though Carriles couldn't always tell where things stood with the alien. Finally, she said, "It wouldn't be unprecedented."

Izaiah stepped forward. Carriles hadn't even noticed he was there, but in this moment, he was glad the alien-chef-spy had joined them. "Like Oneida, I have the right to contribute. And I think you should grant them this."

"Why?" Telio asked.

Izaiah smiled. "I lived among them, too. I learned their styles of preparing foods. Some of it was almost . . .

palatable. I also got to see their better moments. Some of those moments are small, in comparison to the size of their mistakes. But they're no less important."

"If we repair the ship, we can be back home within a few months," Carriles said. "Then we can sell this to the Interstellar Union, let them know what happened after their membership application to the Mutual was rejected—and what we can do to fix it. If you'll just give us that chance."

"We won't have to wait a few months," Telio said. "Follow me."

Telio led them back to engineering. As they approached, Carriles heard a riotous sound bouncing off the metal corridors of the ship. His shoulders tensed, and he turned the corner, expecting to see that all hell had broken loose.

Instead, he found Robinson and Montzar leaned over a console.

And they were laughing.

The two of them looked up and saw they had company. Robinson stood to full height and slapped Montzar on the back, sending the alien scientist staggering a little.

"Hey, Jose," the chief engineer said, "this guy is all right. Really know his shit. Apparently, he can fix our engines and tune them up so we can be home in about an hour."

"An hour?" Carriles asked, getting a little dizzy. He tried to calculate the distance and the speed they'd need to travel. He couldn't come up with an exact number, but it seemed like more than enough to rip the ship apart like tissue paper. "I know what you're thinking," Robinson said. "That we're going to end up as little puddles of goo. Hey, Montzar, explain the bubble thing."

Montzar nodded. "We're taking what you've been using—the gravity drive—and essentially wrapping the ship in a bubble of negative gravity energy. The positive energy around that will provide a cushion, and rather than fly, you'll effectively slide your way back. It's a little complicated . . ."

"Yeah, it's complicated, but if it works, it'll be pretty damn cool." Robinson clapped his hands. "And if it doesn't, we'll all be dead so quick no one will know the difference. So, let's all pour some drinks and kick the tires on this thing. I want to see if it works."

"As much as I'd love to share a drink, we can't imbibe alcohol," Montzar said. "It would be quite deadly."

Robinson shrugged. "Well, that aside, you lot ain't so bad. What do you think, boss?"

Boss. It took a moment for Carriles to realize that Robinson was looking at him.

Carriles looked around the ship. At the engineering team, at Telio, Vicks, and Izaiah. At the chance to fix this.

"I think we should tell Corin Timony we'll be home pretty soon," Carriles said.

Robinson clapped his hands. "Excellent!"

Carriles turned to Telio. "And we'll have the Interstellar Union call an emergency meeting, right now. That gives us a little bit of time to negotiate, you and me, to come up with a way to make this happen."

"Agreed," Telio said. "Let's get to work."

NEW DESTINY

INTERSTELLAR UNION HEADQUARTERS

Carriles met Timony's gaze and felt a wave of relief wash over him.

For so much.

He was home. The drive had worked better than expected. Aside from a brutal headache and some mild nausea, the new quantum drive was a massive leap in technology. The first thing they'd noticed, as the *Mosaic* entered New Destiny space, was the Mutual warship, casting the city into a deep well of shadow. Everything about the Mutual, Carriles mused, looked sleek—spherical and smooth, and not how he'd imagine a ship or tool or anything. It was unsettling.

But they'd arrived. They were here.

Carriles couldn't really believe it. He hadn't expected to be back—even before the whole mission went sideways.

He'd left Vicks and Robinson on board the *Mosaic*, to not only study the unfathomable updates that had been made to the ship's drive but to keep Delmar and his acolytes under watch. The last thing Carriles needed was for the former captain to escape and make an already risky gambit more so.

Carriles had to lean in on everything he'd seen his mother do. He had to become a negotiator, a diplomat. Carriles had to figure out how to sell this idea—that the Mutual would not only let Earth and its colonies live but enter the Mutual as a probationary member—to the Interstellar Union, without losing the various member countries to a spiral of bickering and backstabbing.

On paper, it seemed like a no-brainer: we don't get annihilated and get a part of what some of our more excitable members wanted to steal for free, with more to come in time. But if Carriles had learned anything from his mother, it was that diplomacy was a nuanced and complicated art, one that involved equal amounts of appeasement and force.

Sometimes if you leaned too hard in one direction, the whole house of cards could come tumbling down.

For this to work, they needed Tobin. He'd already helped quell the riots taking place across New Destiny, addressing the crowds through the public address system and explaining that the ship outside the dome didn't mean them any harm. It was a lie, of course, but it had worked. At least long enough to allow every cop and Bazaar operative to retake control of the streets.

But it wouldn't be a comfortable arrangement. Despite his name, Carriles didn't have the clout to stand in front of the IU and argue a case in favor of humanity. The IU wouldn't even let him in the room. The political landscape was especially precarious, with the death of the ship's first officer, Wu, and a handful of other crew members, and reports of the Americans firing on the Chinese contingent of the *Mosaic* mission. The Russians, too, were probably gearing up for a fight.

Tobin could fix it. He had to clean up the mess he'd created. Timony and Carriles had enough dirt on him to force his hand and get him to play nice, they figured. Nobody was better at wheeling and dealing in the halls of the Interstellar Union than Tobin, no matter how big a scumbag he might be.

Carriles hesitated as he stepped into the large Interstellar Union conference room. Timony stood at the doorway, her eyes locked on him. Tobin was seated at the far end of a massive glass table, wearing a shit-eating grin, despite the woman standing over him like a sentry. Her features were similar to Izaiah's, so Carriles presumed this woman was the Mutual spy he'd briefly met years before, Oneida.

Carriles felt something on his arm, and realized it was Timony, her fingers gently squeezing, as if she was trying to reassure him that he was home, that he was safe.

"It's good to see you, Jose," she said with a nod, her eyes wide.

Were they watering, Carriles wondered?

"Uh, same, yes—I wish it was under better circumstances," he stammered. "I should have done more. I should have—"

Timony offered him a grim smile. "Let's talk about it later."

"Nice work," Oneida said, raising her voice from across the room.

"On what?" Carriles asked.

She shrugged. "The redemption of your entire race." There was no sign of humor or sarcasm in her tone. Carriles was beginning to enjoy the flat delivery of the Reosians. It was refreshing in a world where everything anybody said tended to be snide or cutting.

"Thanks," Carriles said.

He stepped forward and looked at Tobin, that grin still plastered on the senator's face. Carriles wanted to smack it off.

His mind flashed back to that strange hour of transit, during which his entire body had felt discombobulated and pulled apart, the *Mosaic* hurtling back home. He'd spent most of the time in Delmar's quarters, the only personal space equipped with a wire terminal, alternating between hashing things out with Telio and talking to Timony. The latter felt natural. Like old times. Two friends strategizing a play in the park.

But it was also fraught. Everything had to not only work but it had to work perfectly for them to have a chance at success—at survival. A misstep would be dire on a galactic scale.

No pressure, Carriles thought.

Because of Tobin's standing in the Interstellar Union, they needed him to sell the plan to his colleagues. He and Timony had agreed that, despite the man's sins, this tenuous deal Carriles had struck with the Mutual needed every bit of support it could get. So they'd let him keep his position, they decided, but they'd make it clear it came with one big caveat.

This was the first step in a long journey, Carriles knew.

He took in a short breath and started to speak.

"Tobin, I think we can all safely agree you're a piece of shit," he said, looking down at the disgraced senator. "But even you have to understand what needs to happen. Not just for your survival, which I realize is your primary concern, but for humanity in general. No more games."

Tobin didn't respond.

"The Mutual is going above and beyond by allowing us provisional membership. The only catch is—if we fuck up? We're out. It could make us their enemies. Which, as you probably saw when that giant ship was hovering in orbit above New Destiny, could be very bad," Carriles said.

"This is where you come in," Timony said, stepping alongside Carriles, both of them looking down at the man they had once admired. "This is where you make up for everything. For the double crosses, for the betrayal—for what happened to Slade. This is your shot at redemption."

"What do I get?" Tobin asked, a slight smile on his face.

It was unnerving. Despite everything, Tobin was acting like he'd won.

And maybe he had.

Timony spoke next.

"You get to stay in power," Timony said, her teeth gritted. "But I will be watching. So will Oneida. She keeps working for you. She's going to be the Mutual's main point of contact. In a year, if we keep our noses clean, the Mutual will convene a meeting to discuss full membership. In the meantime, they're going to help us with New Destiny's power issues." She leaned down toward Tobin, putting her palms flat on the table and getting closer to his face. "You will play ball with them. You will say *please* and *thank you*. If you screw us over, I will end you, and gladly accept whatever consequence I'm given."

Carriles could tell this was hard for her. He wondered what he would do, if he had to basically give his protégé's killer a pass for the greater good. He doubted he'd handle it with the resolve Timony was showing here.

"You're out of cards to play," Timony said. "Either you

help us here, or we blow the lid off everything you were doing. The Interstellar Union would not take kindly to discovering one of its most-lauded elected officials was running a shadow government and making executive decisions on his own."

Tobin let out a dry, self-satisfied laugh.

"Fine," he said with a shrug. "I'm glad you came around, Corin. I knew you would. You're like me. A pragmatist."

Timony flinched, and every muscle in her body went taut. Carriles held his breath, terrified of what she might do next.

She reached into her pocket, coming out with an ID badge. She turned it around, one side covered in patches of brown, dried blood.

"This was Slade's," Timony said. "Her death is on your hands. I'm beginning to think you're incapable of caring about the damage you cause, but I hope one day the impact of her death hits you. What you did."

She slapped the ID badge on the table.

Then there was a subtle buzz from the ID badge, and Timony's hand shot back. She grabbed it with her other hand, like she'd been shocked. A concentrated beam of light burst from the badge. As they all watched, the light solidified.

The holographic image was static at first—black on gray. But then it came slowly to life, and Carriles felt a chill run through him as he made out not just what—but who—they were looking at.

A woman. Tan skin. A gash on her forehead. Blood streaming slowly down the side of her face. Her breathing short, labored. She was looking directly at them, but lying on the ground. Carriles hadn't seen that many people on death's door, but he was certain this woman didn't have much time left.

"Slade," Timony said, her voice cracking with emotion.

"Timony . . . Corin . . . if you're worth your salt, and if you find my dead-ass body, you'll know to grab my badge . . ." She started coughing violently, wincing at each movement. "Don't . . . don't have a lot of time, so I'll cut to it."

Another series of coughs. Wet. Bloody. The noise of New Destiny around her. Timony and Carriles moved in closer to hear better.

"Tobin set me up, okay? He told me to kill you, and when I told him I wasn't going to go through with it, he double-crossed me," Slade continued. "It wasn't the Russians. It wasn't the Chinese. It was him. Him and Delmar and Sandwyn. And god help me . . . I agreed to help."

Her eyes closed, as if she'd fallen asleep—for a second, Carriles thought Slade was dead, but then her eyes fluttered open again, a look of surprise on her face—like someone waking from a nightmare.

"No matter what Tobin says to you, believe this: Adan was pushing back. He got cold feet. Realized what a shitshow it all was. He tried to stop it. He was good, Corin. That's why he died. Why he was killed. Tobin and Delmar made the call. They had him dosed. I found out a month ago. I should have told you. I didn't. I'll never get the chance to make that up to you."

More coughing, a streak of blood in the corner of her mouth. Slade wiped it away before continuing.

"I hope you find peace. I hope you find a little vengeance first, though. Guess you're the best now. With me dead, it's an open road to the top." Her eyes fluttered. "You're a good spy, T. But you were a better friend."

And then she was gone.

The image lingered—of Slade's face, as if she'd fallen asleep—then flickered off without ceremony. The conference room was quiet except for the sound of Tobin's labored breathing. But not for long.

"You killed him," Timony said, the words so low they were almost imperceptible.

But Carriles was close enough to hear the godlike level of anger in them.

She leapt forward and grabbed Tobin by the shirt collar, pulling him toward her. Timony yanked a blaster from some hidden holster in her coat and pressed the barrel to Tobin's sweat-coated forehead. "You killed Adan. You piece of sh—"

"No, please, don't—listen to me, you can't trust what she was saying," Tobin said, his words pouring out of him desperately. The grin was gone. The steely reserve evaporated. He was scared now. "I didn't have Slade killed. I didn't order Adan killed. That was all Delmar—I was just trying to make the best of a bad situation—you can't . . ."

Timony pressed the gun harder to his temple.

Carriles shot another glance at Oneida, who was still in her spot—on the far wall, looking on.

And he remembered they were being judged.

"Tell me the truth, Tobin," Timony said, crouching down, the barrel pointed squarely on his forehead now, their faces close. "Tell me the truth if it's the last thing you do, okay? I don't want to kill you without you having a clear conscience."

"No, no, please, I—"

Carriles knew Tobin still had a role to play. But he also understood that this one moment could destroy every ounce of goodwill they'd struggled to broker with the Mutual.

He knew that Timony's grief and rage were like a slumbering volcano. But volcanoes wake up at the worst possible times.

He stepped forward and placed a hand on Timony's shoulder. He didn't pull her back. He didn't say anything. He just wanted her to know he was there.

That she wasn't alone.

She turned slightly. Gun still on Tobin's forehead. Her eyes on Carriles.

"He's not worth it," Carriles said.

Carriles watched Timony's face. Watched it contort from steel-hard to broken, her muscles fighting back the tears, her eyes and mouth wincing against the feelings she couldn't bury anymore.

"Adan . . ." she said, looking back at Tobin—her sadness back to rage for a second. She turned back to Carriles.

"Adan was a good man," Carriles said, his hand still on Timony's shoulder. He crouched down, to be with her at eye level. Inches away from each other. "He wouldn't want you to do this, either. To throw everything away. Don't do it for vengeance. Do what's right for the rest of us. Do it for *yourself*."

A few seconds passed. Timony and Carriles's gazes locked on each other, the only sound Tobin's belabored, moaning breaths and the ticking of a distant clock.

Then Timony placed the blaster back in her coat.

"New deal," she said, leaning toward Tobin, who pushed himself back in the chair, trying to create distance between them. "You go in there, you make this deal happen. And you retire. Give Oneida your seat, as a sign of goodwill to the Mutual. If you don't"—she gestured toward the ID card—"that video goes out to every inbox in this city."

Tobin nodded in response. Quickly, desperately.

Defeated.

Before Carriles could say anything else, he felt his entire body being pushed back as Timony leaned into him, her face hot against his, streaked with tears. She buried herself in his shoulder—the sobs short but strong—the tears of someone who didn't cry often, who didn't allow herself much time to feel anything but what she was paid to feel.

Carriles wrapped his arms around her.

Without looking up, he felt Oneida step closer to them. Felt her shadow looming over them.

They both looked up, Timony wiping at her eyes. Carriles didn't dare look at Tobin. Afraid of his own rage. Afraid of the damage he would do to this man who'd destroyed so much in his own twisted quest for power. Carriles and Timony pulled away from each other as Oneida spoke.

"So I'm a senator now?" Oneida asked.

Carriles smiled. "That work for you?"

"Not ideal, and I may have to look among our ranks for a more permanent replacement, but the Mutual will see it as a powerful peace offering," she said. Then she turned to Timony. "You showed great restraint."

"If I'd killed him, would I have fucked everything up?" she asked.

Oneida slowly nodded her head.

Timony leaned down to Tobin one last time, and raised her fist. Carriles watched Tobin wince, eyes shut tight, as he waited for the punch to land. Instead, there was a loud bang. Timony pulled her fist back from the table and backed up a few paces, her good hand rubbing the knuckles that had slammed the table a few inches from Tobin's traitorous body.

Then Timony stormed out.

Carriles and Oneida shared a glance. The alien woman looked almost relieved. Carriles wondered if he should let Timony go, let her be alone with her anger and regrets. He knew what that was like. But he also realized he'd left her alone for too long.

He gave Oneida a slight shrug as he followed Timony through the door.

Whatever happened next was out of his hands, anyway.

Better to be there for his friend.

NEW DESTINY

TEXAS 2

Timony gazed at the flickering neon sign above her. She'd made this walk so many times before. Often from work. Sometimes from home. But always with a purpose. This time shouldn't be any different.

Yet it was.

She'd planned it as she choked out one final deal to save humanity, lifting Tobin's wallet as he cowered in fear. If she couldn't kill him, she'd at least enjoy a good drink on his dime.

She deserved it.

Deserved to walk into Alamo, wave over Tadeen the bartender, slide Tobin's credit card across the bar top, and order from the top shelf. The real-deal whiskey, imported from Earth.

That's what she *wanted* to do.

But today felt different. She felt raw. Alive.

It wasn't a moment she wanted to drown in booze.

She heard the footsteps behind her, but she didn't turn to face them. She knew who they belonged to.

"So," Carriles said. "Long day, huh?"

This had always been their spot. It made sense for Carriles to find her here. She wondered if he was surprised to not see her inside, halfway through her second drink.

"You could say that," Timony said, turning to face him, an empty smile on her face.

"First round on me?" Carriles asked.

"No," Timony said with a slight shake of her head, her eyes on the sign again—the second *a* in the bar's name flickering off permanently. "Not tonight."

She pivoted and started to walk. She could feel Carriles catch up with her, their steps synchronized as they wandered down the empty street.

"We going for a walk now?" Carriles asked as he sped up to keep pace with her.

"Yeah, maybe," Timony said. "Just felt like I needed to . . . I dunno, do something different. The same is what got us into this mess, right?"

Carriles cleared his throat. He was going to say something important, Timony thought. He always did this, even after all this time.

"That must have been really hard," he said. "Letting Tobin . . . survive."

"In the moment . . ." Timony trailed off, chewing on her thoughts. "Yes, but with a little bit of distance . . ." She shrugged. "He's losing his power. For a man like him, that's a fate worse than death."

"Yeah, it is," Carriles said. "Look, Corin, I get that this has been a mad rush to the finish, and I just want to say, now that we have a moment to ourselves . . ."

Timony put up her hand. "I know what you're going to say. Forget it. It's forgiven." She stopped as she said the words, then turned to face Carriles. "I've been mad at you for a long time. I've been blaming my downfall on you. Everything on you. Like it was your fault. You didn't shove Boost down my throat. And if I was in your position, I would have jumped at the same job on *Mosaic*."

"It wasn't fair, though," Carriles said. "You got knocked on your ass and I landed on my feet."

"Way of the world," Timony said with a wry grin. "We play the hand we're dealt." She started walking again, then pointed a finger at the sky. "Game just got a whole lot bigger. I think we're past the point of petty squabbles."

She spun around, facing Carriles now, leading him in a different direction. She wasn't sure where, but it felt like the right way to go in this moment. "Nice job, by the way. Saving the human race."

Carriles laughed. "I think we both nailed this one."

"What was it like?" she asked, still a few steps ahead of him. They were turning on Butler Avenue, heading toward the center of New Destiny.

"What was what like?"

"Being one of the first humans to stand on an alien planet," she said, leaning toward him as he caught up to her, her eyes excited. "Making contact. Arguing in front of a fucking alien tribunal with the future of the human race hanging in the balance. Y'know, mundane shit like that."

"You made contact, too," Carriles said. "Oneida."

"Not the same," she said. "Don't deflect."

Butler Avenue ended and Timony kept walking, through a tiny stretch of grass and toward a stone structure that was at the center of a large traffic circle. She hadn't expected to come here, but somehow knew it's where they'd end up.

She let her fingers glide over the large plaque at the center of the structure.

"We going sightseeing?" Carriles asked. "You never struck me as the sentimental type."

"Things change, I guess," Timony said. They both looked down at the image of the New Destiny colony—the collection of domes, the tunnels in between—etched into stone. The words under it in bold, blocky letters.

NEW DESTINY COLONY—
A SECOND CHANCE FOR HUMANITY

"You were saying?" Timony said, her fingers sliding over the words, resting on HUMANITY.

"I was?"

"What was it like, Jose?" Timony said, turning to face Carriles. She knew her eyes were watering. She didn't care. She'd been so tired. So broken for so long. It felt nice to feel something for a change.

Carriles pulled back slightly before taking a deep breath. Calm seemed to wash over him.

"My whole life, I stood in my mom's shadow," he said. "It protected me. I never felt the urge to step out of it, because why? It made life easy. I've lived a good life, and I haven't always deserved it. I've had things handed to me. I'm still chewing on why I did what I did. I just . . . thought it was time to earn my keep." He shrugged to himself. "Does that make sense?"

Timony smiled. And she realized that, yes, Jose Carriles was the one to stand in judgment on behalf of all humanity. It wasn't because he was brave. It wasn't because he was smart. He was those things, too. But most of all, he was humble.

That's all it took to save them. For now. All it took was a little humility.

"Tobin told me he sent you because he expected you to fall in line," Timony said. "But it's easy to be wrong when you can't see past your own cynicism. He didn't know you."

"He was wrong about you too, Corin," Carriles said. "You were always the best at anything you did. Honestly, in my toughest moments up there, I just asked myself what you would do. What my mom would do. That got me through it."

"Do something," Timony said. "It's better than nothing."

She felt her throat grow thick, and she turned her face away from Carriles, so he couldn't see her face.

Carriles gave her a moment. Eventually, he cleared his throat. "So what comes next?"

"Damned if I know. I guess we try to make this whole thing with space aliens work."

"Not that," he said. "You."

Timony hadn't even thought about that. She'd been so caught up in the threat of annihilation. It was easy to focus on today when there didn't seem to be a tomorrow. She leaned against the large plaque. She liked how strong it felt next to her.

"I want my old job back," Timony said. "That kind of work is going to be more important than ever now. The Mutual sent in spies. Which makes me think that, despite all their big talk about peace, they're subject to the same kind of political bullshit we are." She looked out at the city—at New Destiny's sprawl—and toward headquarters. "I suspect it'll take a little legwork to earn back the trust of the Bazaar, but today is probably a big mark in my favor."

Carriles smiled. "I can put in a good word. Son of a senator . . ."

"Oh, shut up," she said, then thought about it for a moment. "Actually, fuck it, whatever works. I may as well enjoy some of that Carriles high life. What about you?"

Carriles looked up at the dome, his eyes losing some of their focus, as if overwhelmed by the vastness above both of them. "My gut wants to fly. Pilot's gotta pilot. But there's also a part of me that wants to do more than just push buttons. It felt good to lead. I think I was pretty good at it. Plus, there's a whole big universe out there that we'll now have access to. I intend to see it."

"Captain Carriles has a nice ring to it," Timony said, playfully punching his shoulder. "Maybe I'll get to join you for some of it."

"Always room for you on my ship." The words seemed to come naturally to Carriles. She let her thoughts wander to that theoretical future. Aboard the *Mosaic*, together. Exploring. She smiled and watched as Carriles contemplated the plaque again. "You think the people who installed this had any idea what was to come?"

"Don't think anyone did," Timony said, joining Carriles as he looked down at the rusted slab of metal—a piece of a history that was still being written. "But that's usually how we learn. We make a big mess, clean it up, and try really hard to make different mistakes the next time."

Carriles placed a hand on her shoulder. "Keep walking? It's a nice night."

Timony took in a deep breath before shaking her head. "Nah. I want to get into the office early tomorrow. Plus, I need to ditch Tobin's wallet."

Carriles's brow scrunched up as he realized she'd stolen it.

"Before or after you almost killed him?"

"During. Asshole deserved it and much more. I thought he owed me a drink." She pulled the wallet out of her pocket to examine it. "But it didn't feel as fun once I got outside."

She stepped toward the curb and dropped the wallet down a sewer drain.

Carriles laughed. It was a light, breezy laugh. Timony hadn't laughed like that in a while. It was nice to hear, at least.

"Fucking Tobin," Carriles said with a sigh. He nudged Timony with his elbow. "I'd say we should get a bite, but I plan on going home and sleeping for the next three days."

"Oh, to be the son of a senator . . ."

Carriles frowned, and Timony smacked him on the shoulder. "Don't be so sensitive."

They turned around and made their way back through the recycled air of New Destiny, still uncertain as to exactly where they were going. As they walked, the two of them tipped their heads back, looking at the dome, then through it. Timony didn't know what she was looking for, but the darkness of space, just barely visible beyond the artificial night sky, suddenly looked a whole lot deeper.

Carriles took her hand and gave it a squeeze.

"This is going to be fun," he said.

"Yeah," Timony said. "I think it will be."

ACKNOWLEDGMENTS

FROM ROB

Thanks to Alex, for shooting me a text one day that probably said something like: “Hey man, want to jam on a sci-fi novel?” And here we are. I feel very lucky to have such a patient and talented collaborative partner. The fact that we’re still pals after writing a whole book together is testament to our friendship!

On behalf of me and Alex, thanks to Josh Getzler, our agent, and his assistant, Jon Cobb, as well as the entire team at HG Literary. Also, Team Blackstone: Addi Wright, Cole Barnes, Marilyn Kretzer, Nikki Carrero, Rebecca Malzahn, Rachel Sanders, Tatiana Radujkovic, Josie Woodbridge, Andy Kifer, and anyone else we missed (sorry!). Big thanks to Candice Edwards for the amazing cover!

Finally, thank you to my daughter, Abby—this book dreams about a better place in the universe for humanity, and she’s where I looked for that inspiration.

FROM ALEX

Huge thanks to Rob for helping bring this idea to life. Rob's the ideal cowriter: talented, hardworking, and low on ego. As always, the best idea always won, and we were able to put our heads together to create a story that felt both fresh and familiar—evoking our favorite things while melding with our voices. The end result is a book that reads like something apart from our own, solo work—which is the goal. Neither of us could've written this book alone.

The idea for *Dark Space* (*Star Trek* meets John le Carré) was born out of a passion for epic sci-fi—*Star Trek*, *Star Wars*, *The Expanse*, *Battlestar Galactica*—and wanting to weave an espionage story through that kind of universe. I owe a big debt to some of my favorite contemporary speculative fiction authors, who proved to be consistently inspiring and amazing: Zoraida Córdova, Justina Ireland, Charles Soule, David Mack, Dayton Ward, Una McCormack, Cavan Scott, Michael Moreci, Michael Jan Friedman, Keith R. A. DeCandido, John Jackson Miller, Ben H. Winters, Lauren Beukes, James S. A. Corey, John Scalzi, Mary Robinette Kowal, Charlie Jane Anders, and many more.

The novels of John le Carré—particularly those staring the stuffy, middle manager George Smiley, loomed large over this novel, and I'm grateful for the months spent revisiting them while writing *Dark Space*.

As always, I'm thankful to the readers, librarians, booksellers, reviewers, and tastemakers who support and celebrate our books. Without you, these books would not exist.

I'm forever indebted to the many author friends and

colleagues I've met over the years—particularly Kellye Garrett, Amina Akhtar, Liz Little, Wanda Morris, Shawn Cosby, Yasmin Angoe, Sandra S. G. Wong, Alafair Burke, Laura Lippman, and so many more. In a business that is always competitive and often confusing, it's a great balm to know they're in my corner.

I owe everything to my family—especially my wife, Eva, and our two children, Guillermo and Lucia. Thank you for keeping me grounded, focused, and loved.